OCCULT DETECTIVE
MAGAZINE

#7 (May 2020)

Edited by

John Linwood Grant & Dave Brzeski

CATHAVEN
PRESS

OCCULT DETECTIVE MAGAZINE #7

ISBN: 978-1-9160212-2-8

http://greydogtales.com/blog/occult-detective-magazine/
occultdetectivemagazine@gmail.com

Publishers: Jilly Paddock & Dave Brzeski

Editors: John Linwood Grant & Dave Brzeski

Logos & Headers: Bob Freeman

Cover by: Sebastian Cabrol (http://phoarto.com)

Interior design by Dave Brzeski and Jilly Paddock

Uxmal art © 2020 ODM/Mutartis Boswell
Pause For Station Identification art © 2020 ODM/Luke Spooner
The Case of the Signet Ring art © 2020 ODM/Bob Freeman
The White Sickness art © 2020 ODM/Autumn Barlow
Dash Thy Foot art © 2020 ODM/Russell Smeaton

Published by
Cathaven Press,
Peterborough,
United Kingdom
cathaven.press@cathaven.co.uk

CONTENTS

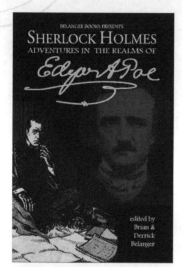

EDITORIAL

One of the things that the late Sam Gafford and I were sure of, when we founded an occult detective magazine in 2016, was that we wanted to explore this sub-genre with open minds and open hearts. Nothing – as long as it had both a supernatural, strange or weird element and an investigative one – was necessarily out of bounds. And we started out in that spirit because there was an initial fear that we would be swamped with similar old-style takes of Victorian and Edwardian sleuths, or overwhelmed with noir PIs whose best friend was either a bottle of Jack or a .45. Did we still want those types of stories? Of course we did (they can be terrific), but the magazine was not to be merely a safe house for standard tropes – it was intended as a jumping off point.

To our delight, many talented writers have proved to be up to the challenge, and so Dave Brzeski and I have been able to continue that original, exploratory approach. We have published both modern weird fiction and pulp adventure, classic-style supernatural tales and historical fiction going as far back as the start of the Christian era. Even the struggles of some jaded PIs. We have been to Paris, Alexandria, and Mumbai; Africa, Australasia and Japan. So the issue in your hands now is therefore more of the same, and also not the same –   new characters, strange settings and imaginative interpretations of the term 'occult detective'.

Following S L Edwards' interview with writer Jonathan Raab last issue, we have a new and very dark Sheriff Kotto story by Matthew M Bartlett and Jonathan Raab. Aidan Hayes introduces us to the start of a young occult detective's career, and we add a surprising tale of a PI trying to serve a writ on Satan in Hell, by Julie Frost.

Tanya Warnakulasuriya provides a fresh contemporary tale, one set in London with Guyanese folklore undertones, whilst Paul StJohn Mackintosh brings us one of our most unusual investigators as he shares the story of Scotland's only insurance claims adjuster for ghosts. And for those who like the old one-on-one struggle with demonic forces, we have Nancy A Hansen's unabashed occult investigator with a difference, Chandra Smoake.

In the spirit of exploration mentioned above, we travel round the world with D J Tyrer's story of spiritual sickness in the coastal villages of South Africa, Debra Blundell's innovative tale of a pre-Conquest Mayan agent for the Smoke Throne, and another story of Brandon Barrows' Japanese priest-investigator, as last encountered in Issue 5. Nor do we forget our roots. To round off the fiction, we bring you two classically-set pieces, with the return of writer Aaron Vlek and her erudite and arcane character Geoffrey Vermillion, plus the first appearance here of a character from the pen of Colin Fisher – the Occultress, facing the supernatural in British India.

As usual, we have a range of non-fiction and reviews. Dave Brzeski examines the unconvincing exploits of Grimm, an occult detective from the golden age of American comic books, and we present two articles which tease with connections that are so close, but not quite there. Bobby Derie explores the complexities of inter-relationships between weird fiction writers in the days of Robert E Howard, and Steven Philip Jones offers a timely piece on the not-quite-occult events in the work of Clive Cussler, who died earlier this year.

Finally, speaking of connections, we should mention an anthology coming soon from Belanger Books, and edited by John Linwood Grant – *Sherlock Holmes and the Occult Detectives*. Over two packed volumes, Holmes the sceptic finds himself working with occult detectives new and old, including Van Helsing, John Silence and even Mary Morstan, Dr John Watson's wife! We're sure that the huge success of the campaign for this project was due in some part to the enthusiasm of readers of *Occult Detective Magazine*.

As ever, thanks to our great artists, who bring so much to the magazine, and be assured that next issue will be different again... but always *ODM*.

John Linwood Grant

NOTE: This issue is dedicated to the late Susan Biggers, wife of Cliff Biggers. Cliff is of course our current sponsor, and has been instrumental in ensuring that we were able to continue.

IN MEMORIAM:
SUSAN HENDRIX BIGGERS

(OCTOBER 1, 1950- JULY 22, 2019)

I knew Susan for 51 years. I was married to her for 48 years. I still cannot fathom how I was so lucky. Susan shared my interests in science fiction, fantasy, horror, mysteries, comics, and music. I met her because of her letter of comment that appeared in Batman #199. I took a chance and called every Hendrix in the phone book, asking for Susan; I found her on the fourth try. In spite of her better judgment, she agreed to meet me. From there, a friendship grew into a romance that led to a marriage three years to the day after our first meeting.

Having a partner who shares, understands, and supports your interests—what a gift! Our work in fanzines (including an award-winning SF/fantasy/horror review fanzine, *Future Retrospective*, which relied heavily on Susan's discerning skills as an astute critic) brought us into contact with writers like Frank Belknap Long, E. Hoffman Price, George R.R. Martin, Chelsea Quinn Yarbro, John Farris, and many others. That fanzine background inspired my 33-year career producing the weekly *Comic Shop News*, as well as my fiction writing. And Susan was there with me, encouraging and supporting me all the way.

"When you find something you love, you have to do it." I still hear those words of encouragement ever time my fingers touch the keyboard and a new story begins to appear on the screen. I remember the pride she displayed as she saw my work in the pages of *Occult Detective Quarterly*. I know she would be just as proud today to see how *Occult Detective Magazine* has carried on the tradition of *ODQ*, and she would be very happy about the small part I have played in keeping Sam, John, and Dave's vision alive.

Cliff Biggers, April 2020

UXMAL

DEBRA BLUNDELL

Below the smooth white roads and crowded plazas of Tikal lay a hidden, three-sided chamber, where nine solemn figures sat cross-legged on a broad dais. Fire pots cast wavering light across the elegant murals along the walls, making the painted figures there appear to writhe and tremble. The seated individuals, three women and six men, made up the entire membership of the *Butz' Tz'am*, the Smoke Throne. Mayan kings and queens, nobles and chancellors, imagined themselves the controllers of political and cultural matters in their respective territories; in reality, the society of the Smoke Throne convened regularly to address certain issues of trade and affairs of state that the conventional rulers were unaware of and, often enough, unprepared to deal with.

The current meeting was winding up the evening's business. A round-faced, plain-featured woman spoke in the flickering light. "Anything else before we adjourn, friends?"

A thin man with jade earspools gestured slightly.

"Yellow Turtle?"

The man cleared his throat. "It has come to our attention that something extraordinary has occurred in Uxmal." He shifted on his cushion, frowning. "A rather large, odd-looking pyramid has appeared in the central plaza."

"Appeared?" This from another member, a man with one eye and a missing ear.

"Appeared, yes, overnight." The crackling from the fire pots seemed loud in the close space. "My sources tell me that it was, um, *generated*, by a magician who happens to be a dwarf. And who has assumed the throne of Uxmal."

It was a moment before the woman spoke again. "Obviously, you have this on good authority."

"Obviously. And there is a possibly related matter... scores of citizens have gone missing from the area recently. Maybe a hundred or more."

The one-eared man asked. "Corpses found? Or did they just vanish?"

Yellow Turtle shrugged. "No trace of any of them, so I'm told."

"This is clearly unnatural, and therefore unacceptable," stated the round-faced woman. "Have you a suitable operative available to look into it?"

Yellow Turtle nodded. "We have an agent in Uxmal now, one Mo' Tok', but he is too well-known at court there to make obvious inquiries. One of our best men, Chaan Ch'amak, is just back from that dreadful business of the fish-woman on the Chanputun beach. He has a flair for extraordinary situations, and I'd say this qualifies."

A tall, graceful woman across from him nodded. "That's the same fellow who dealt with the Fire Monkeys."

"The same. I will dispatch him to Uxmal at once, if we are all agreed?"

Murmurs of assent followed. Yellow Turtle took up a brush and wrote out a coded message, then sent for his assistant. "Get this dispatch to Chaan Ch'amak in Dzibilchaltun by the fastest runner. Pay extra if you have to."

* * *

The trees were behind us now and finally we could see it clearly, the pyramid that shouldn't have been there. The four of us stopped there, the whole of Uxmal around us, the splendidly decorated municipal buildings, the ball court, the fine main plaza. Buildings clustered atop the highest terrain, farms in the distance, people everywhere. And jutting up on one side of the plaza, the grotesque mountain of stone the locals were calling the Temple of the Magician.

I had been hearing plenty of stories from fellow travelers about the pyramid and its creator, but it was a jarring sight in person. I glanced around to gauge the reactions of my companions to the curious edifice. Naabi was staring intently at the monstrous building. Behind her, the twins, Hun and Itz'in, were taking it all in, their handsome matching faces gleaming with sweat and anticipation. "Naabi," I asked gently, "does that building look like something you might have seen in... the place where I found you?"

She continued staring, silent in the relentless heat. The most unnerving feature of the pyramid was its rounded base, almost elliptical in form and totally unlike the magnificent tiered constructions prominent in any major Mayan center. Although the temple at the top and the shrine just below were decorated in the distinctive ornate style that distinguished Puuc region architecture, it was not enough to lessen the outlandish foreign impression of the thing. The beautiful embellishments depicting mighty Chaac, the rain god, and the intricate latticework could not disguise the overall sense of alien design. After a while Naabi turned her eyes to mine and gave a somber nod, dark memories clouding her gaze. *If only she could speak*, I mused, *we'd know a great deal more. Ah, well...*

"That thing was definitely not here last time," muttered Itz'in, nodding toward the pyramid. Hun sniffed in agreement. The twins had accompanied me through Uxmal some sixteen months previously. We'd been on Smoke Throne business then too, disguised – as now – as purveyors of salt.

People passed by in both directions, and most of them paused to stare suspiciously at us, especially at Naabi. Naabi *was* something to see. The left side of her body was entirely covered in fine-lined, sky-blue tattooing that seemed to glow from the surface of her brown skin. Blue body paint was common enough, but Naabi's vibrant tattoos *permeated* the skin: twisted geometric forms that confused the eye, stylized animals with too many limbs, figures that might be dancing people or gods, and everywhere tangles of aquatic vegetation that made you look away if your gaze rested too long upon them. In contrast, Naabi's right side was unblemished, and although she modestly wore the pretty embroidered white dresses my good wife Eleven Bee made for her, she made no extra effort to cover her decorated flesh from inquisitive eyes.

When I dragged her along with me out of that nightmare hell-fissure in Ouaxactun, she had cried out once in shock, but that was as much sound as she had ever made in my presence. I had seen quite a lot during my forays into those adjacent worlds, where mind-bending monstrosities staggered and howled; because she could not speak, I could not know what horrors young Naabi had witnessed there, nor for how long. Little wonder the girl had been struck speechless.

"Let us press on," I suggested, "before we attract a crowd."

Itz'in and Hun re-shouldered their heavy packs and set off again. The twins were fine-looking boys with athletic frames, good breeding evident in their comportment and fashionable hair, meticulously arranged in braids and tails at the peak of their long skulls. Women old and young alike gazed after them lustily wherever we went. It was enough to make an average-looking man like me a trifle jealous.

Naabi deliberately pulled her gaze away from the impossible temple and followed them.

I was hoping I could remember where the residence of Mo' Tok' was without asking directions. Uxmal looked essentially the same as the last time I was here (except of course for the fresh pyramid at city-center), but my memory had dulled a bit in my mature years, as Bee gently reminded me whenever it suited her. We stayed on the main *sacbe*, one of the raised white paved roads, passing through tracts of houses, small plazas, and swarms of people everywhere. I timed our arrival to fall on market-day, thinking more crowds would minimize the novelty of our little band, but we still attracted stares. I led us north through the center of town and found a connecting lane off which I believed Mo' Tok's' estate lay, and another half-hour of heat and crowds brought us tired and hungry to our destination. My old friend had substantial holdings, extensive gardens of medicinal plants, sheds and storehouses, animal pens and fruit trees. It was all very impressive.

A small unit of guards challenged us at the gate. I produced a stamped clay tag on a leather cord, which would identify me to my old friend. Mo' Tok' and I had fought side by side in our youth, not in bloody raids on neighboring communities but against beings, *things*, which most ordinary people never guessed existed, except in stories and in nightmares. He and I were part of the same covert society and I knew I could depend upon his hospitality and sanctuary.

The overseer of the estate appeared, and though frustrated by the fact that he could not read the glyphs on the tag, evidently he had seen such markers before. We waited a bit more in the fly-filled heat, and after a time the fellow hurried back, tag in hand.

"Venerable Chaan Ch'amak and party are most welcome to the house of Ajaw Mo' Tok', Lord Macaw Blade! Follow me please, we will await him inside."

We were a bedraggled lot, dirty and slouching from weariness. The overseer led us across a broad courtyard dotted with fruit trees in planters, officiously waving aside servants sweeping the pavement. We arrived at a broad, shaded gallery where a contingent of Mo' Tok's household staff bustled about, bearing cups of cool water and *balche*, relieving us of our packs, bringing cushions for sitting. Servants waved huge feathered fans to get the stifling air moving. The soft textiles and cool tiles made a fine welcome, and beautiful youths materialized with basins of scented water to wash the road dust off our burning feet and tired arms. Comfortably seated, we were presented with dishes of *poc chuk*, roasted vegetables, and fruits with honey. I was almost dozing off in a haze of pleasure when I heard the deep rumbling of our host's voice.

"Chaan Ch'amak, Sky Fox, my brother the Ghoul Breaker! Your presence brings joy into my home!"

I arose to clasp the arms of my old friend. The twins stood up respectfully as well, and perceptive Naabi followed their example.

"Please relax, refresh yourselves! You've been a long time on the road." He was a fine figure of an aristocrat: long-skulled with a slender nose beaked like a hawk, his hair done up lavishly with rare shells, jade beads and feathers, clad in rich garments more suited for the court than a hot day at home. I smiled: *you always were a bit of a dandy!*

"Mo' Tok', my old friend! Many thanks for your kind hospitality! Let me introduce Hun and Itz'in, who have joined my humble household. And this," I pulled her gently from behind me, "is Yax Janaab, my ward. Naabi we call her. My good wife and I have taken her into our family as well." Naabi kept her eyes on the floor, bowing uncertainly.

" 'Hun' and 'Itz'in', eh? *'One'* and *'Younger Brother'*? How droll! You fine fellows and the lovely waterlily maiden are all welcome to refreshments and rest, while I steal away the old man and catch up with all the gossip!"

The two of us relocated to a broad, open room, deep in cooling shade with cushions and jugs of *balche*. We were quite alone here and could talk freely.

"So what's with the girl?" he asked eagerly, pouring us drinks. "And those strapping twin lads! Some noble's bastards, I'll wager, fobbed off on you to raise! Tell me I'm wrong!"

I grinned. "The boys' mother, I'm told, was a diviner who caught the eye of the illustrious Singing Frog Hill, the king's chief advisor at the court in Chichen Itza. The boys themselves displayed some uncommon abilities at puberty, glyph-casting, fire-witchery, mimicry, that sort of thing. A fair-minded man, their noble father did not consign them to the bottom of a *cenote* but made some discrete inquiries instead. We were glad to take them in."

"Then they double as bodyguards. Lucky you! And the mysterious waif?"

I felt my expression darken. "I was on a mission, deep in the forests of the south. A ghoul from beyond Xibalba was wrecking a remote settlement far down in the southern forests. I tracked it to its entry-threshold and, armed with my songs and my talismans, I entered after it. A more horror-ridden place I have never seen, my friend! It took all my skills and wit to destroy the fiend, and as I was making ready at last to depart the foul place, I spotted what appeared to be a human huddled near the portal. She reached out to me as the veil between the worlds began to close. On impulse, I grabbed her hand and dragged her with me."

"That could've been... *disastrous.*"

"Yes. I don't know where she came from or how she came to be marked so precisely on one side, but someday maybe she can tell me."

"She can't speak at all, eh? And the skin design – not to be indelicate, but are they...?"

"All over? My wife tells me the tattoos are on every spot of flesh on the left side. Don't indulge your curiosity by looking at them too closely. That can lead to unpredictable consequences."

"I'll remember that! Well, you made good time getting here." He took a long drink from his cup and refilled it. "Here's what you came to learn, friend, and a strange tale it is. The most common version of the story is that

Nich te', an old crone who used to make a living selling water, small charms and trinkets by the *sacbe* to Kabah, found a peculiar egg by the side of the road, took it home, and covered it with leaves to incubate it. Eventually the egg hatched, revealing not a chick or a lizard, but a baby. This was supposed to have taken place early last year."

"Similar to the story I heard all along the way here."

"This 'baby' grew alarmingly fast. In two months, it had a full beard and the features of a grown man but stopped growing at waist height. Clearly it was not a natural dwarf nor a small person. More like a *ch'at*, a goblin."

"I've seen some truly bizarre things, but I've never encountered a goblin," I smiled.

"Nor have I, until I laid eyes on this one. He's peculiarly misshapen. Revolting-looking. Obviously, he obtained some skill in enchantment from his adopted mother, for soon enough he was seen in the main plaza, performing all manner of tricks and inexplicable feats. I myself saw him pull a fish out of the dirt at his feet. A *sea* fish, alive and thrashing. Eventually the dwarf-magician's antics came to the attention of the king, Lord Shield Jaw. He invited the *ch'at* to the palace and what transpired after that is vigorously disputed. What *is* known is that within a few days of the dwarf's stay at the palace there was a falling-out. Lord Shield Jaw became apprehensive of his little guest, and advisors suggested the king get rid of the dwarf by setting a monumentally impossible task and using his failure as excuse to have him exiled. The king agreed."

"Like spontaneously bring forth a pyramid in the middle of Uxmal?"

"Sounded foolproof. It wasn't. The king publicly challenged the dwarf to build the grandest, tallest pyramid in all the Puuc lands in one night; if he succeeded he would be king. The dwarf agreed. Next morning, early risers were astonished to see that architectural atrocity casting a shadow over the palace. No one saw it materialize, but it is whispered that the goblin's sorcerous mother helped him out."

"It's an evil-looking thing to be sure. What happened next?"

Mo' Tok' scowled. "The next day the stunned king challenged the dwarf to a duel with bundles of hardwood, thinking to dispatch him outright with a blow on the head. The Lord Shield Jaw struck him hard, but the dwarf lived on. Not a scratch."

"Why didn't the king's courtiers stop the whole thing right then?"

"Too late, the plaza was choked with onlookers. They had to hold the king to his bargain or face an outraged mob. On his turn, the dwarf landed a solid blow to Lord Shield Jaw's pointy skull. And now we have a *new* king who's clearly not from around here."

I let that sink in for a moment. "I hear since then there have been a number of missing citizens?"

"Many. Scores of them. No one has investigated the matter, for fear of reprisal if the dwarf is somehow responsible. Old people, young people. Babies. Warriors. Uxmal is a pretty big place, but nearly everyone knows someone who's vanished."

I sighed. "Right. How close can we get to him, this goblin king?"

"Not very, he's remarkably keen on personal protection." Mo' Tok' frowned. "Understandable, what with all these disappearances."

I snorted, in a way my good lady considered uncouth and frequently asserted. "Tomorrow we will see how close we can get. I'd like to see Naabi's reaction to the sight of him. She has an understandable *feel* for the unnatural. Beyond that, I don't know where to start. If we were further east of here I would be seeking caves and *cenotes*, looking for a water connection. If that dwarf's not from an egg, which is surely as preposterous as a surprise pyramid, he's likely from one of the worlds beyond Xibalba, and water often provides access between our existence and the other."

Mo' Tok' looked thoughtful for a moment. "Come see something."

I followed him out into the sunlight, through courtyards and across the gardens behind his main house. We stopped in the middle of a sloping paved area. In its center lay a gaping hole lined with well-laid masonry and half-ringed with stonework. "This is a *chultun*. We don't have *cenotes*, the giant limestone wells from your area, or rivers of any size, so preserving fresh water is a perennial problem here in Puuc country. We've built these underground cisterns everywhere, and we depend upon them for catching and storing Chaac's precious gift of rainwater."

I stood at the edge of the hole, looking downward. "How far down do they go?"

"Some of them are quite deep. Occasionally diggers have punched through to limestone caves far below the…"

But I had stopped hearing him. I understood where the rupture might have occurred in the skin between our world and that other, profane, malignant realm. Maybe somewhere along the road to Kabah, an old water-seller named Nich te' had dipped into a *chultun* with such a watery breach, seeking to refill her pot, and there found the loathsome egg that she hatched into a monster. Or instead of it hatching from an egg, *some loathsome, unspeakable act had spawned it…*

I shuddered at the obscene vision I had conjured in my mind. All I wanted now was to cleanse the rest of the sweat and dirt from my skin, and have a rest in Mo' Tok's shaded sanctuary. We returned to the house. Naabi, I was told, was visiting the pottery workshops on the estate and the twins had ventured back into town to flirt with the local ladies and poke about for gossip.

I stretched out on a mat on the cool tile floor and sleep came swiftly. As always, when I am traveling, my wife Bee came to me in a dream. She was sitting on our little terrace, sewing.

You forgot to pack your rash balm, husband.

"I know. I had to buy some from a vendor along the way. No comparison to your fine salve, of course. I miss you."

I should hope so. But it's only been a week.

"Seems like a month. Two."

How is my pretty flower?

That was what she called Naabi, just as she had named her more formally *Yax Janaab*, Blue Waterlily. Among all the twisty-angled symbols and disconcerting figures that seemed to float on the girl's skin there were more depictions of waterlilies than anything else recognizable. If Naabi had ever had another name, she could not speak to say it. Had those marks been put there to protect her? Punish her? Why only cover half her body? I might never know.

The day I brought that wild-haired, blue skinned child home with me from my harrowing mission, Bee had claimed her as her own. She had spent the day bathing her and braiding her hair and feeding her and murmuring softly all manner of comforting words and healing songs. Bee never pressed the girl for details but simply treated her as the daughter we'd never had. Naabi was devoted to me, but she worshipped my wife.

It was something we had in common.

"Naabi is attracting some attention, as you'd guess, but people seem more concerned with the fact we're possibly dangerous strangers. A lot of people have disappeared. And yes, there's a big new ugly pyramid in town."

Bee's image shimmered like sun on a waterfall mist. *You must be careful, Ni Juntan.* Even after so many years my old heart still beat faster when she called me 'My Beloved'. *I wanted to tell you something important that I know, but don't understand. I know that when you see the flame turn to green, you must look up. I don't know why, I only know that I must tell you.*

Bee was often the recipient of visionary knowledge. I had no way of knowing what her warning referred to.

"I will remember, my dear."

Be careful, Chaan. Find out what's happening to the missing and hurry home all intact. I will show you how much I missed you when you return.

"I'm a lucky man," was my last thought before the black oblivion of sleep consumed my mind.

* * *

I was awakened too soon by a rough shake on the shoulder. "What?" I grumbled. It was Hun.

"Lord Mo' Tok' sent me to wake you. The Goblin King wants an audience with you and Naabi! He sent his guards to bring you to the palace!"

Nothing wakes a man up faster than a demand from a goblin king. Naabi appeared in a fresh white dress and a fine necklace made of ceramic beads, all on loan from one of Mo' Tok's womenfolk. She looked at me inquisitively.

"So, daughter, we have been invited to visit with King Dwarf. What do you think?"

Her eyes narrowed, and she made a face. I laughed. "Yes, I feel the same way. Now we may get a little closer to the situation and come away with some new information." I looked around to Itz'in and Hun. "My boys, I am glad the invitation omitted you, because I need you to procure a few things we may need later."

I was planning on a 'later' I was not entirely certain of.

"Get some beeswax. Small torches. A better mirror than the one I brought, three if you can manage it. With luck we won't be long." I smiled at the troubled looks. "Don't worry, likely a bored king has just heard about a lovely lady with curious body art and wants to see it for himself."

Now faces showed doubt as well as concern. "Don't fret, I'm not completely helpless, you know." I caught myself rubbing the tiny amulet of sky-silver that my father had placed under the skin of my right wrist when I was a boy. And Naabi was not the only one with cryptic tattoos, only mine were more discretely placed.

We set off with the king's men, Mo' Tok' coming with us to make introductions. *Or to show off his expensive feathers and finery at court*, I grinned to myself. The hike back up the *sacbe* this time was oppressively hot, and bruise-colored clouds glowered to the west. Though a solid downpour was always considered a gift from Chaac, impending rain coupled with the heat made the air thick and hard to breathe.

At last we reached the palace forecourt, facing the pyramid across the plaza. What looked like an overdressed child stooped in the center of a row of courtiers and officials, resplendent in bright body paint, nose ornaments, feathered headgear, fine appliqued garments, and carefully cultivated expressions of disdain. We neared the dais and respectfully kneeled on the broad steps.

"Great King!" Intoned Mo' Tok', "May I present my old soldier friend from Dzibilchaltun, Chaan Ch'amak, Sky Fox, along with his ward, young Yax Janaab." Mo' Tok' made a bow low enough to let the longest and costliest of his headdress feathers sweep the pavement, then politely retreated. The misshapen form of the king lurched forward toward us. The back of my neck prickled and the hair rose on my arms; *unnatural little monkey*, I mused.

"I heard there was an exquisite creature come to town, one with skin decoration that could only have been created by the gods. I wished to see for myself!" he croaked. "Tell me, Master Sky Fox, how did she come to be adorned so?"

"I cannot say, great king, and neither can she. She cannot speak."

"Extraordinary! The designs have a light all their own, don't they?" Behind him I could just see one of the noblemen, exceptionally tall and with a wary air, edge forward curiously. With a flopping gait, the king came closer and pushed forward his face to get a better look at the meandering leaves and stems of the waterlilies twisting across Naabi's left shoulder and neck. If his gaze lingered long enough, I knew the stalks and blossoms would appear to undulate, as though under moving water. The king's greedy eyes followed the luminous lines around to other images – double-winged bats, clouds over an empty field, a temple on fire. Naabi watched the dwarf through her eyelashes.

I desired very strongly to knock the leer off the little man's malformed face with my fist. I resisted the urge. "Daughter, turn about and show his majesty the fine tattoos across your shoulder blade." Naabi dutifully did as I said (was that the trace of a smile on her lips?), and modestly shrugged down her *huipil* sleeve, exposing her back. There, the uncanny precision of the borderline between natural bronze flesh and ornamentation was even more distinct. The king beamed at the exposure of more skin, until his gaze landed upon the singular illustrations on Naabi's back. There was a three-trunked tree that became five-trunked if you followed the branches around, and a spotted iguana biting its tail that appeared to rotate in the direction opposite from the track of your gaze, its four legs becoming more tails. Elsewhere, a woman's face morphed into that of a monstrous jaguar and back to human, laughing maliciously at what you knew were your own depravities.

Whatever the Goblin-King saw in those unearthly designs no one can guess but the effect upon him was ferocious. He jerked backward up the steps with a blood-freezing howl, eyes glaring, twisted mouth agape. In another moment he was convulsing in the throes of a violent fit. The tall courtier motioned for attendants to subdue the spasming creature, and he was hastily taken inside the palace.

"His majesty is blessed with these occasional bouts of... *ecstasy*. Take no notice," said the courtier dryly. "Seriously, *no notice*. I trust your visit to Uxmal has been enjoyable, profitable, whatever, and now I wish you a swift and safe journey to wherever you call home. I suggest you depart before the rains start."

* * *

Departure would have to wait. It was close to midnight when Hun, Itz'in, and I left Mo' Tok's' villa. The anticipated rain was now falling in undulating sheets and sporadic lightening provided just enough light to keep us from falling off the *sacbe*. When we reached the base of the pyramid I clapped both boys on the shoulders reassuringly, but they seemed eager enough for the undertaking. Naabi had been displeased at my insistence that she stay behind while we made our foray into the goblin's pyramid, yet she relented somewhat when I explained what Bee would do to me if I allowed anything to happen to her 'pretty flower'. The twins and I arrived sodden at our destination and began the steep, slippery climb up the west stair front of the façade. My plan was to seek entry into the shrine situated just below the long temple at the pyramid's pinnacle. It was dreadful to behold in daylight, the doorway cleverly fashioned into a monstrous mouth. Anyone crossing the threshold was effectively entering the savage, gaping jaws of Chaac himself. Ragged flashes of lightening intensified the terrifying effect.

Wheezing, wet, and shaking with the exertion of the climb, I sat down at the summit to rest for a moment. After I'd caught my breath, we felt our way cautiously through the entrance, which seemed even darker than the surrounding night. Just inside, Itz'in produced from his pack a fist-sized clay ball, miraculously dry. He cracked the magical ball open, revealing glowing embers inside. With them we lit the torches we'd packed and stared around us. In the center of the stone floor was an ominous black rectangular hole and the walls were covered in painted murals. But unlike typical scenes of noblemen and ladies, warriors and gods, all in majestic settings, these were different. These were vile depictions of sickening fiends engaged in the most nauseating acts, gorging themselves on—

"Don't look at the artwork, boys." My voice sounded shrill in the humid

chamber. I turned my attention to the hole in the floor. Kneeling, I eased forward my right hand (the one most protected by my sky-silver amulet) and lightly touched the slick, revolting surface, like thick black honey. My skin tingled and I yanked my hand away. "This is it. This is the threshold between our world and that malevolent ancient domain that constantly seeks to contaminate our lands and devour our souls. This is the portal through which all those lost people have vanished. We must close it tonight. Get the mirrors set up, and then we will harness the light and sing forth the secret spirits of our society. No more good citizens will be sacrificed here."

"Oh, you are wrong, Master Fox!" The Goblin King squatted in the dark doorway behind us. "You and your apprentices will make a fine repast for Those Below, with many more to come!"

Great. Just great.

I turned to face him. "Satisfy my curiosity, little man. Did you spring forth from some putrid egg as the story goes, or did your hag of a mother chance upon an entryway to another world while foraging for water?"

"You're good! Yes, poor mother had a scuffle with one of them while rooting around for water near a cistern dig. *They* don't survive long on this side of the void, as a rule. I was spawned to serve as a liaison between the worlds." He cackled horribly, pulling a thin obsidian blade from his belt. "As you can see, I got my good looks *from my father.*"

I had one idea about what to do next and it was a bad one.

"And where is the curious young lady?" he inquired.

"I sent her somewhere safe." His mention of Naabi clinched my decision.

"No, you didn't, Master Fox! When I'm done with the three of you I will find her. *So many things* I want to show her before—"

I leapt and twisted, snatching the vile creature by his arm. A terrifying few seconds of scuffle ensued before both of us plunged through the hole's black surface. The goblin shrieked, and I heard alarmed shouts from the twins just as I sank into the thick darkness below.

I have been between the worlds before; my heritage and training as a ghoul-breaker afforded me skills of survival. This portal, however, had opened into an environment I had never experienced. I floated slowly downward in the thick atmosphere, along with a sluggishly-thrashing goblin and a couple of the still-burning torches. I knew we would not be able to cross back through that threshold again; victims flung here would have done as I was doing, twisting, struggling to breathe, like flies trapped inside an insect-eating plant. The fiends on this side of the threshold would have one last meal before the twins closed the entrance forever, as I trusted they would. *At least King Goblin is no longer a threat to my world*. It was a price I was willing, but not eager, to pay.

I waited for the horrors to come for us, watching the torches dim weirdly in the miasma, their yellow light gradually dulling to an unnatural greenish glow. *Greenish… green… when you see the flame turn to green, you must look up*. Where had I heard that? *When you see the flame turn to green, you must look up!* Bee's words to me in my dream…

I looked up. Undulating in the space above me was a patterned, sea-blue radiance piercing the murky space. It looked like… an arm. *It was Naabi's tattooed arm, searching for me.*

With all the strength I could manage I thrust my body upward. It was like swimming through tree-resin, but I stretched for those glowing fingers. As her surprisingly powerful grip closed around mine and I was hauled upward and out into the exquisite air of my own world, I heard the dwarf-king's muffled howling intensify and caught a glimpse of things unspeakable swarming up from the depths toward him.

We scrambled madly out of the chamber. Outside, in the faint light coming through the doorway, I let Lord Chaac's sweet rain pour over me, washing the contamination of that evil place from my skin and clothes, to flow diluted and harmless down the pyramid's long staircase. No doubt those steps would wash red soon enough with the blood of sacrificial victims, but that would be in the service of the gods of *my* people, not those who should have vanished from beyond the void eons in the past.

Naabi flung her arms around me and hugged me silently, fiercely; the twins huddled in close, laughing with victory.

"I thought I told you to stay behind!" I snorted. She pulled back and gave me an incredulous look, then smiled.

"At least now we know what those tattoos are all about," teased Hun. "She just pushed her arm through that black muck unscathed, and we held onto her so she wouldn't go all the way in."

Itz'in crowed, "His Majesty the Goblin King, caught in his own trap."

I shuddered. "His Majesty the Goblin King is something's supper by now. Let's get back inside, young ones, we still have some work before us to close that portal tonight. Then tomorrow we must find and close the breach where the water-witch made her calamitous discovery. And *Naabi*—"

She turned to look at me, rain pouring off her half-blue nose.

"Let's not tell your mother about this one, shall we? Hell, what am I saying? I'm sure she already knows."

THE GHOST ADJUSTER: THE GHOST IN THE MACHINE

PAUL STJOHN MACKINTOSH

I don't like to talk about my work. Colleagues gossip about me enough already at our Edinburgh Exchange HQ. I've overhead the whispers and sniggers, caught the furtive glances. I know what they're saying. There he goes, the office pariah: Scotland's only insurance claims adjuster for ghosts.

It's been hell for my private life too. Morag gets no end of snide remarks at the WI and the PTA, and the Kirk on Sundays. Jennie got so fed up with the teasing that she stopped telling her school chums what her dad does for a living. Now she just treats me as some kind of standing embarrassment.

It's a mess, but what can I do? Whenever some lunatic client with this Ghostsafe gimmick package of ours actually makes a claim, they send for me. And I have to go through the whole formal rigmarole of assessing and adjusting the claim, all to demonstrate the utmost good faith.

Govan, my acting supervisor, treats the whole thing as a sort of ongoing ex-post moral hazard, like a dodgy business looking for a bail-out. I mean, who the hell would ever think of claiming for this kind of crap if it weren't for the Ghostsafe policy? I believe the only reason that we don't get more claims is that most policyholders would be as embarrassed to claim commercial damages from a haunting as we would be to pay out for it. As it is, we've probably been responsible for a big spike in Scotland's reported hauntings. I'd ask the Scottish Society for Psychical Research for the figures if I wasn't wary of feeding their idiot obsessions.

Mostly my job consists of weeding out the fraudulent claims. Weeding out? It's more like torching them with a flame gun. For a nation that prides itself on its brains, Scotland seems to produce more than its fair share of idiots. Probably the star claim was the franchised pub alleging that the noise in its hot water pipes was the voice of a dipso former owner. They're all pretty much like that, though. Well, almost all. The 0.01% that have enough substance to take even slightly seriously can be real sods. Like the case of LinnTel and the haunted rack farm.

I looked up LinnTel when the claim crossed my desk. The company dated from the Silicon Glen glory days, back when Rockstar North foisted *Lemmings* and *Grand Theft Auto* on the world, and the Lowlands looked to have a bright future in the Information Economy. I gather the founders had some smart ideas about rendering, to support companies like Rockstar with their digital animation needs. Then they ran into trouble when the tech bubble burst and their clients started retrenching or going bust, and a new bunch of investors took over the business. Nowadays the company wasn't much more than a glorified rack farm. And now the new management had filed a Ghostsafe claim. They were claiming, well... that their server farm was haunted.

The weather was fine and the air was fresh on the day I went down to the bottom end of the Royal Mile to assess the LinnTel claim. Couldn't imagine anything less spooky. I caught a bus down Grassmarket and Cowgate rather than leg it. No matter how lovely Auld Reekie is, that's more footslogging than I want to do in company time, even though it's downhill all the way. And I'll give LinnTel credit, they picked a fine location: right next to the new Parliament Building, and that weird Dynamic Earth albino hedgehog, in the shadow of Arthur's Seat.

"Look, if it was up to me, I wouldn't have made the claim," the CEO complained when I sat down with him in his office overlooking Queen's Drive. "But the VCs want me to try to maximize yield from the operation, so they made me do it. We've got a couple of big contracts in jeopardy because of this nonsense, and the ownahs want a backstop in case we have to default."

The CEO, name of Thorogood, was a Sassenach, with a heavily disguised Essex accent that made him finish 'owners' with a nah. He had that hangdog air of an usher or footman, whatever his C-suite title: the VCs' flunky.

"Well, I'll do my duty, but I'm sure it won't be hard to invalidate the claim," I reassured him. "I'm sure you've enough worries without this around your neck as well." Always good to have a claimant who's secretly on your side. And I couldn't help but feel a sneaking sympathy for him. After all, he was in the pretty much the same boat as I was.

My bosses kicked off the whole Ghostsafe idea as part of a rebranding exercise, another example of that wretched Americanized image-consciousness that filled Scotland's stations and railways with ghastly stripes and logos after British Rail was privatized. Our new image consultants were concerned that insurance was seen as staid, boring, off-putting. As though anyone expects entertainment value from a business based on risk, loss, injury and death. So they prodded us to come up with initiatives for making commercial insurance seem fresh, wacky, off the wall, and launched an in-house competition for the best ideas. And some bright spark dreamed up the idea of a commercial damages policy for loss of business caused by hauntings or psychic disturbances.

Insurance against ghosts.

As always, these plans take longer to implement than they do to dream up, and by the time our product development team had put together the Ghostsafe policy, the consultants had already flown, taking their fake tans and fat wads with them. The Global Financial Crisis broke, Scotland's financial services sector lurched into crisis mode, and the firm had less money to spare for fripperies. Back to basics, was the cry, now that our backs were against the wall. But instead of just winding up the whole ghost insurance exercise as a bad idea, the board decided that it was too expensive to decommission. And I was the one they picked to run the Ghostsafe policy.

The bastards knew they had me from the moment they called me in to "explain the situation." A new start, they said, a chance to shine, to do something different for a change. Translation: We don't want to use anyone more valuable on a white elephant like this – and if you think a waste of space like you is going to find a new gig in this business climate, think again. A fat pay rise, and a promotion, all because of qualities that would have doomed me anywhere else in the firm. In any firm. They took care to rub that in, just in case I'd missed the point. Near total lack of imagination. No creativity. No capacity for original or independent thought. That's what they pushed across the desk table at me, before they offered me the poisoned chalice. You didn't need much imagination or thought to see what they were getting at. So here I am, jerked around then dropped in shite; just like LinnTel.

The techie who showed me round the server farm wasn't very sympathetic to Thorogood, though. "Aye, the new VCs put him in when they bought out the previous investors," he explained. "He's nae programmer, just a manager type. They've passed the company from hand to hand since the business went tits up, each one trying to squeeze some more oottae it. Not like in Girvan's day, I can tell ye."

"Girvan?" I asked, recognizing the name from the company fact sheet.

"Aye, Girvan, the old CTO. Ye ken he died here?" the hairy techie declared, jerking his thumb towards one end of the vast, dimly lit facility.

That did give me a shiver, though it could have been the endlessly humming air conditioning in that huge dark hall. The long aisles of identical server racks with their glimmering blinkenlights did strange things to your sense of perspective, like a hall of mirrors. I fought an urge to look behind me, or to stick my head round the end of the racks, in case someone, or something, was in the next aisle. I wouldn't have wanted to spend the night in there, not that you could have told day from night in that enclosed space.

"What do you mean, died?" I asked the techie, Kynaston by the namecard on his blue coverall. "Is that where these ghost stories are coming from?"

Kynaston sniffed dryly, as if to show that he, at least, didn't believe in anything more ethereal than the digits flowing through a silicon chip. "Well, ye see, he lost his CTO title whan they switchit the business model from render farmin' tae data minin', but Thorogood kept him on as sysadmin, to keep the place running. He wis still the best, after aw. Then they startit pilin' on the pressure, tae meet their new targets. Girvan took tae spendin' his nichts i' the farm, runnin' on pizzas an' Irn-Bru. Finally, they came i' ane mornin an' found him at his console, dead."

I gasped, professional detachment or not. "Dead? Wasn't there an inquiry?"

Kynaston shrugged in disgust. "They couldnae find anything to implicate management. Nae signs o' overt pressure. Girvan, he wis a loner: nae wife or family, set his own schedule. Management were reprimandit ower it, but there were nae charges. Aw the new kids forgot him an' went back tae work."

"So what's the actual ghost story?"

"Oh, ye can imagine some o't," Kynaston snickered. "Maintenance crews reportin' strange noises; staff claimin' they see some faint figure oot o' the corner o' their een, disappearin' round the ends o' the racks. Amazin' how suggestible humans are. We try tae keep this as close tae a dark centre as we can, sae thon definitely helps the atmosphere."

"Dark centre?" I asked dumbly.

"You know: no lights, minimal human access. Braw environmentally friendly. Saves on the staff, tae. But that's nae really what's upsetting the business. No, the real problem's wi' the ghost code."

"Ghost code?" I goggled. The company's claim had said something about corrupted software, but I had no real idea what Kynaston was talking about.

"Girvan's digital signature keeps showin' up on our scripts. We've debuggit the system multiple times tae tak it oot, but it keeps croppin' back up. Na ane knows why."

"And that's supposed to be thanks to his ghost?" I chuckled nervously.

Kynaston gave me a straight look. "I'm na sayin' ah believe it. But our best programmers can't figure oot whit the reason is. An' Girvan wis a genius: big on information theory. He wad sit here wi' his can o' IrnBru, an' sound aff aboot the limits o' knowledge an' information density, an' hou self-awareness is a quantum phenomenon. Total dobber though, ye ken? I reckon he hung on here cuz he had nowhere else tae go."

"Fine, I'll see what I can do to get this ghost claim issue out of your hair."

I left him in his humming, flickering halls, glad to be out in the open again. Back in the office, I thought hard, and then reluctantly picked up the desk phone to call Quigley.

Quigley is our... well, our reinsurance. Our extra cover for Ghostsafe, in case a client doesn't think we're taking them seriously enough. His appearance would convince them if nothing else. He looks like a human version of one of those Japanese cute dogs, all bulging over-eager eyes. Plus he comes cheap. I think he'd pay us to get him in on the cases if we'd let him. I gather he's even got a bit of a bad rep in the SSPR, which gives you some idea. I mean, if even that bunch of numpties treat you as a social leper, well...

"I've got a beauty for you this time," I told him. "A haunted data centre. Hi-tech as you like. None of your cobwebs and dusty crannies. Let me know when you're free, and I'll fix up a time with them for you to go over the place."

Quigley was less happy when we got to LinnTel, though. "They won't let me bring my gear in," he grumbled. "They claim that radar imaging and ultrasound might disrupt the equipment. Superstitious bunch."

Kynaston stood in his way, adamant, arms folded.

"Call it what ye like," he declaimed. "There wis ae data centre not long ago brought doon by a lood noise. I dinnae want sonar in here."

I didn't feel like causing a scene on behalf of Quigley's nonsense, so in the end we made do with a few video cameras and thermometers. Quigley had a ball with the data centre's CCTV archives, zipping through hour after hour of footage in search of any transient image of the phantom of the rackspace.

"Gloomy, isn't it?" he bubbled. "You know that constant background hum is just the kind of thing to put the human mind into a receptive state, ready to pick up vibrations?"

I didn't answer that the background drone of Quigley's obsessive prattle was just the kind of thing to put my mind to sleep. He tried to foist himself on the LinnTel staff, though, asking me to set up interviews with the alleged eyewitnesses. That finally made me rein him in.

"This investigation is about disruption to the normal business of this data centre," I chided. "None of the statements about any manifestations suggested that lights and noises interfered with their work in any way – if those things even happened. You'll be bloody well interfering with their work if you badger them with questions, though."

Quigley pouted sullenly, then his face brightened like a kid who's just found a bulletproof excuse to get off homework. "If it's the software, I know just the man for the job. Programmed most of the SSPR apps and computer tools, including the image enhancement system. He can get these LinnTel guys onside."

I wanted to say no to Quigley, but I knew that the whole issue of the ghost code would have come up sooner or later anyway. We really couldn't throw the whole case out without going into it. So I shrugged, gritted my teeth, and decided to get it over with.

"Okay, call him," I told Quigley.

The SSPR IT nerd, Daily by name, showed up at my office two days later. That provoked a few more stares and stifled giggles. At least Daily wasn't a total eyesore like Quigley, but he was not the kind to sit down in a conference room in an insurance company and pass unremarked. The lurid green dayglo tee-shirt announcing 'Ghost Hunter' definitely didn't help.

"I've had some experience of digital revenants," he said impressively, then hurried on when he saw how deadpan sceptical my work face was. "I can talk to the IT team at your client, get their version of events, see if there really are traces in the system."

"If you find anything, Mr Daily, I don't want you making a song and dance over it," I pointed out. "If you can fix it, kindly do it. The less said about it the better. We'd much rather find nothing there, never mind any evidence of a ghost."

Daily looked almost as crestfallen as Quigley. Evidently they were two of a kind. I explained the usual contract terms, got him to sign the agreement, and fixed up a time to visit LinnTel.

Thanks to my bloody job, I now know much more about ghosts and psychic manifestations than I do about computers. So when I sat looking over Daily's shoulder at the scripts scrolling down the screen in the LinnTel data farm, they meant nothing to me. At least Daily and the LinnTel nerds seemed to get on with each other well enough: they both spoke the same incomprehensible lingo.

"Well, there's definitely something unco going on," Daily reported, scratching his head. "There are some rogue executables that seem to be hijacking the management programs. Don't seem like any typical malware or botnet software. But it is diverting resources and processing time towards some task of its own. And I've looked at the logs. Each time it's cleaned out, it comes back, always with the same signature."

"Can you find out who's doing it?" I asked.

Daily looked up from the screen and raised an eyebrow at me. Kynaston simply snorted.

"No one's doing it," Daily explained patiently. "It's self-replicating software. If Girvan's signature is kosher, it's probably legacy code left over from when he was still sysadmin. But it's definitely more adaptable, more...

well, alive, than typical code."

"Well, can you get it out?"

"That's not my department," Daily sighed. "I know Girvan's work. Guy was a genius, profiled in *Fast Company*, everything. Had some unique ideas for packing algorithms for flow optimization, based on bird flocking. And these guys have already been all over it. Lucky it doesn't seem to be a Heisenbug."

"Huh? A what?"

"You know: bugs that change their shape when they're studied."

"Oh, for a moment I was worried you were going to say something about cats."

Daily shrugged off the jibe.

"Well, is there any sign that it's of supernatural origin?" I continued lamely.

"All it is is code. Bits. Not ectoplasm. There's nothing there to show any unusual origins. I'll tell you one funny thing though. It only runs at night. During the periods when Girvan was on duty." He let that sink in. Hanging on his words, Quigley let out a small, ecstatic sigh.

"And I guess there's no way they'll turn the servers off for that time, right?" I asked.

Kynaston snorted. "Boss'll gae totally radge. Bad enoo tryin' tae meet his quotas."

"Send me your report and your invoice," I told Daily, anxious to wrap up my day with Quigley in server hell. "That's all I need for now."

Daily's report was just what I had hoped for, actually. It explained the ghost code purely as some kind of legacy from Girvan's time at the helm, with nothing psychic or supernatural at all about it. LinnTel would have a hard time making their claim stick now, and I didn't think they were about to call in a second opinion from other twitches of Quigley's ilk. Me, I was relieved that another crank claim had been, well, laid to rest.

Except that Daily surprised me a few days later, with an unexpected call. "I've been thinking over your ghost code problem at LinnTel," he announced. "And I think I can fix it."

"It's not my problem, it's theirs," I grumbled. "But let me talk to them and see what they say."

I had to take it to Thorogood, partly because I needed his signoff for Daily's fee. He wasn't impressed.

"Look, if you do an exorcism, bell book and candle and all that, fine, but just don't mess with the code," he snapped. "We came to you for commercial damages, not debugging. I have enough trouble keeping our assignments on track as it is. The last thing I need is some code monkey fucking up the system."

In the end, though, he agreed to a consult with Daily, and to a fix, if Kynaston and the other nerds approved it. I wasn't involved in the meetings, but Daily came back to me afterwards and explained his fix in layman's terms.

"Girvan wrote his code to have some autonomous features, so it reacts like a living thing and adapts to changes in its environment," he told me on Skype, against the seedy backdrop of his geekcave. "But it's code with a purpose: it sees everything in terms of the task it was designed for. Everything it comes into, it tries to render."

"So?" I riposted, still a little bit lost.

"Well, I wrote a buffer for Girvan's scripts. It's a layer of interpretive code for the scheduler. Whenever the scheduler receives a thread or other process that's tagged with Girvan's digital signature, or closely resembles one of his scripts, it implements an interpretive layer that convinces the process that it's still working within the old system, performing the work it used to do. Only it's now supporting the main effort. No one's been able to get his code out of the system, so it might as well be useful."

"Will it work?"

Daily shrugged. "I ran it past Kynaston's people. They're okay with it. Anyway, your outfit is off the hook. It's my responsibility, and Kynaston's, if he authorizes it. And there's no reason why it shouldn't work. It can't mess up the management platform anyway."

I could have left it there, but I felt I had to go along out of professional courtesy to see Daily do his little number. After all, LinnTel were still paying their premiums, and I was the one who had made the introductions, even if it was now Daily's show. Only, he said it had to be done at dead of night, to execute at the same time as Girvan's code ran, so he could keep an eye on it in real time in case anything went wrong. Kynaston had to be there to officiate for LinnTel, and Quigley came along for the ride. So the four of us convened in the server farm offices in the wee small hours, with capsule coffee from the office machine, to sit in on Daily's cyber-exorcism.

Daily sat down at one of the laptops in Kynaston's dungeon, with open windows showing reams of text which I took to be the actual processes running through the system.

"Where's your program?" I asked, expecting to see a memory stick or a portable hard drive, or even a CD.

"Oh, I shared it to the cloud," Daily explained casually. "Just have to wait for it to download, then I can run it. There." He poised his finger over the return key, watching the scripts scroll down the screen. "Okay, Girvan's code is running. Everyone ready?"

Kynaston nodded. Quigley sighed fervently.

"Execute." Daily pressed the key. Nothing much changed that I could see. The mix of colours in the scripts changed slightly, that was all. But after a few minutes, the tension seemed to ebb out of the room.

"It's working," Daily said, half to himself.

"So that's it?" I asked.

"My layer is interfacing with Girvan's script just fine," Daily confirmed. "It's optimising the farm's performance and reinforcing the main processes instead of interfering with them. The process gets executed, the work gets done, everybody's happy?"

"Happy?" I echoed. Kynaston kept his mouth shut, but his silence spoke volumes. Quigley nodded like a budgie in a mating frenzy.

"Happy. But it still doesn't answer the basic question," Daily sighed, massaging the back of his neck.

"What's that?"

"Well, whether those are bytes, or bits of Girvan."

"How do you mean?"

"I told you I couldn't get the bugs out of the system. You know I put that in the report; I just didn't say why. I can't tell whether it's the software doing that, or... something else."

He let the implication hang there. I jumped on it.

"But you can't prove whether it is something else, right?" I insisted.

"No," Daily admitted. "Maybe it's still Girvan in there somehow: the ghost in the machine. But all I can see is self-replicating code, doing its work."

That was enough for me. I made sure that Kynaston was happy with Daily's changes, then went to bed.

And indeed, everybody was happy, except perhaps Quigley. Thorogood and his LinnTel flunkies certainly were. After all, we'd sorted out their productivity issue. They weren't too particular about how we'd done it, but that didn't matter much to them. Even the VCs were sort of satisfied: LinnTel would keep running for a little while longer, until the time finally came to write it off as a bad investment. And everyone was spared the expense and the embarrassing publicity of a ridiculous court case. There was no way my employers would have paid up without challenging it in court, after all. So they were happiest of all, which was what mattered most to me.

Only, I can't help thinking of those dim aisles with their flickering lights, like some haunted cloister, and the endless, sleepless background noise of cooling fans. I gather that there are still some reports of phantom presences in the server farm, though nothing bad enough to upset the business. Is Girvan still there, beavering away inside the system, convinced that he's still doing his old job, even happy? Are the bits and threads within the data centre that he'd signed and left behind all pieces of him? All that matters?

Sometimes I think it's a good thing that I've got no imagination. Or at least, so HR says.

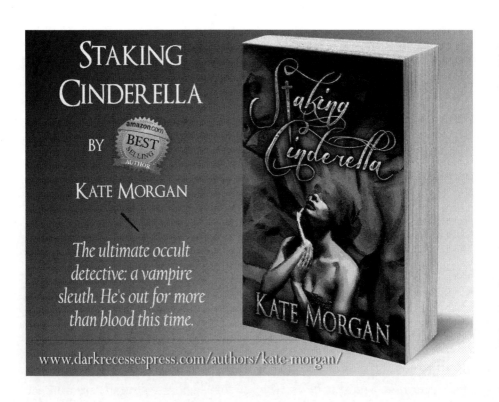

PAUSE FOR STATION IDENTIFICATION

JONATHAN RAAB and MATTHEW M. BARTLETT

The light above the basement entrance to the Cattaraugus County municipal building flickered in vain against the dark of an autumn night come early. Fog flowed down from the great green hills beyond, like smoke rolling off a carrion-pit fire.

Lieutenant Abraham Richards was thankful the county had granted their growing sheriff's department rooms in the derelict basement on the same campus as the jail and the courts. That was one step closer to the powers-that-be acknowledging Sheriff Cecil Kotto's operation as a legitimate one. But on these early autumnal nights when the wind was cold, fog came creeping down from the hills of the state forest, and the coyotes howled at a sinister moon well in advance of the witching hour, he had to admit that the place gave him the creeps.

This was his day off. *Had* been his day off. But being the number two guy on a police force only a handful strong – and working for a guy like Sheriff Kotto, who could slip into hysterics at the slightest provocation and bit of esoteric message-board pablum – he'd learned to be available. It wasn't that much different than being in the Army, really. You were never *really* off-duty.

He reached the concrete steps and ice-cold metal railing leading down to the basement door, the light bulb above ready to give out at any moment. The air was cooler in the shallow stairwell.

Before he could knock on the door, the knob rattled and locks disengaged. The hinges creaked as the door swung in, Kotto standing on the other side, half in darkness.

"*Richards*," he whispered. He leaned forward, the dim light casting his face in a funereal pallor. "Did you get my *message*?"

Richards entered and Kotto quickly shut the door behind him, engaging the locks.

"Something about 'we didn't do any of it, get down to the station.' That sum it up?"

"No," Kotto said. "That doesn't sum it up."

The main room stretched on past the reception area and a pair of duty desks to a conference table that reached back to the far end of the room. Side rooms partitioned off by frosted glass and creaking wooden doors served as Kotto's and Richard's offices, interrogation rooms, and general storage. An electronically key-coded door led to one of the jail's cellblocks, currently occupied by a small number of Cattaraugus County's degenerate shitheels. A green light on the pad blinked in the dark.

"Can we turn some lights on? And whose turn is it on cleaning duty? It smells like a brewery in here." Richards turned his head from side to side, searching for the sheriff. "Kotto?"

A tall flame erupted from the darkness on the far side of the room, orange-yellow spilling out and up from a metal flip-top lighter. Kotto's face appeared, leaning a cigarette into the flame. With a metal clap it was extinguished, and the glow from his cigarette tip bobbed in the dark.

"You know how Judge Crowley gets when the sprinklers go off," Richards said.

"Sit down, Abe."

Richards pulled out a metal folding chair that read 'ST. JOHN CATHOLIC CHURCH' in crooked stencil and sat down.

Across the room, Kotto sighed.

"Over here, Deputy. Jesus."

"This man-in-the-dark routine is giving me the creeps."

"Humor me."

Richards made his way over then took a seat across from the sheriff. On the table was a squat television-VCR combo rescued from a thrift store. Kotto pressed a button and the screen buzzed to life, casting them both in the pale blue glow of the standby screen. Kotto produced a plastic handle of Old Crow and a pair of short glasses bearing the Buffalo Bills logo, then proceeded to fill them both.

"I quit Old Crow. Hangovers are too gnarly."

"A new episode of *Freaky Tales From the Force* aired last night," Kotto said, ignoring Richards' remark and pushing a shot toward him before taking a gulp from his own.

"Right on schedule. Was it the one where we busted those kids pretending to be Sumerian demons in the woods behind the bowling alley?"

Kotto grimaced as he swallowed the cut-rate whiskey, then set the glass back down.

"No. We were due for a rerun. I've been recording the episodes to save them for posterity on an analog format."

"You're a man of the future."

"Just watch. And keep drinking."

The sheriff pressed PLAY.

* * *

Sheriff Cecil Kotto stands on a crumbling county road overlooking a river. The sheriff is wearing his camouflage Army-surplus jacket, his signature wide aviator sunglasses, and the ten-gallon cowboy hat he adopted a few months back. The silver sheriff's star over his left breast pocket glints in the golden light of a fall afternoon. The Allegheny River is framed by tree-covered hills that stretch down to touch the water in vibrant rushes of orange, yellow, and red.

The image is grainy, repeatedly spotted with flashes of distortion or errors in the film. Hisses and pops pollute the soundtrack, and Kotto's words are accompanied by irregular spikes and dips in volume.

"Only a couple of hours until sundown," Kotto says, speaking to someone off camera. He points off to one of the hills stretching down to the water from the north. The camera zooms in and struggles to focus. The trees there are especially robust, with bright red leaves rustling in the wind.

A shrill hiss begins to build in volume. The shot cuts to darkness and silence.

Then Kotto is walking along the road, wearing a hiking backpack and with a shotgun slung over his right shoulder. A deputy in dark blue uniform and sheriff's department ball cap is just ahead of him. Kotto calls out something inaudible and the figure turns, revealing Lieutenant Abraham Richards.

The editing is odd here, shots lingering too long on the out-of-focus movement of Kotto and Richards down the road; short, bouncing shots of the trees along the hills in the distance; blurry zoomed-in close ups of Kotto and Richards as they speak inaudibly to one another – and then of Veronica, the show's producer and secondary camera operator, walking a few feet behind the group. She's speaking to the cameraman and the officers in a series of shots. First on the road, then with Kotto, then sitting next to Richards as she pulls on her hiking boots and shares a laugh with the deputy.

"—dark we don't want to be caught out—"

"—shots of the ridgeline—"

"Can we get—"

"Signal strength growing out of—"

A hard cut to Kotto, Veronica, and Richards standing together in front of a metal trailhead sign. Ahead of them a narrow path cuts up through overgrowth and past tall, skinny gray trees that stretch up like petrified fingers. The camera moves in to reveal the USGS map of the forest in

Richards' hands.

"The trail's two miles up," Veronica says, pointing to a spot on the map. "The tower shouldn't be any more than half a mile from the trail's terminal loop. It'll be the highest point on the ridgeline."

"How do we know it's coming from the tower?" Richards asks. "And how'd it end up on the tapes?"

"We don't, and we're not even sure there *are* tapes," Kotto says. "Except that all the families corroborate that one detail, independently," Kotto says. "Before they went missing, those community college kids got obsessed with listening to a certain cassette tape, either alone or with friends."

The image becomes garbled static with a few frames from the previous shot intercut with what appears to be a figure in a white sheet, two eye holes cut out for vision like a cheap Halloween ghost costume. The figure walks down a dark hallway, directly toward the camera.

The three-shot of the *Freaky Tales From the Force* crew at the trailhead returns.

"—but the given translator's alphanumeric designation can't be in Massachusetts. It's similar to one a few miles away, but a few of the numbers are off. And I did some actual *research*," Kotto says, pulling out a map of his own and unfolding it. Three circles are drawn over the southern portion of Cattaraugus County and northern Pennsylvania. Several red marks dot the interior of the circles. "These are FCC complaints about the signal filed by people in the region. We're looking at a broadcast radius of about eight miles, give or take, depending on the weather, so about 100 miles or more total area."

"Add Kotto's detective work to local legends about this place," Veronica says. "The tower on this ridge doesn't appear on any official maps, including anything put out by the Geological Service. But I know about it. Plenty of people around here do. My *nagyapa* – my grandfather, he used to take me hiking through these hills. Mountains, I guess, although they're old, beaten down by time."

"Hanging out at the Legion about a year ago, I got to talking to some of them old military boys," Kotto says. "A few of them into radio. Turns out, there was a numbers station in the region – used to play a little ice cream jingle, then a girl would start reading numbers. Amateur radio operators recorded a bunch of it, but it went off the air sometime after the first Gulf War. It's been silent since then. Until now."

"Like, secret military broadcasts or spy network, that type of thing?" Richards says.

"Good, you've been studying the research materials I left in your bathroom," Kotto says. "For whatever reason, this one is back online, but it's not the usual spy code stuff."

"Why would some community college students record pirate radio onto outdated cassette tapes and start sharing them with their friends?" Richard asks. "And what does that have to do with them going missing?"

The image cuts out in a wash of static and oscillating noise.

The figure in the ghost costume is closer to the camera now. Ancient and worn leather shoes poke out from underneath the folds of the sheet, which flutters softly. It takes another pair of steps forward.

A clock ticks with voluminous raps, one after the other.

Just out of focus, in the background at the end of the hallway, stands that grandfather clock, partially obscured by the sheet-covered figure in the foreground. Slowly, its wood and glass case door begins to open, revealing the swinging pendulum. A slurry of static emerges from the lower left-hand corner of the frame, working its way up and across.

The sheet flies off the figure, pulled by an unseen hand. The fabric whips and snaps, brought to the floor where it rests.

The shoes stand alone, and nothing obstructs our view of the grandfather clock.

The door on the clock slowly swings back, snapping shut with a soft *click*. The pendulum halts, suspended diagonally for what feels like a lifetime.

Crawling static overtakes the image. Briefly, there's a face in the storm – or rather, a head. Eyes, floating beneath curled horns, staring not at the viewer, but beyond. At something in the room with us, perhaps. Something that we don't know is there.

The shot cuts out and there is a series of brief shots of the group moving up along the trail. It's darker now.

A crackle of electronic interference overwhelms the audio track, and the words of the figures are lost to the noise. Voices, not those of the trio, sweep in from other places, distorted, some faraway and faint, others startlingly loud and close.

... the odor of intercourse and the rays of the planets... gray, black, the color of saffron, hold the eyes like berries in your mouth until the conjunctiva is dissolved by the acidic... savory and... hold the raw cruor between your back teeth, let the words... float... brain. Sacred hair... Dr. Nine-Hundred Ninety Nine takes his due... milky rim of the cosmic... intertwine...

The voices are overtaken by a burst of staccato drums like gunfire and they fall back into the static, ghosts sinking into a fetid pool of grue.

Now the shot is set just behind Richards, who is leading the way up the hill. Richards raises a fist and turns back, moving a finger to his lips. The deputy makes his way back down over the rock-strewn trail to talk.

"Dean, did you hear that?" he whispers to the cameraman. The camera shakes right to left and back again.

Kotto shouts something in the background.

"Quiet," Richards hisses. He looks up, the camera following his gaze. A rat's nest of branches obscures most of the dark gray sky overhead. Shadows of great weight and volume perch above.

One of them moves, the air suddenly thick and rushing. The group cries out as an impossible darkness takes flight with the flapping of great, foul wings.

"What the hell was that? What the hell was that? One of those... friggin' cranes or something?"

"That thing wasn't a crane. Couldn't have been a goddamn crane."

Static.

A hallway, with large bricks freshly painted a calming blue in a shallow stripe along the middle. Two young women standing next to an open door – a classroom, perhaps, or a lab. There are bars on the side of the screen – someone is filming on a cell phone held vertically. The women see the camera and frown.

"Don't put some stupid filter over me," one of them says, holding her hands over her face.

"Never," a male voice says. "I brought you a gift." He holds a plastic rectangle up in front of the phone. Illegible black letters are scrawled across a strip of crooked masking tape.

"It's a cassette!" The woman covering her face opens her mouth in surprise and snatches the tape. "I remember these. I think my dad's got a player in his garage."

"Real cool, analog shit," the man says. "Pirate radio. Try it out."

"What kind of pirate radio?" the woman with the tape asks, her eyes never leaving the cassette.

"Something scary."

"I don't like scary stuff."

"You'll like this."

Static.

A sound like water bubbling up. A mad, helpless volley of laughter. A blaring burst of trumpets.

Static.

The trail leads further up the hill, the bright colors of autumn peak everywhere. Kotto, staring off past the camera. The forest isn't quiet. The forest is never quiet, for those who listen.

There's a pervasive aural wash, a rush of paper leaves moving in the October wind, that underpins everything. A terrible but soothing song deep within the world's foundations. The wind, and the trees and the leaves, and the terrible gray cloud sea overhead.

The camera slowly moves in on Kotto, framed as he is against the ascending trail. His jaw moves while his lips are closed. After a moment he removes his hat and looks at his distorted reflection in the silver star affixed to its center.

"This feel wrong to you?" he asks. Someone shuffles off-camera. Veronica's voice is faint, lost in the rush of wind. The audio levels are all wrong.

Static.

The lawmen have their flashlights out and the camera's mounted light is on. They work together to illuminate the path ahead – which is barely a path at all now, but an overgrown logging road, great ditches and trenches carved by tractor and truck wheels decades ago, slowly being reclaimed by the forest.

Richards has taken the lead again. He curses as he slips in some mud, barely able to maintain his balance. He scrambles up a patch of rocks held together by a black, shiny slime, interwoven with dead branches and hostile earth. He turns to shout something back at the others, but static and a hard cut to a gravestone rob us of his warning.

In this shot the day is bright. There's a soft breeze blowing, tickling the slightly overgrown grass blades and flower petals set against the gravestone. There's a name on the stone, and a short span of years, freshly carved and unworn by the elements. Either the cicadas are screeching in the nearby woods, or a woman is crying off-camera.

Cut to sneakers rushing over a series of cracked and desiccated squares of sidewalk. The camera pulls up to a telephone pole leaning at an ugly angle. Affixed to all sides of it at eye-level are photocopied 'MISSING' posters, the smiling faces of the young women we've seen before – and many more that we haven't seen yet – staring out at us from the past. They have names and nicknames and descriptions and desperate pleas from their parents and friends, all typed up or written in black marker beneath those blurry portraits, the sum total of their short lives distilled down to single sheets of want and pain.

Static.

Back in the forest. This is Veronica's handheld camera, capturing a shot of a purple backpack hanging on to a branch high in the air by a single strap, its zippered pocket open to reveal a college-level *Introduction to Biochemistry* textbook, like a limp tongue hanging at the edge of a dead mouth.

She moves the camera and reveals more backpacks, hanging just out of reach. Shirts, jackets, rain shells, a single sneaker.

"What do you think the odds are that we'd stumble upon this?" Richards asks. "What are the chances?" The question hangs cold in the air.

The perspective shifts to an extreme long shot of the group from a camera mounted high above them. Impossibly above them, unmoving. Lo-fi quality, likely a shot from a camcorder, a VHS-on-TV-on-VHS downgrade rabbit hole.

Kotto says something – too far away to hear – and the group slowly continues on uphill.

The shot lingers as they move further away, but the camera captures the crunching and squishing of their struggling steps over wet earth and leaves.

Waves of distortion begin to move across the screen in regular intervals and a shrill buzzing grows in volume. Shadows stretch out their lengthy arms and legs and lean forward from their dark hiding places among the trees to spy the group as they struggle through the forest.

The waves increase in frequency until that impossible angle is lost, replaced by the slow fade-in of Dean's camera POV once more.

"There, in the break in the trees!" Richards shouts. The camera zooms in and tilts up to spy the concrete building base and metal radio tower that stretches into swirling gray sky. Red altitude lights blink along the superstructure, ominous and staining the hazy air like glowing blood.

The others hurry to catch up with Richards when he begins shouting again. The images and audio jumble together in the rush up the hill.

"Sheriff's Department!"

"I don't see anyone."

"Didn't you hear them?"

The camera settles on Richards standing in front of the door leading into the concrete building. The deputy looks back and forth, shining his high-powered flashlight into the depths of the shadows and overgrowth enveloping the radio tower. The audio is punctuated by flapping distortion – or distorted flapping – and shrill tones as the wind at the top of the hill is whipped into a frenzy.

"They said, 'Sheriff.' I heard it!"

Dean swings the camera over to Kotto and Veronica, who are both staring up at the tower. It stretches impossibly high, its many red lights blinking and glowing against the swirling darkness of the storm. An imperfection in the tape or electrical interference cuts across the image, the audio popping and hissing. For a handful of frames, the tower isn't metal at all, but bone, slick not with rain, but with blood. Blood that falls from the sky in great, heaving sheets of crimson. Instead of wires there are entrails, pulsating with impossible life, slithering almost imperceptibly slow over the superstructure for some mad and baffling end known only to the mad wizard who brought forth such a terror of unreality.

The image goes stark-white, as if the sun emerged suddenly and overwhelmed the sky. The audio drops and there is black, nothing but black.

Then, the chirping of insects, the crackling of wood, a soft wind caressing dying leaves.

Fade in to a group of six young people – the young women from earlier are among them – sitting around a dying fire. They are huddled close to it, arms and shoulders brushing up against one another. Placed on the log in the foreground is a portable radio and cassette player, twin speakers facing the camera and not, oddly enough, the young men and women who have presumably brought it out into these dark woods.

A voice, soft and quiet at first, raising in volume and intensity as it delivers its sermon, the dissonant chords of an out-of-tune pipe organ lifting its own fractured, multitone voice, provides a demented choir as backdrop:

Brothers and sisters, entwined like wires, spilt like wine across motherboards and fatherlands, shattered and disintegrated and spewed into the air to be breathed in by your sons and daughters! Corruption takes hold! Motes in the bronchi! Spreading through the alveoli! Absorbed into the blood – the osmosis of blackness and blight! Diseases handed down like musty heirlooms! The blood goes to the brain as oil to a flame and singes the inside of your skull. Life is a blink of blue light in a carrion-black cave. Existence is madness, nonsense, the scribbling of a lunatic on the moldy walls of a cell within a cell, somewhere a phone ringing, no one calling nothing, no answer, no hope. Hope is a tumor in the marrow, a shot synapse, an error somewhere too deep down in the coding to be located and corrected. You cannot build a house on shifting sands, rear a child in a locked mausoleum...

Great figures of dark and shadow – yes, the ones we've seen before, with spindly limbs of impossible length and thinness – lean in to wrap their terrible appendages around the listeners. The young men and women have slack faces and pale skin, and react not at all as they are lifted high into the trees, leaving the camera-facing radio to preach for us and us alone.

Static.

The team is inside now, presumably within the tower's bunker-like base. Their flashlights cut through the darkness, roving beams of pallor on concrete and cobweb-covered electronic commitment. Blank, curved monitors from decades past stare out at them from panels and workstations long-abandoned.

"Those local HAM weirdos were convinced if there's something weird on the airwaves, it'd probably be coming from here."

"This place is a tomb," Richards says. "There's no power."

"Those red altitude lights say otherwise," Veronica says. She brings her own camera up and the POV switches to hers. She is pointing the camera at the back of the room. The mounted light cuts through the dark to reveal another door, labeled with a military-style stenciled placard that reads 'GENERATOR ROOM'.

"Why don't we try in there?" Veronica says, moving to the door. Her hand emerges from behind the camera to try the black, mold-encrusted door lever.

"Wait, wait."

Richards and Kotto jog over to her, pistols drawn and perched over the flashlights in their off hands. Kotto lines up behind Richards, who waits at the edge of the door. He nods toward Veronica. The producer turns the lever. Metal groans and warbles all around them as if she has just triggered the secret opening to a great and terrible tomb of a Cold War-era mummy.

She pauses, just for a moment, then pulls the door open towards her, revealing a gulf of darkness beyond and a rush of air that turns her news anchor-pretty face into a mask of disgust.

Kotto and Richards rush into the chamber. Flashlight beams cut like knives through the deep black, revealing dust motes swimming in languid air. Richard cuts left, Kotto right, moving to the corners of the room, scanning the dark and unknown.

"Oh, shit."

"What is...?"

"What do you see?" Veronica shouts.

"Bring the cameras," Kotto responds.

Veronica and Dean shuffle into the room. Static and interference mess with both cameras as they enter. We cut back and forth between the two. The images warp and fray, and their auto-focus and auto-exposure settings go flaky, resulting in a parade of color, darkness, and unstable movement.

There are voices in the signal, quiet, but buzzing with reverb and distortion. Even as the images begin to self-correct, leaving only a fingerprint of interference and static and the occasional frame skip behind, we hear those voices. Singing.

Brrrroooaaadcast

From Leeeeds Maaaasss

Paaauuse for staation iiidenttification

Veronica and Dean move their cameras to follow the flashlight beams back to Kotto and Richards, who are moving toward the horrors (*Broooooadcaaast*) congregated at the center of the room.

Boom boxes, Walkmans, cassette players. Portable radios, (*From Leeeeds Maaaasss*) speakers, mixing boards.

Wires connecting them all, co-ax, power, exposed copper wire.

(*Pause for station identification*)

"What the hell am I looking at?" Richards says.

The radio and audio equipment appears to be haphazardly strewn about in a great gyre in the center of the room. But as the cameras and lights sweep over it, wires running back and forth like veins and arteries of some great analog god eviscerated, we see the intentionality, the pattern, the mad design linking it all together. When we hear the first groan of pain, when the cameras turn to the center of the room, the grand design becomes shockingly clear.

"There's people here," Veronica says, carefully stepping over a series of speakers. "Oh, Jesus Christ." She tilts the camera down and switches to manual focus as light splashes across pale, slack faces appearing out of the dark like distant lanterns at dusk. Their eyes are wide and unmoving, their mouths ajar at odd angles.

Dean moves in with his camera, and we get a better sense of scale to the desecration: the bodies here are a tangled mass of limbs and wires, connected and holding on to one another in a pattern that presents itself only from multiple angles and in those long moments beyond the shock of unbelief.

"It's a pentagram," Veronica says, moving her camera from face to face. "Jesus, it's those kids from the internet videos."

"Veronica, I don't want you in the center of that thing," Deputy Richards says, trying to sound confident but not coming across that way at all.

"There's wires in their skin," Veronica says, kneeling down to follow a bundle of cables that splits off and is embedded in three separate (*corpses?*) people. The cables are thick but flexible, coated by a corroding metal, with copper insides exposed at random intervals as if something has been

chewing on them. The cables pierce skin along ankles and wrists, driving into abdomens and wrapping around necks before snaking into the yielding flesh of exposed throats.

"Can we pull them out?" Kotto asks, standing at the edge of the human-and-wire pentagram, running his flashlight back and forth. The beam settles on a large pillar of darkness in the center of the inverted star.

"I don't think so," Veronica says. She is standing over a young woman – the skeptical one from the video we've seen earlier – and gingerly runs her fingers over a small black wire running directly into the girl's trachea. Veronica tenses as her fingers move from rubber insulation down to flesh, expecting a reaction. None comes.

"Her skin is still warm."

"Yeah, they're breathing," Richards says, shining his flashlight down on the man whose head meets the feet of another, forming one of the star's five points. "We need to get EMTs up here. Maybe HAZMAT."

Dean follows the sheriff with his camera, watching the lawman carefully step through the pentagram of missing persons to the obelisk at the center. He tries to focus the camera on the object, which reaches from the floor to the low ceiling. The image frays and is flooded with static whenever he trains the lens on it.

"Can any of you *see* this thing?" Kotto asks. He waves his flashlight back and forth. "I see there's something here, but it absorbs all the light."

"Sheriff, you got any context for any of this?" Richard asks. "Any sort of crackpot theory or obscure occult reference?"

"I think we should get out of this radio tower," Kotto says. "I think we should seal this whole place in with concrete and never look back."

"This is supposed to be the generator room, right?" Dean says, panning his camera from Kotto and the dark-thing to the rest of the room beyond. "I don't see any generators, do you? I don't even see the far wall. How big is this room?"

"This *is* the generator," Kotto says, the courage gone out of his voice. He gestures to the people, the wires, the radios, and the audio equipment at the pentagram's periphery. "We're standing inside the generator."

A sudden buzzing startles the crew. We alternate between Veronica and Dean's cameras. A repetitive warbling and warping can be heard.

The noise grows louder – hissing, an electric-tinged oscillation, underpinned by synthesizer notes and analog tones, drawn out and low, or high and poppy and distorted, a soup of aural detritus from broadcast's bygone era, when signals would cease after the appropriate hours and the whole world became distant and lonely.

Grey light, faint at first, grows into television static reflecting off of the crew's terrified faces, glowing up at them from out of the open eyes and mouths of the missing, those now arrayed into an infernal configuration of power and transmission. The signal is gaining strength; the tower will soon transmit.

There's shouting now, and a flurry of activity from our public access television stars. But maybe there's movement from those locked into the pentagram, too, arms reaching up and mouths spilling out static wash as if it were vomit. The camera angles twist and tumble, and another image bleeds over into this recording, like old-style antenna channels used to cross and co-mingle and create a dual world of voices and sound and color. In this static crossover, we see great black horns, shifting and bucking over a limitless field of stars hanging over the deepest and blackest of midnight hours.

There's gunfire now; it's hard to tell the difference between the discharge of pistols and the popping and distortion of fused transmissions and frenetic images captured on corrupted digital memory cards.

Brooooooaaadcaaaassst

The occasional image gains clarity in the chaos: hands pulling wires out of flesh; geysers of black blood and gore; a procession of robed figures, carrying smoking, swinging censers as they emerge from the far side of that limitless room.

From Leeds, Mass

Richards' face, shouting directly into a camera; the phrase "coming out of the angles" drowned out by gunfire; one of the cameras knocked to the ground, stationary, as a pair of legs and feet are lifted off the ground at the side of the frame. A pained gurgling and a thick spray of blood onto the floor and lens. A veil of red, illuminated from behind by the beam of a dropped flashlight.

Pause for station identification.

* * *

The image flipped from black to blue as the tape wound to a halt, casting the room in a pale azure glow. The VCR whirred and clicked. Kotto leaned over and hit the rewind button.

The bottle of Old Crow had rapidly diminished over the course of those twenty two minutes.

Richards stood up suddenly, pushing away from the table and walking back toward the basement office's entrance. Kotto lit another cigarette.

Outside, the wind harried the trees, disgorging leaves in colorful, dark bursts.

"Has anyone else seen this?" Richards asked. "Any calls in to the broadcast station? The FCC, even?"

"I thought of that," Kotto said. "I called around. Talked to Veronica and Dean. I haven't showed them the tape yet. Not sure I want to."

Richards turned away from the door's window and made his way back over to the table.

"As far as I can tell," Kotto said, putting out his cigarette. "Everyone else saw a rerun."

"You recorded this off the broadcast, right?"

"I did. At my house. I record every episode."

"So this *was* broadcast."

"To my house, yes." Kotto paused to take a long drag from his cigarette.

"Someone made this… movie or whatever, and then beamed it directly to you? That seems impossible."

"Those weren't actors. That's *us* on the tape."

"That wasn't… I would have remembered something like that. It looked like they *killed* Dean."

"Dean's fine," Kotto said, reaching over and ejecting the tape.

"What about the tower? Anything like that in the county?"

"I've been reaching out to my uncle's weirdo radio enthusiasts, talked to the Ellicottville Fire Department – even called the FCC. The guy I got ahold of seemed *real* interested in what I was talking about."

"And?"

"And nobody had anything for me. The FCC guy just took my statement and said he'd be in touch. Nothing since then. I've heard rumors of numbers station activity in this area from time to time, but nothing down near the Allegheny River or National Forest."

"That's a relief."

"That doesn't mean there's nothing there. Abe, we *could* go check it out."

The office suddenly felt much, much colder.

"Did you catch that last bit at the end?" Kotto asked. "The singing?"

"I couldn't make it out. I was a little distracted watching me and my friends get killed by robed maniacs."

"It was a chorus. Kept repeating. 'Broadcast, from Leeds, Mass. Pause for station identification.' "

Richards shook his head. "Does that make sense to you?"

" 'Leeds, Mass.' There's a town in rural Massachusetts with that name. It's about seven hours away."

"You're thinking about going."

"I don't know what I'm thinking," Kotto said, taking another drink.

"I think you should leave this alone."

"Yeah."

The two men sat in silence. Wind rattled the glass window on the main door.

"We shouldn't show this to Veronica or Dean," Richards said. "No way."

"I know."

"I wish you hadn't shown it to me."

"I know. I'm sorry."

"Are you going to destroy it?"

Kotto tapped out his cigarette into an empty cola can.

"Dunno."

"Do you think it's… important? Like, a message? Maybe a warning, or something?"

Kotto nodded, leaning over the table and holding his head in his hands.

"That's what I'm afraid of."

* * *

The cold front brought with it a furious wind, the rushing of air and the tumbling of branches and leaves drowning out all else. Richards' ears burned at the barrage of cold.

The deputy got into his truck, inside which the air was mercifully still. He started the engine, letting it and the heating system warm up a moment.

He placed his hands on the steering wheel and leaned forward. He was tired, much more tired than he was before he arrived. The images on that small screen played back in his memory, warped and indistinct now, but still painful and frightening, jagged angles of light and sound, his own face staring back at him from that screen, shouting a warning from a past or a future or a reality that couldn't possibly exist.

A great shiver ran through him, one that had nothing to do with the cold.

He put the vehicle into drive and flicked the headlights on, then reached over to turn on the radio.

At the last moment, his hand hovering over the console, he thought better of it.

Author's Note

Matthew M. Bartlett's WXXT mythos, first explored in *Gateways to Abomination* and its follow-up *Creeping Waves* has been a constant, looming presence over the independent horror literature scene for years. I knew I wanted my Sheriff Kotto character to encounter it in one shape or another, and with the hybrid novel/anthology *Freaky Tales From the Force: Season One* I gave myself the chance. Matt's contributions here are in the monologue sections from whatever voice WXXT happens to be speaking through. Like me, he's a big fan of *The Blair Witch Project*, which has an obvious, ever-present influence on this story.

Jared Collins and Mississippi Bones wrote the chorus 'Broadcast / From Leeds, Mass / Pause for Station Identification' on their album *Radio Free Conspiracy Theory*, which I had the honor of co-writing. You can listen to it for free via their Bandcamp page.

— Jonathan Raab

THE CASE OF THE SIGNET RING

AARON VLEK

I

Geoffrey Sykes Vermillion was pondering over an ancient Chinese puzzle box in the downstairs study, whilst outside a freezing rain pelted the leaded glass windows with renewed vehemence.

Audrey Hawkwoode glanced up from her book and smiled. "Reminds me of home in the Hudson Valley," she mused, before returning to her worn copy of a book by that noted occultist and colourful character about town, Aleister Crowley. She was still dressed in the leather breeches and tunic from her morning ride, and had barely made it back to the house before the sky opened up and drenched the city.

Allegra Barlow's hands fell away from the harp where she was playing a work of her own composition, a study in four parts dedicated to the Egyptian god Shu, the lord of storms and wind.

"I'd say the old boy was quite pleased with my efforts," she said stretching her fingers and retreating to the fire to warm herself. "Don't you agree, Vermillion?"

"Hmmm?" came the soft reply from the desk.

"I said, I think Shu likes the piece I have composed for Saturday's festivities, don't you agree?" she asked, gesturing to the storm harrowing the town house.

Vermillion put down the puzzle and stared at her for a moment. "Yes, it's an admirable work, I'd say. Although the second refrain lagged a bit and was noticeably repetitive of the first in the last five bars, but I'm sure it will be easy enough for you to remedy. Perhaps a minor key would lend the necessary suggestion of foreboding to hint at the glorious cacophony of the final triumphant volley. This is the lord of storms, Allegra, not the cherub of a gentle spring rain," he concluded, smiling wickedly.

"You're absolutely right, of course." Allegra snapped, bristling at his measured approval where she had expected nothing but a glowing report. Before she could launch a stinging repartee that would remind him just who he was dealing with, a light knock at the door heralded the arrival of Maspeth, Vermillion's manservant.

"A lady to see you sir. No appointment, but she's quite insistent. Shall I tell her to call on the morrow for an appointment?"

"Not at all, Maspeth," Vermillion replied. "Show her in. It must be important to compel the poor thing out in such a deluge."

"Very good, Sir."

Maspeth returned a moment later with a quietly dressed young blonde woman of about twenty-five, her face red from crying and a handbag clutched tightly to her bosom.

The scene might have seemed ordinary to any uninformed visitor. A man and woman of middle age; he of imposing height and bearing and dressed in a severe black suit as was his custom; she, beautiful but austere in her copper bobbed hair, perched like an egret before a magnificent harp, whilst a young ingenue in smart riding attire lay draped lazily over a club chair, book in hand. The truth was anything but ordinary, and nothing was as it seemed.

Geoffrey Sykes Vermillion, traveller, occult detective and master of all things arcane, was known by reputation in society, and presumably this was why the newcomer had sought him out in the middle of a ravaging storm. The lady musician, however, was not his wife, but rather the mistress of Anubis Lodge, an order of occultists rivalling the likes of Crowley and his sometimes questionable entourage; the girl, Audrey Hawkwoode, was Vermillion's protégé, an intrepid student of the occult herself and a seasoned member of his party despite her tender twenty-two years.

"Do come in, Miss...?" Vermillion extended a hand in greeting.

"Mrs Caroline Hilliard," she replied, holding out her card.

"Well, do sit down. How can we be of assistance Mrs Hilliard?" Vermillion asked, examining the card closely. "You are aware of the specific nature of my work, and the sort of cases that constitute my line, are you not?"

"Oh yes!" The woman collapsed into a chair with a defeated air, glancing at the other two women. "If I might catch my breath. I've been walking for hours, I wasn't sure if I should call on you or not." She pushed an errant strand of blonde hair back in place.

"Please, be at ease, madame. May I introduce Miss Audrey Hawkwoode, my assistant and protégé, and Miss Allegra Barlow, my friend and trusted colleague. You may speak freely among us."

"I don't know how to begin, really. You see, it's about my late husband," she said, almost coming to tears.

"I'm very sorry. When did he die and under what circumstances?" Vermillion inquired, motioning to the brandy on the sideboard and smiling when the woman nodded. Allegra retrieved a glass and served the woman as she fumbled in her handbag again and brought out something tied up in a red cloth.

"Well, my husband, Asher Hilliard, died over a year ago in Afghanistan. I was here at the time of his death. We had not been getting on for some months, and since he was buried in Herat in the north part of that country, I saw no reason to trek half way across the globe to attend the funeral."

"Buried in Herat, you say? That seems an irregular turn. Was he posted there, an army man?" Vermillion motioned for Audrey to take notes and was pleased to see that the girl was already scribbling in her case book.

"No, well, he had been some years ago. My husband was a good deal older than I and had his career well behind him when we married. He was in Afghanistan on some matters pertaining to his club, although I don't know much about it. His friends there, his lodge brothers, handled the affairs of the burial."

"Lodge brothers?" Allegra Barlow interjected sharply. "Was he a Mason? Or was this some other sort of lodge?"

"No, he was not a Mason, I know that. My father and brothers are Masons and he was not known to them. I married against my family's wishes you see. As far as this lodge or its doings I have no idea, as they neither involved me nor did I ever attend their gatherings here in London."

"Then what has troubled you so if he is long dead?"

"Oh, Mr Vermillion!" Mrs Hilliard gasped in desperation. "I received this today in an unmarked courier's post," she said, undoing the red cloth and dropping its contents, a signet ring with a large blue stone worked with intricate sigils, into Vermillion's waiting hand.

"And what is this?" Allegra asked, walking up to Vermillion. She took the thing to examine more closely, and then shook her head in puzzlement.

"This was my husband's lodge ring," said the visitor.

"You're sure this is his very ring?"

"Yes, look at the inscription inside the band, our two names entwined. It even has the exact scrape mark from the time my husband took a fall in the street not long after we were married."

"And the significance of it? You have no idea who sent it to you or why?"

"Mr Vermillion, my husband… this ring never left his hand. He was buried with it!"

"I see." Vermillion's eyes narrowed.

"May we keep it for a while, to check the inscriptions and seals?" Allegra asked, handing it back to Vermillion. "I've not seen this particular sigil and it's from no order known to me."

"Oh yes!" Caroline Hilliard's lips curling in disgust. "I want never to see that horrid thing again! Throw it in the river for all I care."

"Well then, Mrs Hilliard, was your husband and this lodge of his involved in the unpleasant sort of occult, perhaps?" Vermillion said, gently urging the woman to get to the heart of her story.

She just sat there, her fists knotted in her lap and her eyes darting to each of them and toward the door as if she might flee at any moment.

"If it's difficult for you to talk about your late husband, again I assure you we are sworn to the greatest discretion in all things."

"I do trust you Mr Vermillion." Her voice was barely above a whisper, her eyes brimming with tears. "I just, well, there are delicate details I've not shared with anyone..."

"I see. Delicate details." Vermillion noticed the colour rising to her cheeks. "Would it help if I left you to speak with my lady colleagues in private?"

She brightened at the suggestion. "Oh yes, would you mind terribly? It's just that I—"

"No explanation required, madame. I shall return." Vermillion rose and left the room closing the door behind him.

"I assure you that Audrey and I are fully experienced in Vermillion's business and are adept along these lines in our own right," Allegra said pulling her chair up closer.

"So, where to begin then?" Caroline said with a sigh. "When I married, I was just a foolish girl. Of course I had never, that is to say, spent time alone with a man, in any sense, any personal sense that is," she stammered, a blush reddening her cheeks.

"I understand," Allegra said with a disarming smile.

"Well, that first night, the night of our marriage, was thoroughly unpleasant but I did my best. There was so much about my husband I dared not question. He was obviously a very wealthy man, but I had no idea what his business was.

"None of my family or friends knew of him or his family in society. He was a complete mystery to us and I'm afraid this made the whole affair all the more thrilling. I fell in love with him, and all too quickly we were married."

"Where did you meet and how did your relationship begin?" asked Allegra.

"I met him in the street if you can believe it! I assure you, I'm not a brazen woman, never would I have spoken to a man I did not know in the street, and never would I have allowed him to take me to lunch that very day, as I did. I was not the sort of woman who sought out silly adventures or anything outside my proper life before that moment!" Caroline shook her head and downed the rest of her brandy.

"When I announced my impending marriage to my horrified parents they demanded I break the whole thing off immediately. A fortnight later we fled to Venice and were married in a dazzling palazzo on the Grand Canal amidst a robed and masked throng out of some carnival dream.

"I was absolutely drunk on it all and prided myself on being so grown up and cosmopolitan. I can assure you, I was neither! But the things that went on in that palazzo mortify me now in memory, while they seemed thoroughly glorious at the time. I cannot speak of them, but I assure you…" Caroline said, choking the words out and stifling a sob.

"There is no need, I can well imagine," said Allegra.

"After several weeks we returned to London, where I was ensconced in my husband's house with a bevy of servants. I rarely saw Asher except on those occasions when he sought out my bed. We maintained separate quarters in that house.

"The curious thing was each time he came to my bed his actions were strange and unlike what I had come to expect from hearing of my sister's wedded bliss. For one thing, prior to our, our coupling, he always made me gaze into the blue stone of that horrible ring I gave you. I had to concentrate on its inscriptions and the strange squiggles and slashes upon its surface. After several minutes of this I would fall into a sort of trance during which I had many troubling dreams about the people we had stayed with in Venice.

"What was also disquieting was that Asher always said a great many things during our coupling, strange sounding words in some foreign language, a sort of chanting that rose to a crescendo as he finished with me, and which filled me with loathing. He sounded triumphant, and so full of hate…"

She broke off and tried to compose herself.

"Then he'd return to his own rooms and I would fall into a dark swoon from which I awoke only late the next morning. On other nights I heard him in his rooms muttering and bellowing out to himself in that same sort of speech he used when we were together.

"After our first year, Asher informed me that he had to go to Afghanistan on business. I did not protest, rather I was relieved to have some respite from the horrid life we had fallen into. Then two months later I received word that he was dead.

"His solicitor informed me that the house and some small inheritance was mine and I was free of him! How I had come to hate that accursed ring, and the man who bore it! I was glad, overjoyed that he was dead and buried with the thing, and I make no apology for saying so."

"I can see why," Allegra said with a scowl. She shot Audrey a glance but the girl sat seemingly mesmerized by what she was hearing.

"Then today, you received this very ring, the ring that was buried with him," Audrey said, finishing her scribbles in the case book.

"Yes, and by what agency and for what reason, I have no idea. I know there's something very sinister in this business, and I'm utterly helpless to defend myself against it. Miss Barlow, can you help me, please!" the woman sobbed into her hands.

"I believe we can, Caroline," Allegra replied, moving to the sideboard and pouring another brandy for the woman.

Vermillion returned shortly with Maspeth and the tea cart. They had a quiet lunch and spoke no further of the ring and the deceased Asher Hilliard. Afterwards Allegra brought Caroline her coat and hat while Maspeth hailed a carriage for her. Then she was gone, leaving Vermillion and company alone in the study to reconnoitre the Hilliard case and plan the next steps of the campaign.

II

The next morning Vermillion, Audrey and Allegra dispersed into the city. Audrey headed to the library in search of references to obscure cults operating in the area, and newspaper notices of irregular doings in Afghanistan. Vermillion sought the counsel of certain discrete barristers and others known to him for any information on the mysterious Asher Hilliard and his ring – or the details of his curious death abroad.

This left Allegra Barlow, mistress of Anubis Lodge, to seek out certain associates, as well as her old friend and mentor, Aleister Crowley. The two crossed paths frequently in London at the man's flat and at his home at Boleskine. She had even briefly touched down at the mage's compound at Cefalu during her early years, before she met her own companions at Anubis Lodge and eventually joined forces with Vermillion. Allegra and Crowley had maintained amicable contact and often ran into each other in society; there they would exchange news of both polite occult society as well as the more dubious escapades of the darker branches of the extended family.

After a late tea and the usual rebuff of the mage's amorous suggestions, Allegra left Crowley to his own devices but not without taking away a very germane bit of information regarding the history of the singular signet ring. She had shown him a sketch that Vermillion had made and the mage's eyes had narrowed tellingly as he examined it closely. Allegra returned to Vermillion's house eager to add some of the missing pieces of their current puzzle.

As for Audrey, before she could return to Vermillion's house with only sparse news of Asher Hilliard, she was surprised in the street by an unexpected invitation…

* * *

Vermillion's interview of various parties had been most telling in its absence of even negligible details. But to Vermillion, it had reeked of the uncanny.

Allegra's tea and biscuits with Crowley had been more forthcoming and the mage had indeed recognized the insignia and inscriptions on the ring. It was the degree ring of a high ranking member of a cult of magicians, he had said, a nefarious hybrid of certain Tantric sects plagiarized by darker circles among the occult backwater. They believed that the subtle essences of the young could be used to invoke and entrap certain powerful denizens of the æthyrs that could be coerced into doing their master's bidding.

"So of course they thrive where they may hide among the protected class," Vermillion said with a sneer. "And where's Audrey? She should have been back before now."

"Indeed. The library is closed now." Allegra frowned. "Give her half the hour, and then we go in search of our wayward girl."

Before the thirty minutes had passed they heard the front door, Audrey's greeting to Maspeth, and then footsteps on the staircase. They waited but she did not join them.

"Strange," Vermillion said.

"I'll go check. Perhaps she is changing for dinner. She knows we're waiting."

Five minutes later Allegra rejoined Vermillion in the study.

"She found something, but she's so tired she just wants to sleep,"

"Strange again."

"I asked her where she had been but she brushed me off and told me not to wake her for dinner."

"Dash that! I'm going up there."

"Geoffrey, no, let her sleep. Something is amiss here; my skin prickles. I'll look in on her later."

"Alright then." Vermillion glanced toward the staircase. "My dear Allegra, would you join me in my meditations tomorrow?"

"Of course."

"I'd have a closer look at who we're dealing with before things become any more bothersome."

"Agreed."

III

Just after the steeple nearby had struck the quarter hour of three o'clock in the morning, the front door of Vermillion's town house shook with the angry pounding of someone demanding entrance.

"Vermillion!" the caller bellowed. "You really must keep your house in better order! Come down at once! You too, Allegra!"

Allegra and Vermillion threw on dressing gowns and scrambled toward the front door, almost knocking down a groggy Maspeth as he struggled into his jacket, flattening his hair as he pulled open the door.

"A Mr Crowley and, and Miss Audrey to see you, Sir," he said rubbing his eyes.

The figure of Aleister Crowley, still dressed in evening attire, greatcoat and top hat, barged through the front door, shoving Audrey in before him and glaring at the household assembled in the entryway.

"Aleister?" Allegra frowned as she stared at Audrey.

"Crowley! Blast it man, what's the meaning of this? And Audrey? What the devil?"

"It's my fault, I went back out. I couldn't sleep and I needed some air—" Audrey began. Vermillion shot her a glance that paralysed her for a moment – and then she ran upstairs and slammed the door of her room.

"You'll be damn happy I was on the prowl later than usual and saw her," Crowley began.

"That'll be all, Maspeth," Vermillion said, releasing the befuddled manservant to return to his bed.

"In here, Crowley." Vermillion barked, indicating the library off the entry hall. Once they were all seated there, brandies in hand, he looked to Crowley. "And now let's have it."

"I saw her walking down the street alone, staggering a bit, as if she'd been in her cups much of the evening."

"Never!" Allegra cried. "She was in bed well before midnight and she takes no spirits beyond the goblet or two of wine with dinner!"

"I thought she must be some tart on her way back to her rooms after a night's roll," Crowley said matter-of-factly; Vermillion snorted and turned his head in disgust.

"The way of the world, old stick – you might wish to leap down from your pilloried perch from time to time and dust off your backside. But by and by I caught sight of her face and recognized the girl. Now here's the rub. She was soon in the company of two men. I didn't recognize the blokes as part of your set, so I went to spy with my little eye and what I saw, I liked not at all.

"As soon as they saw me hail Audrey with a hearty doff of my hat they took off. And here we are, you're welcome, good night, and many thanks for the fine and dandy to warm my gizzard," he concluded, rising to take up his hat and cane and slip back into his topcoat.

"I see. Good man, Crowley, I'm in your debt, I'm sure," Vermillion said, patting him on the shoulder but not relinquishing the look of concern.

"As am I, Aleister," Allegra echoed and Crowley glanced at her, his eyes a-twinkle.

"I'll bear that in mind, madame," he said, raising her hand to his lips and kissing it lightly.

And with that he was gone, leaving Allegra and Vermillion sitting in silence. After some minutes, Allegra rose and went to a small carved wooden case she kept in the bookcase.

"She met with two men in the middle of the night? This troubles me greatly Geoffrey," she began, opening the box.

"As it does me!"

"She escaped the house after we were asleep, telling no one. Vermillion, there's more afoot here than an obstinate girl and a midnight frolic. I would see what the æthyrs make of this." She placed the ancient tarot deck on the table.

Vermillion nodded and left the room without comment, leaving his friend and colleague to consult the voices that rode the haunted winds and companioned her mind and spirit.

* * *

Allegra had laid out the cards and was taking stock of the curious arrangement when for the second time that night a violent pounding echoed through the front hall. Glancing at the clock she saw it was well past four. She bolted toward the door, calling for Maspeth to attend from his first floor apartment, and the man was soon at her side, this time his pistol at the ready.

Opening the door and placing himself as warden against any physical intrusion, Maspeth staggered in surprise as the limp form of Caroline Hilliard fell into his arms.

"To the sitting room," Allegra barked as she flung open the doors. Maspeth carried the woman to a place near the hearth and laid her down, retreating to the front door to see if anyone else was about on the street. A flurry of voices from above sounded, and then Vermillion and Audrey stormed into the room, staring.

"What in god's name is going on in this house?" roared Vermillion as he strode to the figure draped insensate across the divan. "Is she hurt?"

"Oh my," the Hilliard woman said groggily and then opened her eyes in surprise. "Oh, Mr Vermillion, Miss Barlow, I'm so sorry to intrude upon you, but, the most horrible thing has happened. I... I must ask for my husband's ring back, immediately, now if I might." She sat up and pushed her dishevelled blond hair back from her face.

"Tell me everything." Vermillion ordered, and Allegra winced to see no trace of sympathy on her old friend's face, but rather irritation.

"Earlier this evening a man came to see me!" she muttered and burst into tears. "He said that if I wanted to ever..." Her voice trembled with fear, and then she blinked and collapsed unconscious onto the divan.

"Maspeth, get her upstairs," Allegra said. "Put her in the Ivory Room. Vermillion, let her sleep, she's beside herself and there's no point in putting her through any more tonight. We'll sort this out in the morning."

"Good night then," Audrey said, her voice little more than a whisper as she went upstairs.

"The cards?" Vermillion inquired.

"I laid them out but they were a mess, a jumble of things and would take a devil of doing to make sense of them."

"Indeed, and I grow less interested in this matter by the hour. You put the read to the Hilliard woman in the morning, and if you think it worth our while we'll continue, otherwise we bid her adieu." He turned on his heel and left the room.

Allegra hated it when he got into one of these moods. He could retreat into himself for days; his power became implacable, cutting like a sword anyone who got in the way as he removed the offending situation, and people, from his sphere. She knew when to dig in her own heels, when to bring her own sober wisdom to bear and make him see reason, and when to let it go. She was of a mind herself to counsel Mrs Hilliard on the morrow to seek the help of the police, and not an occult detective.

She retired to her room and didn't sleep for an hour. It seemed she had only just shut her eyes when there was a gentle but insistent knocking at her bedroom door and then Maspeth's voice called out in alarm.

"Miss Allegra, Mr Vermillion is calling for you. It seems Mrs Hilliard has vanished while we slept, and Miss Audrey is gone as well – again!"

Vermillion was waiting for her in the drawing room. His cold features and clenched fists were those of a man wholly bereft of any patience and sympathy for the events that had descended upon his household.

"Sit down Allegra," Vermillion said gesturing to the small round table near the fire as he closed and locked the door. She seated herself and he came and joined her, taking her hands in his and looking into her eyes. She immediately relaxed and clasped his hands firmly, knowing what was to follow.

Vermillion's lips moved wordlessly for a few moments and his breathing slowed. Allegra closed her eyes, and then a moment later she felt her astral soul quiver like a flame and then leave her body. She ascended beyond the room, beyond the house, out and away above the city. Opening her eyes Allegra knew that her friend and partner in things arcane could see with her eyes, could feel what she felt of the æthyrs flowing over her subtle body.

"Where is Audrey?" She felt his voice break over her like a roll of thunder. "And the Hilliard woman, are they together? What is afoot here, Allegra? Seek! Find! Reveal!"

Allegra Barlow looked down at the city, a vast warren of lights, heat, and the buzz and hum of machines newly brought into being in a dying world as it gave birth to a new. She soon saw two warm red pulsing glows of warmth that were familiar to her among the city's throng, one so much more than the other. She could feel the essence of Audrey in a dwelling far below, and Caroline Hilliard was with her. They were alive and unharmed. But just before the location of the house began to emerge through the mists, she felt a jolt and was drawn away...

She gasped and her eyes shot open. "I could not quite—"

"No matter." Vermillion fetched her a brandy. "I have enough now. We're off then, to bring this case to a speedy close, to retrieve our own, and to bring its culprit to swift justice!"

IV

Inside the hour Vermillion and Allegra were charging up the staircase of a very fashionable town house in an otherwise 'not quite as fashionable as it once was' quarter of the city. Just as Vermillion was about to rap brusquely on the door with the head of his cane it swung open. An exotically-dressed young man attired after the current Ottoman fashion bowed curtly without expression and ushered them to the nearest room, where the shadows of a roaring fire danced upon the walls. Geoffrey Sykes Vermillion had never set foot in this residence before – but Allegra Barlow had.

The lord of the house stood warming himself by the fire wearing a fine scarlet lounging jacket trimmed in black velvet, a pipe highlighting the broad smile that animated the roguish face.

"Vermillion, Allegra!" the man bellowed, bowing to the arrivals and gesturing for them to take seats where they would. "So good of you to complete our little party. I was about to send for you!"

"Crowley! What are you playing at here?" Vermillion roared. "Explain yourself immediately. And these two!" he concluded, glaring at Caroline Hilliard and Audrey Hawkwoode who sat nearby drinking tea and playing backgammon.

"Audrey?" Allegra said in utter confusion. "Are you alright?" she asked, knowing the answer and seeing the proof of it.

"Do sit down, you two, and I will explain all. First, let me introduce my own student, Miss Maude Kingsley." At this, the former Caroline Hilliard raised her cup in toast and smiled as Audrey grinned.

"So you were having us on, I see," Vermillion said, helping himself to a snifter of Crowley's best and not being challenged for the boldness. Allegra declined and they sat down to consider their host.

"Yes, you see it's very important for Miss Kingsley's training that she master the arts of subterfuge and the sciences of appearing wholly other than she is when necessity demands it. Indeed, is not the creature you see before you much transformed from the timid widow who tearfully laid out her sorry tale of woe before you?" Crowley asked, beaming with pride. The girl sat transformed in black silk harem trousers and a scarlet tunic. Her long black hair lay in a tangled plait to her waist while the matronly blond coif of Caroline Hilliard lay on her dressing table upstairs.

"You and Allegra were perfect for the gambit for so many reasons. Neither of you would suffer too much discomfort at the ruse, and it was not designed to persist beyond its usefulness." Crowley explained. "No harm done as they say," he added, glowing with satisfaction and delight at having put one over on Vermillion. "The two of you would not fail to rise to the cries for help from a beleaguered widow, and there were certain details of the story I was certain would elicit your keen interest, Geoffrey, if I might be so familiar." This last was met with a curt nod from Vermillion.

"And?" Allegra said tersely.

"And your friend Vermillion here is just so damned full of himself! I thought it good fun to have some innocent sport with him on the side. Fair enough, don't you think old chap?"

"Perhaps," Vermillion mused. "Shall I tell you when I was first onto this farce, if not perhaps its author?

"Surely you jest! I saw the look in your eyes when you raced in here, alight with righteous indignation to rescue these damsels in distress!" Crowley roared.

"Yes, and is not my own art also incumbent upon not seeming to be as I am? But nevertheless... when Mrs Hilliard, or Miss Kingsley as it happens, first appeared on my doorstep I rose innocently to the bait, I'll not deny that.

"But when I left her to the counsel of Allegra and Audrey and went to the hall to see to other matters, I noticed her outer cloak and umbrella were almost completely dry. How odd, I thought. Just moments before she had been bemoaning her long wander through the storm that plagued us the whole day. Clearly the woman had been deposited at my door in a carriage, and had not arrived on foot as she claimed. Odd indeed, don't you think, Aleister?" Vermillion inquired, the hint of a smile on his lips.

"I'd say so, old stick. Do go on."

"So we proceeded apace, though I didn't share with Allegra my initial unripe suspicions."

"Prudent. Continue." Crowley goaded, thoroughly enjoying himself.

"Then there was the matter of the ring. That curious and troubling ring that seemed to bother our young guest to near hysteria. She took special pains to point out a deep scar on the ring's band, ostensibly from a fall in the street that her husband had suffered. It was clear to the naked eye, without benefit of a glass, that the scar was new and not possibly sustained some two years or more ago, again, as our young guest, your student, had claimed.

"So my hackles were up for the game and I made a great show of grasping at the bait. I inquired at my club and a few others where I enjoy entry and showed the ring around. None were the least bit familiar with such a notorious treasure. Then I visited every jeweller of note in the city. Again, none had ever laid eyes on the thing or its like even for repairs, and not one of them valued the obvious paste at above a few quid.

"An unlikely bauble to be held so dear by men of supposed great wealth and material and arcane prowess. By now I was indeed hooked and not in the intended way, I am sure." Vermillion paused to refill his glass and that of his host.

"Well, Vermillion, what about me?" Audrey inquired. "Weren't you the least bit frightened for my safety?" She seemed disheartened that Vermillion admitted to no concern that she had not once but twice mysteriously disappeared from the residence.

"Oh Audrey, you have come so far and yet have so far yet to travel on your journey. When Allegra and I left the room to see to this young vixen's safe departure, I glanced back into the room and saw Maude (as we now know her to be) immediately begin whispering in your ear. I saw that grin you get when you think you are being sly and was immediately onto the pair of you, though I did not surmise just then what exactly I was onto.

"Then Crowley here returns with you in the middle of the night under peculiar circumstances and my suspicions ripened further. But I had to see the pageant through to the encore, did I not?"

"Oh," the girl sighed as though she had just been robbed of her dessert.

"I knew two things," Vermillion continued, standing and assuming his professorial pace before the fire. "One, it was not like you to misbehave in this fashion, so irresponsibly, and to conceal your comings and goings. And two, knowing what I know of the wards and seals set upon every inch of my house, I was certain no one could have absconded with you physically, nor could they have drawn you out on a glamour. You had to be in on it with this young woman. Knowing you would never do or allow me harm, I assumed it was some sort of folly." For a moment Audrey looked totally devastated. "You will one day be as clever as our friend Miss Barlow, I'm sure of it, but that day has yet to come!" Vermillion added and Audrey turned a deep scarlet.

"And what about me? When did you plan to let me in on the caper? You knew I was suspicious enough to lay down the cards," Allegra said incredulously.

"I had to determine that you were not playing some nefarious part yourself in an attempt to fool your dear old friend!" he said, waving a finger at her. Allegra just shook her head and gazed at the ceiling. "I could not be certain who amongst my household had been enlisted in this prank. Not even the virtuous Maspeth was above suspicion."

"Good, good, go on then," Crowley prodded.

"The rest was fairly innocuous if tedious," said Vermillion, and Crowley raised his eyebrows in objection. "Once I had determined that the affair was harmless if irritating, I sought to wind things down. I had used my own channels of inquiry off the board, so to speak; a servitor whom I retain for such matters. This creature assured me there was no such order in existence as my would-be client described. No foul play at work in my house, no parlour tricks to rob me of hearth and home and fortunes, no danger at all lay on the horizon for me and mine. That's when I relaxed and played my hand at leisure."

"And that hand was literally mine!" Allegra said laughing in disbelief. "We did the mind joining; you saw where Audrey and Maude were – and you blocked my sight just before I could see exactly which house sequestered the girls! Then you waited until we were on the man's very doorstep to let me in on what was happening. Vermillion, I'll have words with you when we return to the mansion!" She spoke sternly, but tossed him a smile. "And you Aleister, that was quite a performance you put on two days ago when I came to solicit your help!"

Crowley closed his eyes and bowed again. "One endeavours as one can. I too like to keep my fingers nimble in the theatrical arts."

"So you had me for a moment, I'll concede you that," Vermillion said pointing a finger at Crowley and winking. "But the ruse was so quickly unveiled."

"Very good then, sir, very good!" Crowley roared. "So we have taken the measure of one another, you and I, and we've learned a thing, have we not?"

"Indeed we have. Without the mirth, magick is not a thing to be trifled with!"

"And are we forgiven?" asked Audrey, holding Maude Kingsley's hand.

"For now," replied Vermillion with a mock growl.

The party laughed and retired to the dining room where the gentleman in the Ottoman garb had laid a magnificent Turkish feast. Long after sunset the party broke up and Vermillion and company returned to the mansion.

Geoffrey Sykes Vermillion and Aleister Crowley did not become friends that day, but each had taken the other's measure, for future reference.

DIRK PITT: OCCULT DETECTIVE?

STEVEN PHILIP JONES

"Any ghost catching is strictly a side-benefit."
Dirk Pitt, *Pacific Vortex*

Is Clive Cussler's bestselling adventure hero Dirk Pitt an occult detective?
Nope.

Pitt is neither a detective, nor has he encountered a genuine supernatural threat. A marine engineer and Special Projects Director for the National Underwater Marine Agency until he replaces his boss and second father, Admiral James Sandecker, as NUMA's Director, Pitt has nevertheless been unraveling strange mysteries since his first published adventure *The Mediterranean Caper*, which was nominated by the Mystery Writers of America for Best Paperback Original of 1973. Pitt's techno-thriller exploits – Cussler is often cited as one of the genre's modern founders with authors like Tom Clancy (*The Hunt for Red October*) and Craig Thomas (*Firefox*) – have included the

V3179 / $1.25

A treacherous ex-Nazi, a cunning drug connection, and scientific sabotage in the hottest new superthriller of the year!

The Mediterranean Caper

Clive Cussler

discovery of the Library of Alexandria, Atlantis, and the real-life Captain Nemo's *Nautilus*, and they almost always contain some Gothic elements. These include allusions to tombs and graves, bad weather underscoring dire situations, melodramatic language, premonitions, doppelgangers, and, perhaps most importantly for occult detective fans, overt (created through special effects) or implied (suggested rather than fully revealed) supernatural representations.

Take the doomed *Manhattan Limited* from one of Pitt's earliest adventures *Night Probe!* (1981). This phantom train, which makes its "spectral run over the old track bed" in New York's haunted Hudson Valley, is apparently about to barrel over a cornered Pitt before it vanishes before his eyes. And speaking of vanishing, the President of the United States, his Vice-President, and several passengers and crew members do just that while aboard the heavily guarded presidential yacht *Eagle* in *Deep Six* (1984) after an impossible fog bank rolls over the vessel while it is docked at historical Mount Vernon.

Intrigued yet?

Pitt unearths the rational explanations behind these chilling enigmas, just as he does in *Cyclops* (1986), which starts with his corralling an antique dirigible that drifts into Key Biscayne. The dirigible is the *Prosperteer*, which has been

missing with its billionaire owner Raymond LeBaron and aircrew for ten days; but when Pitt looks inside the gondola he finds, in place of LeBaron and his men, "a

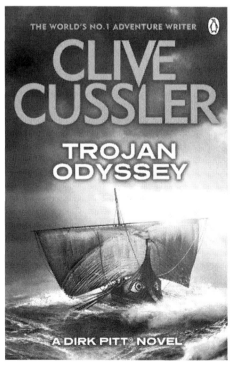

macabre crew" of putrefying corpses who have "flown from some unknown grave... in a charnel airship on a ghostly mission." As for ghostly missions, in *Trojan Odyssey* (2003) Pitt and the crew of the NUMA research ship *Poco Bonito* become the latest vessel to be attacked in the waters off Nicaragua by a Flying Dutchman: the cursed pirate ship *Scourge* and its legendary captain, the "Wandering Buccaneer", Leigh Hunt. Pitt again exposes the explanation behind this apparition, but not every weird encounter in his adventures are explained away, leaving open the possibility that the supernatural exists in Cussler's literary world.

In the prologue to *Flood Tide* (1997) for example, Katrina Garin is freezing to death in a life raft after the passenger ship, *Princess Dou Wan*, sinks. All looks lost until her dead father appears to Katrina to tell her that she is going to survive, mere moments before Katrina's future husband, Ian Gallagher, sights land.

Hallucination? A dream? Coincidence?

In Cussler's first novel, *Pacific Vortex* (not published until 1983), Pitt, who believes "only what I can see, smell, and touch," recounts a report from a NUMA zoologist who was recording fish sounds off the Continental slope near Iceland at a depth of ten thousand feet when he picked up noises like someone using a pencil to tap a code on the microphone – later translated as a mathematical formula – followed by shrieking laughter.

Pitt follows that with another reported incident that happened only nine months earlier where the instruments on two NUMA oceanographic ships seemed to detect the sound of a vessel traveling at a speed of one hundred ten miles an hour at a depth of nineteen thousand feet in the Kurile Trench off Japan, only to have the same thing happen to another NUMA ship working off the Cayment Trench (Cussler probably meant the Cayman Trench) off Cuba. (The 2005 film adaptation of Cussler's *Sahara* references this event in a newspaper clipping seen briefly in its opening credits. The headline reads "NUMA Digs Deep in Kurile Trench" and a subhead "Team claims they detected [the next few words are obscured by a shadow] moving fast at a depth of 14,000 feet").

Pitt confesses that NUMA's scientists and engineers are not in the habit of researching "unexplainable discoveries" and when events like these occur they are "purely accidental, and afterward, they're quietly filed away," a policy that would sound all too familiar to Carl Kolchak.

Maybe NUMA ought to consider opening up its own X-Files unit?

In Pitt's most famous adventure, *Raise the Titanic!* (1976), a hubristic curse reaches out from the past to affect the present. This curse destroys a half-crazed mining engineer and grandstander named Jonathan Hayes Brewster, who inexplicably seals himself inside a safe in one of the White Star liner's cargo holds while the ship is sinking, and seven decades later it infects obsessed physicist Gene Seagram, whose efforts to create a new missile defense system for the United States necessitates salvaging the *Titanic* and whatever Brewster died with inside that safe. By the time the resurrected liner docks in New York Harbor, Seagram is a shell of himself and living on the fringe of

madness, his eyes "dulled with the lost and vacant stare of a zombie". Pitt shows Seagram a mirror so the physicist can see how he is destroying himself, but when Seagram looks "another face slowly emerged. A strange face with the same haunted eyes". Brewster's face.

Again, hallucination? Insanity? Only Seagram and Brewster know for sure.

Pitt's most elegant and impactful encounter with the weird takes place earlier in *Raise the Titanic!* when he and NUMA comrades Al Giordino and Rudi Gunn at last discover the resting place of the sunken White Star liner, a scene infused with allusions comparing the vessel with The Lady in the House of Sleep (e.g. Briar Rose or Sleeping Beauty). The Titanic is *"cloaked* in the eerie stillness of the black deep" with her forecastle still "set on a southerly course, *as if she were still pathetically struggling to reach out to touch the waters of a port she had never known*" (my emphases). There is "a morbid beauty" about her, and all things considered the ship, like the enchanted Briar Rose, is in remarkably good condition in spite of the passing years, a comparison that extends to the White Star liner and Sleeping Beauty's fellow inhabitants. When the Prince enters Briar Rose's castle the entranced residents resemble waxen images of a great celebration in progress, while, in contrast, as the lights of the NUMA submersible *Sea Slug* "danced over" the *Titanic's* "ghostlike superstructure, casting long spectral shadows," Pitt, Giordino, and Gunn "could almost see" the ghostly passengers and crew as they were on the day the ship sank:

The passengers walked her decks: the wealthy, the famous, men in immaculate evening dress, women in colorful ankle-length gowns, nannies with children clutching favorite toys, the Astors, the Guggenheims, and the Strauses in first class; the middle-class, the school teachers, the clergymen, the students, and the writers in second; the immigrants, the Irish farmers and their families, the carpenters, the bakers, the dressmakers, and the miners from remote villages of Sweden, Russia, and Greece in steerage. Then there were the almost nine hundred crew members, from the ship's officers to the caterers, the stewards, the lift boys, and the engine-room men... Would, perhaps, the bones of Captain Edward J. Smith remain somewhere in the shadow of the bridge? What mysteries were there to be discovered within this once colossal floating palace if and when she ever greeted the sun again?

This haunting encounter may have influenced a proposed scene for the 1980 motion picture adaptation of Cussler's novel that was never filmed. Storyboards recently recovered by the movie's foremost historian, Jonathan Smith, include an unscripted scene (INT. SEA CLIFF S.C. 189) where a woman's ghost drifts through the submersible *Sea Cliff* as it nears the *Titanic*. It is also not hard to suppose that this scene with its "dining saloons and staterooms flooded with lights and crowded with hundreds of light-hearted and laughing passengers" likewise influenced the heavenly climax of James Cameron's 1997 film *Titanic*, which, like Cussler's novel, revolves around a mystery uncovered in a safe aboard the doomed vessel.

A reoccurring supernatural element in Pitt's adventures (some critics call it a conceit) that is highly anticipated by the series's fans, is a cameo by Cussler in which he appears to Pitt and other attendant characters – none of whom remember any earlier encounters they may have had with Cussler – long enough to aid Pitt in his mission. These walk-ons began in *Dragon* (1990), but the 1998 short story "The Reunion" expands this element into a tale wherein Cussler crashes "a twenty-year celebration of NUMA and the people who built it" at Pitt's home, which is sequestered in an old hangar on the southern border of Washington's National Airport. Some of the partygoers, however, have assumed room temperature long ago, and in a deliciously macabre twist, Cussler eavesdrops on some of Pitt's vanquished adversaries as they commiserate their denouements:

Min Kroyo, though frail and ancient, still had eyes that burned with evil... ["] If you recall, I was sent hurtling down the elevator shaft of the World Trade Center from the hundredth floor."

Arthur Dorsett, as ugly as any man created, grinned through yellow teeth. "Consider yourself lucky. After Pitt crushed my throat, he left me to be consumed by molten lava."

Foss Gly spread his huge hands expansively. "After beating me with a baseball bat, he jammed his finger in my eye socket clear through to my brain."

Topac Amaru, the Peruvian terrorist, scoffed. "At least he didn't shoot off your genitals before killing you in total darkness, deep in an underwater cave."

Yves Massarde, immaculately dressed in a white dinner jacket

with a yellow rose in its lapel, stared vacantly into the bubbles rising in his champagne glass and wondered aloud, "How could Pitt be even more brutal and vicious than the worst crew of villains ever created?"

The gray-haired stranger [Cussler] leaned between Gly and Qin Shang and said, "It was easy."["]

The only characters that recognize Cussler during this story are Pitt's future bride, Congresswoman Loren Smith, who 'met' Cussler in *Inca Gold* (1994), and, for once, albeit briefly, Pitt, who asks his creator, "Why is it when we meet I'm never supposed to remember who you are?"

The simple explanation: "Because I plan it that way."

In other words, it's Cussler's world and Pitt is just living in it.

Pitt's adventures will often also include Gothic settings such as caves, underwater caverns, mines, secret rooms, and hidden passages like the undersea lairs of Delphi Moran in *Pacific Vortex* and Bruno von Till in *The Mediterranean Caper*, the subterranean Luftwaffe bunker in *Dragon*, the underwater graveyard in Lake Orion from *Flood Tide* (Pitt's discovery of which remains one of the series's most chilling moments), and the embedded lost ships *Lax* from *Iceberg* and *Pilottown* from *Deep Six*. Cussler will pepper scenes like these with phrases that conjure a Gothic mood, and he is never better at this than in *Raise the Titanic!*, beginning with Pitt's introduction during a rescue on the Arctic island of Novaya Zemyla, where the hero "materialized from the white mist" of a blizzard. Pitt's next appearance takes place during another tempest, an electrical storm in Newport Beach, where Pitt comes across like an avenging spirit when a lightning flash unexpectedly reveals that he is standing near Seagram and he laughs in unison with a thunderclap. When the time comes for Pitt to make his exit at a tiny British graveyard, he "entered a shroud of mist and disappeared."

To quote Pitt from *The Mediterranean Caper*, "Shades of Edgar Allan Poe."

The fact is that adventure stories featuring Gothic elements are nothing new. Classic adventure writers like Sax Rohmer, Edgar Wallace, and Frank L. Packard injected Gothic elements into many of their stories, and even Clarence E. Mulford could not resist writing "The Ghost of the Canyon" (1935) for cowboy hero, Hopalong Cassidy. When Cussler incorporates Gothic conventions into his stories, he is following a literary tradition of perpetuating the Gothic genre for another generation, but like Dashiell Hammett in *The Dain Curse* (1928) and Daphne du Maurier in *Rebecca* (1938), Cussler's sole intention is to evoke the Gothic. He never does more than dabble in it.

As Ebenezer Scrooge might say, there is more of gravy than of grave in Cussler's adventures.

Even so, occult detective fans can still enjoy reading how Pitt solves ostensibly supernatural threats, and if he fails to substantiate the existence of the occult, the possible existence of the supernatural is never totally dismissed. It is a shame, however, that Cussler, who possesses a deft Gothic touch, never writes about some of those unexplained discoveries that NUMA quietly files away. The prolific British author Dennis Wheatley enjoyed tremendous success marrying the technical aspects of the supernatural to the pace of the thriller in the Duke de Richleau series which includes *The Devil Rides Out* (1934), and it is intriguing to wonder what kind of horror-adventure classic Cussler might have created had he set his mind to it.

Clive Eric Cussler (July 15, 1931 – February 24, 2020)
R.I.P.

THE THING IN THE BEDROOM

W*LL**M H*PE H*DGS*N

The circle of initiates about the roaring fire in the King's Head bar had sadly decreased of late, entertaining though the conversation had always been. For one thing, the roaring fire had been superseded by a mournfully bonging radiator; even the popular Mr Jorkens had ceased to come when the landlord installed his third Space Invaders machine. On this particular evening there was little sparkle in the conversation, and far too much in the foaming keg beer: only Major Godalming, Carruthers and old Hyphen-Jones were present, and, passing by an easy transition from gassy beer to chemical warfare and military reminiscences in general, the Major was well into his much-thumbed anecdotes of the earlobe he lost to Rommel, the duelling scar acquired whilst in Heidelberg on a package tour, and the ugly kukri wound he'd received in Bradford.

Carruthers and Hyphen-Jones yawned their appreciation and choked down their beer; half-formed excuses about not keeping the wife up too late seemed to be trembling in the air like ectoplasm, when a shadow fell across the table.

"My round, chaps?"

The speaker was tall, handsome, rugged: from his built-up shoes to his shoulder bag he was every inch an English gentleman.

"Smythe, my dear fellow!" the Major cried. "We'd given you up for dead!"

"And well you might," said Smythe. "It happened to me once, did death – you may remember me telling you about that hideous affair of the haunted percolator? For a short while, then, I was clinically dead. It was nothing. There are things much worse than death, worse by far…"

"Murrage's keg beer, for example?" suggested Carruthers.

The subtlety of this hint was not lost on Smythe, who took the empty glasses to the bar and in a mere twenty minutes returned with three beers and a stiff gin-and-tonic for himself.

"Cheers," said the Major. "Now where have you been these last three months? Living abroad with some woman, I suppose, as you did for half a year after laying the ghost in that 'Astral Buffalo' case? Ah, you randy devil."

"Not so," Smythe said laughingly. "For one reason and another I've merely been visiting a different class of pub, a different sort of bar, as shortly you will understand..."

"Well, dammit man, what was this case?" the Major boomed. "What was so much more terrible than death? You've changed, you know. The experience has set its mark upon you by God! Your hair! I've only just noticed it's white!"

"Just a little bleach, my dear Major... I fancied myself as a blonde. But let me tell you of the case which must rank as one of the most baffling and sinister of my career... an appalling case of what I can only call occult possession."

"We had that last year," said Carruthers, scratching his head. "That business of the giant bat of Sumatra: or was it the giant cat? One frightful influence from beyond the world we know is very like another, I find."

Smythe settled himself more comfortably on his favourite stool, smiled, and opened a packet of potato crisps in the characteristic manner which told his friends that another fascinating narration was on its way – and that they were expected to buy drinks for the raconteur all the rest of the evening.

"As you know, I've gained some small reputation in matters of detection, the occult and the odd tricks of the mind..." Here Smythe distributed the customary business cards and mentioned the 10% discount he offered to friends. "And so it was that Mrs Pring brought her terrible problem to me, on the recommendation of a bosom friend who'd heard of my ad in the Sunday Sport colour supplement. Mrs Pring—"

"Ah, you incurable old womanizer," wheezed Hyphen-Jones. "Did Mr Pring find you out?"

Smythe gave him an austere glance, and coldly ate another crisp. "Mrs Pring is a widow of late middle age and forbidding aspect, whose home is in the moderately appalling seaside resort of Dash. She lets out one room of her house under the usual bed-and-breakfast terms; personally I think the enterprise would be more successful if she did not apparently stuff the mattress with breakfast cereal and serve its former contents in a bowl each morning, but this is to anticipate. The story that Mrs Pring told to me three months ago was, like so many of the tales told in my office, strange, terrible and unique.

"Over the years, you see, my client had noticed a curious statistical trend as regards the people who stayed with her. She keeps a very detailed set of books, two in fact, and there was no possibility that her memory could be deceiving her. In brief: many gentlemen (to use her term) had undergone bed and breakfast at Mrs Pring's and for some reason which I find inexplicable had returned in subsequent years. Some women did the same: the odd point which caught Mrs Pring's attention was that young or even relatively young women tended not to return. In fact they tended to leave abruptly, with various noises of embarrassment and outrage, after no more than one night in the room.

"That Mrs Pring took several years to notice the phenomenon is perhaps best explained by her delicate state of health, which is only sustained by almost daily trips to buy medicinal liquids not sold by chemists. That Mrs Pring was properly alarmed by her discovery is shown by the fact that for a whole year she actually provided butter rather than margarine with the breakfast toast: it made no difference. What d'you make of that?"

"I suppose," said Carruthers slowly, "that some terrible tragedy had been enacted in that fatal room?"

Smythe looked startled, and dropped a crisp. "Well… yes, actually. However did you guess?"

"My dear fellow. I've been listening to your curious and unique tales for upwards of eight years."

"Well, never mind that. Mrs Pring evolved a theory that that all too unyielding mattress was infested, not with elementals as in that fearsome Wriggling Eiderdown case, but with what in her rustic way she chose to call incests. As she put it, 'What I thought was, those bleeding things might be partial to young ladies what has nice soft skin… anyway, I reckoned I'd better have a kip-down there meself and see if anything comes crawling-like, bedbuggers or flippin' fleas or whatever…'

"With uncommon fortitude, Mrs Pring did indeed pass a night in this spare room of hers. Her account of it is very confused indeed, but she remarked several times that something had indeed come a-crawling… but as to its nature or actions, she continually lapsed into a state of incoherence and embarrassment. The same embarrassment, you may note, with which her lady lodgers would so hurriedly leave."

The Major said: "And the next morning, I suppose, she came straight to you and asked for something to be done about it?"

Smythe studied each of his friends in turn, until Hyphen-Jones misinterpreted the dramatic pause and scurried to buy more drinks. "In point of fact," Smythe said quietly, "she first attempted to investigate the phenomenon more closely by sleeping in that room every night for the following six months. It seems that no other manifestation took place during all that time, as she informed me with some suppressed emotion; after a while she dismissed the experience as hallucination and thought little more of it until the first week of the new holiday season... when no fewer than three young women stayed a night and left without eating the margarine they'd paid for. One of them murmured something incoherent to Mrs Pring about a ghost that needed to be laid. It was then that Mrs Pring decided something must be done: and after checking that my fee was tax-deductible, she placed the matter in my hands."

"Why d'you suppose the Pring female only saw whatever-it-was the one time?" inquired Carruthers.

"My theory had to take into the fact that this was a chauvinist haunting, as you might put it, with a preference for young ladies quite contrary to the Sex Discrimination Act. The inference would seem to be that Mrs Pring, who is a lady of what is called a certain age, very rapidly lost her appeal to... let's call it the manifestation. Picture her as a glass of that repellent keg beer: one sip was quite enough for any person of taste."

"I'm beginning to get a vague but quite monstrous notion of what you're leading up to..." the Major observed slowly.

"It's worse than you think," Smythe assured him. "I know I shall never be the same again after the night I spent in that room."

"But..." said Hyphen-Jones querulously, before Smythe silenced him with a single charismatic gesture which tipped half a pint of beer into his lap.

"An exorcism seemed to be in order," said Smythe, "but first I had to know what I was up against. You recall that ghastly business of the Squeaking Room in Frewin Hall... the exorcism had no effect whatever upon those mice.

When closely questioned, Mrs Pring retreated into blushes and giggles: I saw I'd have to keep a vigil there myself, and see what astral impressions my finely-trained nervous system might glean from the surroundings.

"Thus I travelled first-class to Dash, and Mrs Pring accompanied me back in (I'm glad to relate) a second-class carriage. The resort was as depressing as I'd foreseen, rather like an extensive penal colony by the sea; Mrs Pring's house corresponded roughly to the maximum security block. Anyway, I steeled myself against the appalling Presence which pervaded the place... chiefly a smell of boiled cabbage... and readied myself to pass a night within the haunted room. I assured Mrs Pring that I never failed... have you ever known me to tell the story of a case in which I failed?"

Hyphen-Jones looked up again. "What about that time when... ouch!" Some paranormal impulse had helped the rest of his beer to find its way into his lap.

"So I assured her, as I said, that I never failed — ah, little did I know! — and that whatever dwelt in that room was as good as exorcized. I fancied, you know, that she looked regretful – as though admitting to herself that a favourite aunt who'd committed several chainsaw massacres should probably be locked up, but admitting it regretfully. So, one by one, I ascended the creaking stairs to that room of dread. The dying sun peered through its single window in a flood of grimy yet eldritch radiance. But there was nothing sinister about the place save the peeling wallpaper, whose green-and-purple pattern set me brooding for some reason on detached retinas. I waited there, as darkness fell, all lights extinguished to minimize the etheric interference…"

"And what happened, old boy?" cried Carruthers. "What happened to you?"

"Precisely what I'd expected: nothing at all. Whatever haunted that room was staying a male chauvinist pig to the very last. The only moment when a thrill went through me was when I heard a clock strike midnight far out across the town… the witching hour… the moment when my consultation rates switched from time-and-a-half to double time. Presently dawn came, and, this being the seaside resort of Dash, it wasn't even a proper rosy dawn: more like a suet pudding rising in the east. An appalling place.

"Over breakfast, when not pitting my teeth against Mrs Pring's famous vintage toast, I questioned her closely about the room's history. As you know, we occult sleuths can deduce a great deal from the answers to innocuous-seeming questions. After some routine enquiries about whether, for example, she regularly celebrated the Black Mass in the room in question, I subtly asked her, 'Mrs Pring, has some terrible tragedy been enacted in that fatal room?' She denied this loudly and angrily, saying, 'What kind of a house do you think I bleeding well keep here? I've had no complaints and no-one's ever snuffed it on my premises, not even Mr Brosnan what had the food-poisoning, which he must have got from chips or summat brought in against me house rules… you'll not get no food-poisoning from my bacon-an'-eggs sir.'

"I was tolerably well convinced that I wouldn't, since after noting how many times Mrs Pring dropped the bacon on the floor I had taken the precaution of secreting mine under the table-cloth (where I was interested to find several other rashers left by previous visitors). After a short silence during which she tested the temperature of the tea with one finger and apparently found it satisfactory, Mrs Pring added: 'Of course there was always poor Mr Nicholls all those years ago.'

"We occult sleuths are trained to seize instantly on apparent trivia. Casually I threw out the remark, 'What about poor Mr Nicholls?'

" 'Oh, 'e had a terrible accident, he did. Oh, it was awful, sir. What a lucky thing he wasn't married. What happened, you see, he caught himself in the door somehow, which I could understand, him being clumsy by nature and having such a... Well, lucky he wasn't married is what I always said, and of course 'e wouldn't get married after that. I heard tell he went into the civil service instead. Oooh sir, you don't think...?'

" 'I do indeed think precisely that, Mrs Pring,' I told her solemnly. We occult sleuths are, as you can imagine, sufficiently accustomed to such phenomena as disembodied hands or heads haunting some ill-favoured spot, and I've even encountered one disembodied foot... you remember it, the 'Howling Bunion' case which drove three Archbishops to the asylum. I conjectured now that the unfortunate Mr Nicholls, though it seemed that most of him still lived, was a man of parts and haunted Mrs Pring's room nonetheless.

"Upon hearing my theory, the landlady seemed less shocked and horrified than I would have expected. 'Fancy that,' she remarked, with a look of peculiar vacancy, and added, 'I ought to 'ave recognized him, at that.' I did not press my questioning any further."

"What a frightful story," shivered Carruthers. "To think of that poor Mr Nicholls, never able to know the pleasure of women again."

"In that," said Smythe in a strange voice, "I share his fate."

There was a tremulous pause. Smythe licked his lips, squared his shoulders. "I must have a trickle," he remarked, and departed the room amid whispered comments and speculations as to whether or not there was something odd in the way he walked.

"My strategy," Smythe continued presently, "was to lure the manifestation into the open so it might be exorcized by the Ritual of the Astral League. You need damnably supple limbs for that ritual, but it has great power over elementals, manifestations and parking meters. But how to lure this ab-human entity into sight? Mrs Pring no longer had charms for it, which was understandable and I could hardly ask some innocent young woman to expose herself to what I now suspected to lurk in that room.

"In the end I saw there was only one thing to be done. During the day I made certain far from usual purchases in the wholly God-forsaken town of Dash, and also paid a visit to a local hairdresser's. You remarked, did you not, my dear Major, that I'd gone ash-blonde with fright? I cleared the furniture from that bedroom and made my preparations... having first instructed Mrs Pring to remain downstairs and presented her with a bottle of her favourite medicine to ensure she did so. Now the water in that town, I suspected, was not pure: instead I consecrated a quantity of light ale and with it marked out my usual protective pentacle. This was a mark-IX Carnacki pentacle, guaranteed impervious to any materialized ectoplasmic phenomena specified in British Standard 3704.

"In the early evening I carried out the last stages of my plan, undressing and changing into the clothes I'd bought – amid some small embarrassment. There was an exquisite form-fitting black dress with its skirt slashed almost to the hip; beneath this dress, by certain stratagems well known to us occult consultants, I contrived a magnificent bosom for myself. I need scarcely trouble you with the minor details of the sensual perfume guaranteed to send any male bar the unfortunate Mr Nicholls into instant tachycardia, or the pastel lipstick which so beautifully complemented my eyes, or the sheer black stockings which I drew over my carefully shaven legs, or..."

"All right, all right," said the Major, gulping hastily at his beer. "I think we get the general idea."

"Be like that if you must. I waited there in the huge pentacle, in a room lit only by the flickering candles I'd acquired from the occult-supplies counter at the local Woolworth's. As I stood there I could see myself in the mirror screwed to one wall (presumably because Mrs Pring felt her guests might well smuggle out any six-by-four-foot mirror that wasn't screwed down): I was magnificent, I tell you, a vision of... oh, very well, if you insist.

"I waited there with the tension mounting, waiting for whatever might (so to speak) come, and the candles gradually burnt down. The room filled with bodings of approaching abomination, as of a dentist's waiting room. Suddenly I realized there was a strange luminescence about me, a very pale fog of light that filled the air, as though Mrs Pring were boiling vast quantities of luminous paint in the kitchen below. With fearful slowness the light coagulated, condensed, contracted towards a point in the air some eighteen inches from the floor; abruptly it took definite shape and I saw the throbbing, ectoplasmic form of the thing that haunted this room for so long.

"It was larger than I'd expected, perhaps nine inches from end to end; it wavered this way and that in the air as though seeking something in a curious one-eyed manner; the thought occurred to me that it had formed atop the bed and centrally positioned, or at least would have done so had I not previously removed the bed. Even as this notion flared in my mind like a flashbulb, the Thing appeared to realize there was nothing to support it now: it flopped quite solidly and audibly to the floor."

"Audibly?" Hyphen-Jones quavered. "With a thud, or a clatter, or...?"

Smythe darted an impatient glance at him. "With the sound of a large frankfurter falling from a height of eighteen inches on to wooden floorboards, if you wish to be precise. The horror of it! These solid manifestations are the most terrible and inarguable of spiritual perils: it's definitely easier to deal with an astral entity which can't respond with a sudden blow to your solar plexus. And worst of all, something which might have sent my hair white if I hadn't already dyed it this rather fetching colour, the Thing had now fallen inside the pentacle, with me! Again, imagine the horror of it, the feeling of spiritual violation: already my outer defences had been penetrated.

"The ab-human embodiment reared up, questing this way and that like a cobra readying its strike; and then it began to move my way. I utterly refuse to describe the manner in which it moved, but I believe there are caterpillars which do the same thing. If so, they have no shame. I knew that a frightful peril was coming for me... it's always horribly dangerous when something materializes inside your very defences, though this wasn't perhaps as bad as in that Phantom Trumpeter case: you remember it, where the spectral elephant took solid form in my all too small pentacle? But in this particular situation I felt I was safe from the worst, at least."

"Why were you safe from the worst?" asked the fuddled Hyphen-Jones.

"I was relying on a matter of anatomy," Smythe said evasively, and left Hyphen-Jones to work it out. "Still, I was too confident, as it happened. The only safe course was to get out of that room and perhaps try to bag it with a long-range exorcism from the landing. What I did was to experiment with a little of the consecrated ale left over from making the pentacle. I flicked some at the crawling Thing as it snaked its way towards me, and... well, it must have been peculiarly sensitive. It positively dribbled with rage, and vanished in a burst of ectoplasm.

"I believed the Thing must have withdrawn itself for the night, abandoning its rigid form and returning to the nameless Outer Spheres. Again, I'd fallen into the trap of over-confidence. I was still standing there in my fatally gorgeous ensemble when once again that luminous fog filled the air about me and... no, I can't bring myself to describe what happened then. Certain of the older grimoires recommend that practitioners of the magical arts, black or white, should ritually seal each of the nine orifices of the body as part of the preliminaries. I believe I now know why."

"My God, you don't mean...?" said Carruthers, but seemed to lack the vocabulary or inclination to take the sentence further. Hyphen-Jones appeared to be counting under his breath.

"Well, I'll be buggered," the Major murmured.

Tersely, Smythe explained how, pausing only to waive his fee and advise that Mrs Pring should sleep henceforth in the cursed room while renting out her own, he'd departed without so much as changing his clothing.

"So my life was transformed by that Thing in the Bedroom," he concluded gaily. "Now let me tell you of my newest case, one which I was formerly reluctant to investigate. The matter of the haunted chamber in the Café Royal, where the shade of Oscar Wilde is said to (at the very least) walk…"

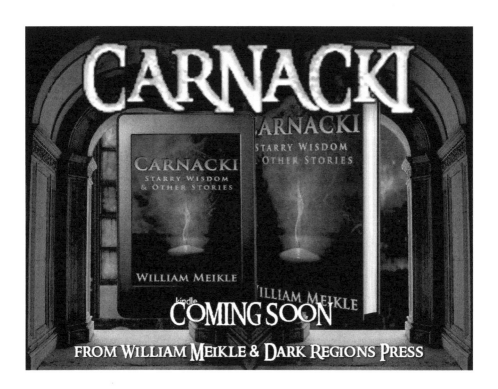

THE WHITE SICKNESS

D.J. TYRER

"The sangoma is coming! The sangoma is coming!"

The shouts rang out across the green hills before the newcomer came in sight of the clustered huts of the umuzi. Boys, with knobkerries waving in their hands, abandoned the cattle they were minding and ran ahead of the old woman to announce her arrival.

A man who might have been a warrior, but whose muscled frame was wasted and face lined with weariness and fear, stepped out of one of the huts to receive her.

The woman, the sangoma, was stooped and shrunken with age, yet walked with a determined stride, leaning heavily upon her staff. Despite the warm weather, she was tightly wrapped in a jackal-hide kaross as if against a chill and there was a shawl of tattered cloth draped over her shoulders and head.

Reaching the man, she raised her head to look at him, revealing an ebony face so wrinkled her keen black eyes were almost invisible.

"You are she?" he asked.

"Yes." Her voice was soft and raw-sounding. "You have the sickness here?"

The man gave a slow, defeated nod.

"Show me."

He turned and led her into the shadowed interior of the hut.

"My father, the chief." He gestured at the man who lay, deathly still, beneath a bundle of hides. The man's skin looked as if it were drained of blood, ashen, not a healthy brown, and with patches of what looked like white scaly mould. About his neck he wore a strange object of metal, not beadwork, with four arms extending from a central point. A woman crouched beside him, dabbing at his brow with moist grass.

The sangoma knelt by the chief's side and looked him over, pulling up the lids of his eyes to examine them, placing her head upon his chest to listen to the weak, irregular sounds of his heartbeat and breathing, and then, sniffed at him; sniffed the object he wore.

With the cracking sound of arthritic joints, she rose and said, "Yes, this is the sickness; the white sickness."

It was the same in all the villages along this stretch of the coast. There would be one or two, invariably men, who were seriously ill like this and a general malaise hanging over the rest of the inhabitants and their cattle.

"I need you to assemble everyone outside – men, women and children – *everyone*."

The son of the chief nodded and exited the hut.

The sangoma looked at the chief's wife. "You, too."

As the woman left, the sangoma looked down at the chief again and shook her head, then followed the woman out.

There were two dozen inhabitants of the umuzi, lined up in a double line, on the bare earth of the yard, waiting for her.

Slowly, she walked before them, pausing in front of each person in turn, gazing up into their faces in search of guilt or malice, and sniffing at them for the scent of evil.

With one final sniff of the chief's son, she stepped away.

"Well?" he asked. "Is there a witch here?"

"No." It had been the same each time she investigated the sickness: it bore all the signs of umthakathi, yet there was no sign of the witch responsible.

"I pride myself," the sangoma said, "upon always being able to find the cause of sickness and ill luck, but," she sighed, "this has defeated me."

She struck her staff against the bare ground in frustration, raising a cloud of dust.

"I will find whoever or whatever is to blame."

Turning to look out towards the cloud-strewn sky above the sea, she added, "Go about your business. I must commune with the amadlozi."

The shore was rocky, and she found a large slab where she could sit and gaze out at the churning grey-green waters and the white foam that seemed like fallen clouds, letting her mind roam in search of an answer.

There had to be one: if the disease wasn't caused by a witch, it must be the work of evil spirits, or perhaps an angry sea-dwelling tokoloshe.

Staring at the waves, she allowed her mind to drift away from the immediacy of the physical world, let her soul fly free, up past the wheeling seabirds, towards the herds of fluffy, white sky-cattle, to the domain of Unkulunkulu, from which the amadlozi, the ancestors, looked down upon their descendants.

The spirits of the ancestors were no more than shadows in the bright light of Unkulunkulu, with whom they conversed and to whom they raised chants of praise.

They gathered about her, eager for the proximity of a living spirit, like moths to a flame, yet also agitated and fearful.

"I have come to you from your sons who wail in anguish at the evil which besets them."

"We know, we know. We hear their cries and see their tears. Even here, protected by the shield of mighty Unkulunkulu, we sense the evil that besets them."

"I am a sangoma, one of the best, yet I have smelt no witch. Tell me what is the source of this evil? Is it an evil spirit? Tell me so that I might fight it."

The ancestors seemed to recede from her and she could feel their fear. Whatever it was that was afflicting her people, it was something strange and awful.

"A white death assails our people, the first of many," wailed the amadlozi. "It came from the sea – *from the sea* – and, only the sea shall cure it."

She caught images, fleeting and strange, of something white and waxy tumbling in the surf, of something pale and horrible and dripping wet stalking the blackest hours of the night – and, a shape, four-armed, which she recognised.

"It started here," an ancestor whispered in a voice like the morning breeze; "it started here."

And, then, she was tumbling down, out of the clouds, and back into her body.

The sangoma jerked awake as spray struck her face and a particularly tall and frothy wave tumbled back into the waters below the rock on which she sat.

She had answers of a kind, but only fragments, and the truth of what she faced remained out of her reach.

The sun was sinking behind the hills now, and she rose with creaking bones to walk the short distance towards the umuzi.

"Come, eat with us," said one of the women, her eyes downcast with a mixture of fear and respect; with a single word, a sangoma could condemn anyone to death as a witch, even the greatest of chiefs.

But, right now, she didn't feel mighty, merely old, tired and hungry, and she gratefully followed the woman to a space beside the fire, where she was served uphuthu made of millet, which she rolled into balls in her palm and ate with delight.

Around her, the women of the umuzi watched her warily and relaxed to see her taking pleasure in their simple fare.

There was no singing and dancing, nor any telling of tales; the folk were too weary and downcast at their misfortune, eating in silence. Only moths danced about the flames.

When the meal was finished and people began to drift back to their huts, the chief's son approached her.

"Where would you sleep this night?"

She considered both his question and the one she had silently been asking herself all evening, whether to ask him yet about the item his father wore and the words the amadlozi had said to her.

After a moment without speaking, she decided to keep her own counsel a little longer, and said, "I shall sleep out here, beneath the stars, and seek any sign of misdeeds done under cover of darkness."

The chief's son nodded and retreated to his hut, leaving her to lie down on the hard-packed bare earth of the yard between the buildings.

As a sangoma, she was able to allow her body to slip into the restorative state of sleep, while her soul remained alert to the world about her, able to sense approaching threats and drift about her environs in search of anything amiss.

Although the night was dark to human eyes, to the senses of the unshackled soul it was bright; as she allowed her soul to drift free from her old and aching form, she could see her surroundings with a clarity that would surprise those who lacked her gift.

The huts and the fence surrounding the umuzi and the cattle kraal were shadowy, as man-made objects always were, but she could see the souls of the people and the cattle that they constrained. Only, those souls were not as vibrant as they should be, the chief's least of all. She allowed herself to drift closer to him: it was as if he were a gourd almost emptied of water. Only the object he wore about his neck retained any glow of energy to it and that, in some manner she could not quite comprehend, she knew was baleful.

Moths danced still about the dying embers of the fire, their tiny lives as bright as the flames had been. Outside the fence, she could discern every living thing, both animal and vegetable, from skulking scavengers to bats on the wing.

Then, she sensed something different, out of place.

It came from the direction of the sea, moving almost like a man, yet maggot-white in colour, not the bright glow of life energy, but a sickly, white death.

She kept away from it, for she could sense the malevolent strength of it, and observed it from a distance as it stalked between the huts, within them, before leaving in the direction of the sea, seeming to take a little more from each weakening soul.

Doubtless, it would journey through the night to the other places that had been affected, stealing a little life energy from each living thing.

Like a hunter stalking his prey, she was a little further towards her quarry, but not there yet.

She continued to observe the umuzi and its inhabitants through the rest of the night until the rising of the dawn sun.

Her soul returned to her body and she rose from the hard ground, dusting herself off.

Accepting a little food and drink, she sought out the chief's son.

"Tell me about the object that hangs about your father's neck."

He gave a shrug. "What is there to tell? He found it and took a liking to it."

"What indeed?" she said. "It started here. That is what the amadlozi told me. This place is where the sickness began."

She struck her staff against the ground in anger.

"Something dead and white stalks about by night. Something that came from the sea – and, that object your father wears is connected to it."

The man paled, growing almost as ashen complexioned as his father, and, for a moment, swayed so that she thought he was going to collapse in a faint.

He licked his lips nervously, and then, spoke: "It was three months ago that we found it, an abelungu, one of the dead men washed up from the depths of the sea, tossed up upon the rocks of the shore."

"An abelungu?" The strange pale corpses of men from the sea were a rarity, but she had never heard of such an outbreak following the appearance of one before.

"Yes. But... different."

"Different? In what way was it different?"

"I have only seen one myself once before, and that was a man like me, only his skin was a pale colour quite unlike that of normal skin. But, this one... this one had skin that seemed to shine and had a texture like wax."

"What did you do with it?"

He shuffled a little. "Many men came to look at the strange sight. About its neck, the abelungu wore that object my father took. It had other tokens with it, shiny metal, that others claimed as souvenirs. Then, we took the body and we buried it in a grave not far from the shore."

"Tell me: did you perform qaqa?"

Qaqa: the act of disembowelling a fallen foe so that their soul might escape to join the amadlozi. If it wasn't performed, the belly would bloat as the soul struggled to break free of its fleshy prison and, upon the decay of the corpse, it would set forth seeking revenge.

"No."

Doubtless none of those present had considered it necessary, she reflected, as they hadn't slain the abelungu. Probably the strange and disturbing appearance of the corpse had inspired them to act quickly. She silently cursed their foolishness.

"You should have," she said. "Its soul remained trapped within its body. Still, it might not have come for you, had you not taken the objects from it. They, I am certain, are what drew it back to you, like a moth is drawn to the flame."

She looked at him. "You must give the object to me and send runners to the other chiefs to collect all those other tokens of which you spoke."

"And, then, you shall be able to lift its curse?"

"Of course," she said, wishing she knew what she would do next.

The chief's son brought her the metal cross that had hung about his father's neck and sent his fastest youths down the coast to relay the sangoma's orders.

She prayed all the items would be handed over – and that the youths would all make it back before nightfall; she very much doubted the old chief would survive another visitation.

"Show me where you buried the abelungu," she told the chief's son, "and, bring men with you."

He led her to a hollow not far from the rocky shore, and she directed him and his men to uncover the corpse.

It was unlike any body she had ever seen before and, though she had never seen one of the abelungu in her long life, from the stories she had been told, it was nothing like them. It did retain the general shape of a man and the flesh was a horrible white colour, but everything was swollen and bloated, the face almost featureless it was so swollen, the limbs grotesquely stout and the belly hideously distended.

But, it was the waxy sheen to the skin and its strange damp appearance, as if it were sweating a colourless paste, that repulsed her most. The rest of the abelungu washed up upon the shore might be considered humans of a sort, but, whatever this was, she couldn't believe it was ever human. It was monstrous. Even prior to death, she was certain, it was inimical.

The flesh of its belly had begun to split. The spirit was not yet able to break fully out of its prison, yet a little of its malevolent essence had already seeped into the world. Soon, when it had gathered enough life energy, it would be free, unleashing who-knew-what evil upon the living.

She shuddered.

"Now, what do we do?" asked the chief's son with a weary sigh.

"First, we wait for the other items to be returned – I must have them all to effect a cure – and, then, I shall deal with this vile thing."

She just wished she knew how... what had the amadlozi said? The sea would provide the cure... She wished she knew how.

Throw it back? Would the waves carry it away?

Her instinct was to burn it: Flames could eradicate many evils and the burning of the right herbs drive them off.

Then, it came to her...

"Send women to the seashore and have them gather as much weed from the rocks as they can – the drier the better."

The women of the umuzi hurried away, accompanied by some of the youths, eager to assist the sangoma in any way they could. To the youngsters it all remained abstract, a game, but the sangoma settled wearily upon the hard-packed earth in a cross-legged position and attempted to focus her mind against what was to come.

Long shadows reached eastwards towards the sea as the sun began to vanish behind the hills.

She looked up from her meditation. They were running out of time. Soon, night would grip the land and the white spirit would rise from the dead once again to drain the last of the chief's life-force.

The first of the exhausted runners had returned with the tokens taken from the abelungu. They were small discs of silver. Some had been punctured and strung on leather thongs to wear about the neck or wrist. Each, to her inner sight, was infused with a baleful energy.

She accompanied the youths to where the body lay exposed.

"Place them on the body," she said. Already she had laid the golden cross upon the chest of the bloated corpse. The runners laid the discs about it.

The sun continued to sink behind the hills and she took up a position, leaning heavily upon her staff, to watch over the body while the shadows lengthened.

As the evening rolled in like the waves upon the shore, the abelungu seemed to shine more, as if it had stolen the light of the day for itself. And, as she watched it, she was certain she could see the vile spirit writhing about in its swollen guts, growing ready to break free.

It was nearly time.

The last of the runners returned just before the sun finally vanished and tossed the last of the tokens across the waxy white flesh.

A substantial mass of weed had been gathered and laid into a pile nearby. Some was still damp – she just hoped it would burn...

"Pile it about the abelungu," she told the women. "And you men, bring torches."

The spirit was churning now, ready to be born out of that rotting belly and into the night, to take vengeance upon the living.

"Hurry!" the sangoma shouted. "Hurry!"

They quickened their pace, covering the corpse in the weed, concealing it from view.

"Burn it," she told the men.

They tossed their blazing torches into the pile.

There was a crackle and sputter as the damp seaweed began to catch, flames struggling to form. There seemed to be more smoke than fire. Would it work?

The sangoma dropped to her knees, still clutching her staff: This was it – her struggle was about to begin.

Above her, she could sense the amadlozi looking down upon her, willing her to victory. Silently, she called upon them to lend her their strength.

Within the flames, a sickly white light glowed, somehow brighter than the red fire. Beneath the burning weed, white flesh cracked open and the spirit seeped out towards her like a tide of pus. It stank of disease and death.

It swept over her like a tidal surge.

She felt as if she were drowning in filth...

She had to fight. Calling out to Unkulunkulu and all the ancestors, she struggled against it, calling upon the fire that burned within herself.

"Go!" she shrieked. "You do not belong here! Return to the stagnant depths that birthed you! You do not belong here!"

It was impossible: she was drowning, sinking down into a vile white void...

She had to rise. Rise or drown.

Flames burst from within her and were joined by fire falling from heaven as the amadlozi sent their aid to her, burning away the disgusting white liquid that cocooned her as the morning sun burns away the mist.

It vanished and she collapsed onto the ground, gasping for air. The rancid smell of smoke filled her lungs and she began to cough.

Looking up, the sangoma watched as the last white tendrils withdrew into the pyre where they were burned up alongside the foul flesh that had birthed them.

From the umuzi, the chief's wife came running, shouting joyfully: "He is awake! He is awake!"

The last light of the sun vanished and night surrounded them. The flames flared, then began to die.

"It is over," gasped the sangoma. "It is over."

As if coming out of a stupor, the people slowly began to cheer.

With difficulty, she stood.

"When the morning light comes," she said, "take the ashes and whatever is left and throw it all into the sea – send the evil home."

She turned and began to hobble back towards the huts.

"As for me, I need to sleep..."

SMOAKE AND MIRRORS

NANCY A. HANSEN

When you are an independent woman of small stature, whose skin is darker than the average person on the street, you learn that it's quite important to have some sort of claim to fame. Chandra Smoake was the epitome of a someone who had raised herself from outsider obscurity to the very fringes of social respectability.

She was bustling up the stairs of a brownstone on Holbrook Avenue where there had been a disturbance of the sort which interested her. It was always tough meeting new clients, and so she had dressed carefully. The hat was tasteful and not too large; a straw bucket with some ribbon and a rather long and vicious hatpin of ivory carved with esoteric protection symbols. The two piece suit was smartly tailored, though the skirt was not as narrow as was fashionable; the matching pumps had low block heels that were easy to run in. Practicality trumped style in her business, for one had to be able to move about rather quickly at times when things got intense. A canvas tote full of necessary oddities was over one shoulder, a purse decorated with needlepoint celestial images held firmly in a gloved hand. That hatpin and the Moroccan silver filigree *Hand of Fatima* pendant were the only outside indicators that this short, plump woman was something more than outward appearances would suggest. Chandra Smoake was a well-traveled and well-paid occult investigator, and she was both businesslike and exceedingly competent.

The address she had scribbled on a matchbook said #97 was the building she was looking for. She grabbed the brass knocker and gave it several vigorous bangs against the plate.

The middle-aged, tall and slender woman who came to the door looked like she hadn't slept for a month. Her eyes held that hollow gaze of the grief-stricken in war zones. "What do you want?" she asked listlessly.

"I am Chandra Smoake," she announced smartly as the woman opened the door a crack. "Are you Mrs Vera Hadley?"

"Oh… I wasn't expecting you so soon," the woman said, flinging the door open. "I just thought you'd be—"

"White? Well, I am partially, on my dear departed father's side," Chandra told her in her businesslike, matter-of-fact American English tone, though her voice still had a trace of her mother's Punjabi accent. "Now that we have that out of the way, am I still welcome?"

"Yes, of course, do come in. I'm sorry, I'm just overwrought," the older woman explained vaguely. She led the way through the foyer, moving listlessly past the narrow staircase that led to the upper floor and continuing on down a brief hallway.

Chandra looked around curiously as she trailed behind, and more importantly she *listened* to the whispers that no one else could hear. The spectral voices clamoring for her attention were particularly loud and rather strident. Many of them were filtering down from upstairs, and she was already getting uneasy feelings about the house as she tuned them out.

She followed the woman into the kitchen, where Vera Hadley busied herself heating a kettle on the range and setting out china cups and saucers with tea bags.

"Have a seat, Miss Smoake. Would you like some tea?"

"I would love a cup, if it isn't too much bother." Chandra carefully put her things down on one end of the Formica and chrome kitchen table and pulling out a matching chair, settled herself. Once the hot water was poured, she danced her tea bag in it, and after removing the bag, added a single dot of sugar. She looked over at her hostess, who was drowning her tea in cream and sugar. Goodness, what was the point of that?

"If you don't mind, I'd prefer to get down to business while we sip away. Now what exactly happened to your daughter?"

"It's a long story," the woman said, with a sigh that seemed to collapse her into a hunched position. Chandra opened her notebook and after writing a heading on a new page, looked up expectantly at the woman across from her, pen poised to take notes.

"Let's start at the beginning, shall we?" she said. "What makes you think you have a case of demonic possession?"

* * *

It appeared like the typical sort of thing. The girl was just entering adolescence and with the changing body came the sort of mood swings that open up a doorway to the unseen world. You can't medically treat or exorcise a child for being a teenager, but you can control what they are exposed to, if you know where to look for it. Chandra Smoake did. Yet she asked many questions and got only answers that lead to more questions...

"When did all this begin?" Chandra queried the mother.

"Somewhere just after my daughter turned fourteen and... um... well you know, she became a woman." Like most Americans, she seemed very uncomfortable talking about menstruation.

"What sort of out of character behavior did you notice?"

"Not too much at first, though this rock-and-roll, sock hop stuff is certainly a very bad influence," Vera Hadley said in a disapproving tone. "Donna used to be such an obedient girl and a good student, but almost overnight her attitude changed. She began to give us trouble over the smallest things and she would talk back and use slang. Her grades dropped off, and she was always going on and on about boys!"

That actually sounded pretty normal, but Chandra managed to suppress a wry smile. Whatever was cohabiting with the Hadley family in that building was not particularly humorous. "And as far as you know, she never dabbled in anything occult, such as Ouija boards, Tarot cards, candle spells, and so on?"

"Definitely not!" Vera Hadley exclaimed in a shocked tone. "I would not allow such foul nonsense into our home."

"Good," said Chandra, and marked that down. Those sort of things were not safe for the unenlightened, no more than a gun was a toy. Both came with dire consequences if you had no idea how to use one.

"So when did you move here, and why?" she asked the woman.

"My husband Matthew worked in the furniture sales department of Findleys for years," Vera answered with pride, for it was one of the biggest local chains, "and back then we lived in a two bedroom apartment. When he got promoted to sales manager we bought this place. Donna was only nine, and we worried that she'd miss her old school, but she seemed perfectly happy here. It's a pleasant neighborhood, and she had made friends with some nice girls before all this occurred." She was obviously fighting to keep her voice from quavering at the thought of how things had changed since then.

"I see," said Chandra, wondering what exactly had led the Hadleys to where they were now. "What have you done in order to help your daughter? I know from your message, she saw both doctors and specialists."

"We tried everything they suggested," Vera Hadley told her. "We took Donna to our family physician when she started mutilating her skin and talking about imaginary people; he referred us to a psychiatrist. She was hospitalized and they tried several medications; she seemed to be doing so well, they sent her home. Within a week she was back to screaming out in her sleep, throwing things, hurting herself, and babbling nonsense. *Five times* we've had her hospitalized, and even the electroshock therapy didn't stop it. Just be on the safe side, we had the local parish priest bless her with holy water, and we aren't even Catholics!

"Every time she comes home, it's the same. She's fine for a day or so, and then the whole ugly cycle begins again. I lost our last child to miscarriage because I was so distraught, and Matthew won't even talk to me about it. He blames Donna for everything and he wants her to be permanently committed. I can't stand the thought of my only child in an institution with... crazy people. We fight about it all the time, and it's tearing our marriage apart!"

The distraught woman lost her battle with tears and covered her face with her hands, sobbing in a heart-rending fashion. Chandra Smoake bustled over and poured them both more tea, giving her some time to compose herself.

Vera Hadley eventually looked up, her lipstick smeared into a clown-like grimace. "I'm sorry to break down like this but I just can't bear it anymore—"

"That is perfectly understandable. Any mother would feel the same way. Now how do you want to proceed?" Chandra asked quietly.

"I want my daughter back home where she belongs, Miss Smoake. Only Mathew cannot hear about any of this because I'm afraid he'll divorce me. I have a little money that my husband doesn't know about. It isn't a lot, but if you can somehow fix this, I will gladly give it up."

"We'll talk about payment once I've looked around," Chandra said with a thoughtful glance at the time. She had to be out of there before the husband came home or he would likely throw her out. It had happened before. Most women were more open to the occult than men were. "With your permission, I should like a tour of your home."

"Please, anything you need," Vera said in a shaky voice.

* * *

Perhaps it had been the palpable distress of Vera Hadley or the distracting whispers of the spectral voices that had caused Chandra to be less than observant about the interior of the house when she had first come in. She was far more thorough about noting things now, paying close attention to details both corporeal and on the spectral plane. Like a lot of older residences, the Hadley family home had its share of 'psychic sludge', leftover energy from almost a hundred years of occupation.

The kitchen seemed like a sanctuary, which was probably why Vera Hadley had instinctively headed directly to it. The rest of the home was charming and rather tastefully furnished as well as scrupulously clean, but it did have the usual brownstone emphasis on plenty of dark wood, large windows, and steam radiators that made hissing, clanging, and whistling sounds. Rather disconcerting when you were home alone or trying to sleep, no doubt.

"You seem to have a lot of mirrors," Chandra noted. There was at least one in every room except for the kitchen and the hallway, though the foyer had one right by the door when you came inside.

"Yes, my husband has brought home several from work that were unclaimed or returned. He says they make the place look brighter. Is that some sort of problem?"

Chandra thought about it a moment. "Generally speaking no, providing none of them were antiques from an older home. I suppose there is a chance that one of the returned items picked up something…"

The brownstone also had a long history of tenants before the Hadleys bought the building. Some of them had never left, but that was nothing new to Chandra, as she had dealt with residential spirits before. Most of them were benign; lost souls who tended to hover in places they had occupied in life. Often enough, occupants in the material realm had no idea they had otherworldly entities. In the worst case scenarios, there were the usual mischievous to antagonistic poltergeist activities.

What was happening in the Hadley house was something else altogether. Most of the spectral inhabitants were agitated because 'something else' had joined them and was declaring lordship over all. That was an indication that whatever had entered the scene was a higher vibration entity from what Chandra termed the *Malevolent Plane*. It was clearly demonic, and had no tolerance for the mortal inhabitants of #97 Holbrook Avenue. She could not get a read on it by simply working her way through the pecking order of spirits in the home, because whatever this thing was, it was both powerful and self-protective. But she could sense it, and the strength of this one had made the hairs on the back of her neck stand up. The upstairs was definitely its realm, and the area in and around the daughter's bedroom felt cold, tense, almost humming with pernicious intent.

This was not going to be easy.

"By my analysis, your daughter's problems lie here in the house, not in herself. That is where I will be doing my work. When is your husband usually home?" she asked Vera Hadley as they trooped back downstairs and stood at the front door.

"By 5:30 most weekdays and all day on the weekends. I'd prefer you not be here when he's around. I'd have trouble explaining your presence, even if it were something benign like... a bridge club member..."

Chandra knew she was trying to politely explain his bias against people who weren't strictly Caucasian. She sighed, because you couldn't fight prejudicial thinking; it was up to the individual to change his or her beliefs.

"I understand, and I can work around his schedule. Here is my card with my contact information," she said, handing it over. "Please let me know if you are interested in having me back, and what would be the best time to do this. It will require several hours and some setup time beforehand. We'll talk about what this costs then, but I assure you, I *can* at least make your home safe for your family," Chandra added as she caught the woman's eye before taking her leave.

She didn't believe she'd ever hear from Vera Hadley again. The woman was more concerned about her husband's reaction to her last-ditch effort to save her daughter from a lifetime in a mental institution than she was to actually living like a normal human being.

Some people had far more constricted lives than she did. Chandra actually pitied them. She was free to be who she was, without pretension or having to conform to any rigid social mores, by virtue of the fact that her services were often so badly needed.

* * *

The call came surprisingly fast, just two days after she had left the Hadley household. Young Emma Gilbraith, Chandra's understudy and erstwhile housekeeper, met her at the door when she came in from giving a lecture on parapsychology at the local university. It had started well enough, but there were too many skeptics...

"Miss Chandra," Emma said, taking her mentor's jacket and hat and hanging them in the hall closet, "You had a call late in the afternoon. A woman named..." she dipped in a pocket of her dungarees, and pulled out a pencil and notepad. Brushing blonde bangs out of big blue eyes, she read, "Mrs Vera Hadley. She says she is free on next Tuesday if you'd like to come over and clean out her house." Emma turned an inquisitive look on Chandra. "She didn't say what happened, but I got the impression that you'd been there previously, and there's been another 'event' since. So I'm guessing she's not trying to hire you as a maid, right?"

"That assumption would be correct, dear," Chandra told her as she turned on the jet under the tea kettle. "Actually, I was thinking about her today, because I had a unit on spirit ingress that drew criticism bordering on derision, and she's got a rather powerful 'houseguest' from the Malevolent Plane bothering her daughter to the point of mental breakdown. Going over my notes, I now have a better idea about how it came in. Come have a cuppa with me, and I'll tell you all about it."

"Sounds like something totally off the wall then!"

"Precisely," Chandra answered, but wished sometimes these young people came with a translator. She was quite fond of Emma, who was reliable and not very squeamish. Things got messy at times. "I want you to come along with me Tuesday, because I suspect I will need your help with this one; it's big, belligerent, and powerful. I am going to have a devil of a time ousting it because it has found its way into the spiritual fabric of the building, yet I am still unsure how it got in there in the first place. It has also connected with the daughter somehow, but she doesn't seem to be the reason it manifested. There has to be a portal it has been using to get to her. I just haven't found exactly where that is yet – though I will."

"Cool!" said Emma as she dropped into a chair and sipped her tea. "Tell me what I have to do."

* * *

Tuesday morning at 9:30am Chandra and Emma stood in the foyer of the Hadley residence. A very frightened and white-faced Vera Hadley wrung her hands as she explained to them what had happened a few days prior.

"I went up to Donna's room to dust and sweep. I felt odd as soon as I got in there, like I was intruding or something. I just want the room to remain clean! As I was moving around I thought I saw something out of the corner of my eye. It was... it was too big to be a rat, and we have no pets, but it scooted across her floor more than once. I would turn to look at it, and it was gone.

"Then some of her books came tumbling out of the bookcase – I didn't think too much of that because I had been moving things around to clean beneath them. But when the door slammed shut I panicked..." her voice trailed off and she shivered. "The window was closed, so there was no breeze, and it seemed locked or stuck. While I was struggling with that, the ceiling bulb and bedside lamp both popped and glass sprayed everywhere. I finally wrenched the door open and ran out of there; but I turned my ankle and almost fell down the stairs, I was so terrified. Now my husband thinks I'm having a nervous fit, and he wants me to see the doctor too."

She buried her face in her hands and Chandra's heart went out to her.

Whatever had taken up residence in the Hadley home was purposely targeting the women. "Your husband has never seen any of these things happening, Mrs Hadley?" she asked quietly.

"No, he thinks I've gone off my rocker, as the young people say. I can't live like this, I just can't!"

She was near hysteria. Chandra took firm control of the situation. "Emma dear, take Mrs Hadley into the kitchen and make her some tea. I'm going to have a look around upstairs. Do not forget what I said about the shrouds, dear, because that should be dealt with as soon as you're able. I'll call you if and when I need you."

"Do you have a good supply of towels or bedding we can make use of?" Emma asked the woman.

"I... I believe so, but whatever use would they be?" Vera Hadley asked in an uncertain voice.

"She just wants the mirrors all draped. That should sort of calm things down," Emma explained without saying too much. She knew Chandra didn't fancy chasing the entity from room to room.

"I'll give you whatever you need," the woman told her, and headed resolutely to a hall closet with Emma behind her.

"We will leave the mirror in the daughter's room uncovered, I'll be working in there," Chandra called after them as they began raiding the linen closet while she was checking her bag of supplies. Whatever it was that had invaded the Hadley home, Chandra was determined that it was leaving that very day!

* * *

Halfway up the staircase, Chandra felt pressure building in her head and chest, as well as an angry buzzing in her ears. The more benign entities in the household were wailing in discord or whispering for her to go away. Many of them were unfriendly, but whatever had become the overlord of the spiritual realm at #97 Holbrook Avenue was decisively hostile and had grown stronger since her last visit.

Chandra pressed her lips together and frowned, but she resolutely continued up those stairs, though it felt like she was climbing a mountain with increasingly thin air. This shadow creature was malicious and it obviously fed on fear; she was determined to oust it before it gained any more strength. It knew she was there – and why. It was going to be an epic battle of wills just to evict it from the Hadley home, let alone send it back to the other side of life's veil.

The one encouraging thought was that while the demon had taken up residence in the building, it had not completely bound to Vera Hadley's daughter. The mother had said she was doing well in a controlled, clinical setting, and only relapsed at home. To have to exorcise the girl before dealing with the actual entity channeling through her would have made things far more difficult, and young Donna Hadley could be permanently injured in the process. Still, that meant that *something* somewhere in that Brownstone was harboring it, and that item needed to be identified and purified – possibly even destroyed. The question was, exactly what was it linked to?

Certainly the high amount of spiritual intensity in the building was making it far easier for this thing to manifest, for the bigger, more aggressive entities had no qualms about siphoning energy off their lesser counterparts. Once Chandra identified the portal it was using she would shut down that conduit and then have a chance of capturing and sending it away permanently. It would be wise to clean the rest of the vagrant spirits out afterward, so that nothing like this ever happened again.

Donna's room was where she set up, because it seemed like that had been the focal point of most of the manifestations. She decided to work in front of the big arch-shaped mirror on the dressing table. Nothing seemed particularly sinister about it, but if the amount of mirrors in the place were aiding manifestations as she suspected, this was one of the largest looking glasses in the entire home.

Out of the tote bag first was a wooden cigar box repainted black with leaded paint that had some finely ground iron and charcoal in the mixture, and equipped with a variety of helpful items. She quickly opened it and after moving a scatter rug, followed the carefully drawn design on the underside of the cover and chalked out a large sigil of protection on the floor encased within a pentagram. She laid candles at the cardinal points and a shot glass of holy water flanked by an abalone shell with a bundle of sage that had been lit and was smoldering, sending up cleansing wisps. It was all surrounded by a hexagon of coarse salt large enough to stand inside; that took care of the four elements of fire, water, air, and earth.

Black box and tote bag within reach, Chandra took a moment to calm and center herself, and then voiced the evocation, choosing words which came easily to mind and had personal meaning. Focus of will and a strong personal conviction were everything.

Already she could feel the ominous magnitude of the demon's presence.

Chandra spoke in a powerful undertone that seemed to resonate in the room.

"I stand in the protection of The Living Earth.
Nothing and no one can harm me here.
Manifest foul thing, for I demand your presence.
I would speak with you before you are banished."

The cruel, raucous laughter her opening provoked was almost deafening, though she heard it only in her mind. The candles guttered and nearly went out, and the salt blackened. The stench of death and decay that filled the air and overpowered the cleansing scent of sage was very real, and almost choking. It was enough to make a less secure or savvy person want to cover her ears and run blindly from the room to where she could breathe without that foulness filling her nostrils. Chandra had enough experience to know this was just a preliminary test of her resolve and that the demon would not be able to keep up that robust of a pretense for very long without actually manifesting before her. So as the room grew darker and shadows loomed, she stood her ground, though she realized now that this being was even more substantial in the world of the living than she had expected.

It wanted something. They always did.

Obviously the entity had been holding back its energy to see just what kind of offensive attack she could offer. Chandra was not about to take that bait. She would continue to provoke it until it actually appeared, because that was when they became most vulnerable. Face to face was always the best way to deal with a malicious spirit, though it was generally the most dangerous way as well.

"Parlor tricks, how very quaint," she taunted it. "What else have you to share with me before I send you back to the Void?"

The answer was a snarl and a feeling like Chandra had been walloped in the abdomen. It bent her double and she went down on all fours, breathless and retching. She managed not to spew on the floor, but it was an effort. Even while her body recovered from the attack, her nimble mind raced.

Clearly a higher level demonic, judging by its ability to assault her without having to manifest. That it could reach her through the protective circle with at least a psychic attack was not encouraging, but it did explain why it had such a profound effect on the Hadley women. Interesting that it never bothered the father though. There had to be some reason for that.

It also seemed reluctant to leave its sanctuary to confront her, if the mirror was actually what was harboring it. That indicated a level of wariness about her own abilities. Chandra knew that she had to get it riled up enough to appear in that mirror.

That was when she might need Emma, who was rather cool-headed under pressure. For the time being though, she would work alone. Drawing it forth without endangering herself would call for a higher level of defense. Once Chandra had recovered her equilibrium and the room stopped spinning, she snatched up five blessed cards depicting the four archangels, who were powerful spirits of defense, along with a personal favorite high-level entity she liked working with. She set them in between each of the five candles marking the points of the pentacle and then chanted her own short version of the Lesser Banishing Ritual of the Pentagram. Using an ebony handled, ivory bladed letter opener as a ritual tool to draw invoking signs, she chanted.

"Behold, Foul Thing!
To left and before me stands Raphael the Healer.
To right before me, Michael the Warrior lifts His sword.
On my left flank awaits Gabriel the Messenger.
Flanking right whispers Uriel the Wise.
Behind me, Diana the Huntress raises her bow.
You shall not harm me or those I protect."

It was a gamble at best because archangels didn't always respond to requests from laity, though the presence of a malevolent entity of this caliber should at least gain their attention. While Diana was always near enough to make her presence known, her powers were limited to dealing with corporeal manifestations.

The demon itself was not in the least bit swayed by Chandra invoking the presence of four archangels and a random goddess. It too was a higher vibration entity, and was quite confident in whatever refuge it had found in the Hadley home. It was not about to be ousted that easily, though it reacted immediately to her challenge.

No laughter this time, but a loud, rumbling growl that seemed to reverberate from the very bowels of the building. It was quickly accompanied by a shock wave that blew out every light bulb on all floors while ringing the phone and doorbell, along with rattling doors and windows. Chandra was staggered and went sprawling backwards; the candles flared up and then blew out in long strings of flame, thankfully not igniting her hair or clothing. She could hear Vera Hadley's shrieks of terror downstairs and Emma's somewhat shaken but still relatively affirming voice suggesting she should step outside for some air and let them handle things.

Emma was a trouper; she was always dependable under duress. Chandra left the frightened woman to the girl's capable hands and scrambled back to her feet in time to see a puddle of bubbling dark gore oozing out of the baseboards and creeping inexorably across the floor at her. It quickly overtook the salt circle and swept the candles and cards aside, snuffing the final wisps of smoke and obliterating the visages of angels.

Ah well, some ectoplasm at last! It was an encouraging sign that the demon had become concerned about her, because manifesting even that amount of non-corporeal energy had to be taxing. Yet none of it seemed to have much to do with the damnable mirror!

"I am not impressed," she stated flatly as the ætheric sludge began to overtake her. "If your idea is to send me packing, you'll have to do better than this." The creeping feeling of the slurry that appeared to be engulfing her sensible low-heeled shoes and rather expensive nylons from Macy's was incredibly disconcerting, though Chandra forced herself not to pay attention to it because it was simply another psychic attack. It felt like she was being overrun by nipping ants with feet of ice. How something could be prickly hot and yet intensely cold at the same time was disconcerting, but she refused to give in to the hysteria, knowing there could be far worse to come.

When the slime turned into ropes of wriggling, hissing snakes coiling about her legs and crawled up under her skirt, Chandra had taken about all she was going to of these overly-theatrical exhibitions.

"That is quite enough now! Either get out here and face me, or I am going to drag your sorry—"

Emma's voice interrupted her. She sounded more than a bit shaken herself, as she called up the stairs.

"Miss Chandra, we've got a... a situation going on down here!" There was the sound of Vera Hadley crying out and some slapping noises. Hopefully Emma wasn't being too hard on the poor woman.

Worry for her apprentice and Mrs Hadley took Chandra's focus off her own plight long enough to break the psychic hold the entity had over her, though it also killed her concentration. The snakes seemed to slump back down into the ooze, which rapidly withdrew, but the feeling of hostility was heightened until she was shaking in anxiousness to leave that room. She rapidly gathered up her things, which other than being tumbled all over, were still intact. The sigil was gone though, and with it the ring of salt. The holy water seemed to have evaporated.

"I'll be back to deal with you," she warned the demon before heading downstairs. She caught the movement of something out of the corner of her eye as she exited the room, but the door slammed shut behind her before she could get a better look.

Chandra shouldered her tote and was making her way down the staircase when she suddenly lost her footing. She grabbed for the railing desperately as something shoved her from behind with brutal force. She instinctively dropped to a sitting position and slid down very ungracefully on her rear end, just glad not to have turned an ankle or otherwise been harmed, though she lost a shoe and those expensive nylons were now rather shredded.

"Are you hurt?" Emma asked as she retrieved the shoe and helped her back to her feet.

"Only my pride, dear," Chandra answered while dusting herself off. "I will admit that this one has me a bit concerned. It is quite strong and well entrenched for something that only recently began making its presence known. I have to wonder what set it off, and I will need your input on that. Other than the more dramatic antics of the Hadley's house guest, what have you noted?"

"Well, all the taps are running blood, and the kitchen is buzzing with a few hundred flies. They seem pretty real, because they can bite," she added, showing Chandra some welts on her arms, neck, and face. "They appeared right after things began to get interesting," Emma added, looking around a bit uneasily. "They were landing all over us within moments."

"How utterly disgusting! Yet that was clever on the part of the demon, to bring in a phenomena from the physical world to trouble us with. What did you do with Mrs Hadley?" Chandra asked as she headed toward the kitchen. There was a low but persistent hum of numerous insects, and something smelled like sulfurous rotten cabbage. She peeked into the kitchen. It was filled with carrion flies – hundreds of them clinging to the walls and ceiling, crawling all over the cabinets and counters. They flew around restlessly as soon as she stepped inside, but settled down once she ducked out again. The rank smell was coming from them.

"She was nervous from the beginning, so right after the... um... big blowout, when we got bombarded by flies, she became hysterical. I grabbed her by the hand, got her coat from the hall tree, and hauled her outside. I calmed her down before I hailed a cab and sent her off to church so she could have some peace. She had her purse with her and I made sure she had the fare to get back home.

"But looking back now, something odd and kind of creepy happened before it got weird..." Emma added. Her pert nose wrinkled, indicating she was disturbed about something and thinking hard.

"Let us take this discussion outside for a moment," Chandra said on a hunch. There was still the buzz of flies as well as the whispering of spirits warning her away. The less this malignant apparition knew about her plans, the better.

They walked back down the hallway and before they stepped out of the front door, Emma wedged a chair in it so that it couldn't slam shut of its own accord and somehow lock them out.

"Please go on," Chandra told her.

"I'd been laying it out with her all along that things could go sideways, so she needed to beat feet out of here—"

"Miss Gilbraith, in English please!" Chandra insisted sternly.

At her mentor's frown, Emma corrected herself. "Sorry, it's been a doozie of a day so far. I meant, I'd been suggesting all along to Mrs Hadley that she should leave the house for a while. I wanted her out before something really scary happened. You always say we work better alone, without extra emotions mucking things up, and she's *waaaay* too high strung. Anyway, just before all holy-heck broke out she agreed to leave, but wanted to check her makeup and hair first. I told her we shouldn't uncover any mirrors, so she fished a compact out of her purse.

That got Chandra's attention. "A compact? You mean one of those purse size rouge or face powder cases?"

"Yeah, that," Emma agreed. "It's a pretty little thing – likely a Stratton, with pink roses on the cover and a mirror inside – but once she opened it, it was like she became a whole other person. Normally, she's kind of a square." At Chandra's frown over the unfamiliar beat term, Emma explained, "I mean she's rather strait-laced, but all of a sudden she's pouting and making these faces and poses like she's Marilyn Monroe. It was embarrassing! So I kind of cleared my throat and she looked up surprised at me, then back down at the compact, and then totally freaked out and dropped it like a hot potato! She kept saying, 'That's not me, I'm not dead!', shaking like a leaf and clawing at herself. That's when things went wonky and the flies came after us. I jumped up and grabbed her because I thought she was going to pass out and hit the floor. I did catch a glimpse of something in the mirror before it went back to reflecting the ceiling, but I haven't a clue what it was because I was trying to comfort her and get her out the door before all those flies ate us alive. They were landing all over us, in our hair and eyes, ears, and noses. It was disgusting!"

Now that was interesting — and useful. "A very astute observation under the circumstances, my dear, considering all you were dealing with. Where is said compact now?" Chandra queried. Hopefully the woman didn't take it with her!

"I made sure she left it on the kitchen table. I did shut it though."

"Good thinking." That would make it far easier to handle. Such a small thing to harbor something so hostile and powerful. Portable and very easily overlooked — quite clever of this thing. "Tell me Emma, was there any manifestation in the kitchen *before* she opened that compact?"

The girl thought for a moment. "No, not really," she finally admitted. "I mean, the lights flickered and then the bulbs popped, but that was it. The bloody tap and the flies came after the compact was open. So that's important, right?"

Chandra nodded. "Most likely, yes. In fact, I believe you might have solved the problem of how this entity got in here in the first place; and perhaps even, *why*. They all need a locus; something to fasten onto that becomes the doorway to our realm of the living. They also tend to have some ulterior motive. I suspect that compact might be the key to what this particular demon wants here as well as what holds its true form, and I'd love to know more about where it came from and how long Vera Hadley has owned it. Unfortunately it's 3pm, and we're running out of time, so I will have to act on assumption and see how that goes. Why don't you go look for Mrs Hadley, Emma; and see what she has to say about the origin of that particular compact. In the meantime, I've got to do everything possible to cleanse this place of the interloper's foul presence. Obviously this entity is well-established here now, and so it is mirror hopping. I must get it to transfer from that compact to the mirror upstairs so that I can isolate and view it in its entirety before I can figure out how to capture it."

"You... have an idea of what sort of thing we're dealing with?" Emma asked with her head tilted to one side, like a dog listening to its mistress' voice.

"I believe I do now, because it made the mistake of tipping us off. I just need a few moments to think of how exactly to go about flushing it out into the open."

* * *

Whenever a spiritual entity tormented someone, as this demonic presence had with the Hadley women, it had an agenda. That sort of exhibition took incredible energy, and until it had a willing human host body, it would not be able to carry out whatever it had come here for. Since it had obviously given up on possessing young Donna Hadley, who was no longer in residence, and was now trying to drive the mother away, it had to be after the master of the house.

Yes, Chandra decided, *Matthew Hadley was the target*. That most likely meant that this manifestation was a succubus; a demon that preyed upon unwary males.

She had to evict it from their house before the husband came home, because he'd most likely throw Chandra out on her ear and then have his wife committed along with his daughter. His level of negativity would enable the demon to bide its time, building strength and sway over him until it had corrupted his reasoning. The pernicious mischief that would ensue did not bode well for any of the Hadleys or their descendants. Once well established, it would plague and subvert their family for generations; attaching itself to one member or another, causing mental issues and ruining lives.

When she set up again for the final battle, Chandra had to still her anxiety and strengthen her will before beginning the summoning. This time it would be housed within an indisputable threat that no otherworld entity could refuse to acknowledge.

She quickly redrew the protective circle with extra defensive runes and glyphs added in, forgoing the candles, the sage, and elemental representatives as well as the pictures of the archangels. Those higher vibration spirits had not been properly dismissed, so they would either have lingered nearby or dispersed on their own – if they had even answered her request for assistance in the first place. With the demon's interference muddling things, there was no telling what might have been about to present itself.

"All right, you nasty fiend," she said, facing the dressing table mirror. "Come out and play with me again. Oh and in case you were wondering what happened to it, I've brought along your temporal world vehicle." She withdrew the compact from her black box, and placed the closed item on the floor before her, threatening to crush it underfoot. "You show yourself now and the worst you'll get is banished back to your level of the astral spheres. But if I can trap you here, and make your existence completely ineffective, you will learn to do my bidding."

It was a calculated deception of course, because Chandra had no interest in mastering and managing such a subversive entity, but the demon didn't know that.

It had the expected effect. The otherworld spirit slowly appeared in the large mirror before her, first as a dim, barely seen humanoid figure, gradually metamorphosing into that of a voluptuous, scantily clad woman. The succubus was both very alluring and incredibly frightening at the same time, for while her body made promises that certainly any man – and perhaps even some women – would find irresistible, there was an alien feral glint in the eyes that said this creature was nothing of the mortal plane. Chandra knew from experience that what she was viewing was a 'seeming', a projected image designed to mesmerize and distract the attention of the unwary from what was blatantly wrong about the creature. That the image was so clear and detailed, with no wavering, said this particular demon was very old, quite powerful, and well experienced.

While she studied it, her mind raced over what she knew of its kind.

The succubi and their counterparts incubi were an ancient, untamed, and initially genderless class of Asmodian lust demons. Their purpose was to tempt and ultimately subjugate humans into copulating with them, in hopes of breeding a mortal world version of themselves. This one was a vain and powerful hunter of mortal male sexual slaves. It would attach itself to one man after another, projecting the outward appearance of a desirably wanton woman while draining them of life energy until they stopped eating, sleeping, and caring for anything other than pleasing their otherworld mistress. Some men would languish for years that way, giving up everything and everyone else they loved and had worked for, eventually dying of personal neglect. The strongest amongst them would be used as bait to bring even more men in to grovel at the whims of the succubus. With an open ingress into the world of the living, there was no telling how many lives it could destroy.

That was just *not* going to happen if Chandra could prevent it!

The demon laughed aloud, its voice low toned and sultry though it sounded as if it spoke in an echoing cave.

"Go away, mortal woman. You are no match for me."

"I wouldn't be so sure of that."

The room dimmed and the air became fœtid and barely breathable, while a buzzing sound that gradually became louder announced that the flies from the kitchen were now on their way. Whatever she fought back with would have to be done quickly because the insects were of the corporeal world, so like cats they would be able to pass right through the spiritual boundary she had set up to protect her from the demon. That they could bite and would soon be swarming all over her would make it impossible to concentrate. And if she left the circle to close the door, the demon would be able to attack her...

The first of the swarm began circling Chandra before landing on her head, arms, and legs. She stooped for the compact but within moments they were crawling all over her face, into her eyes and burrowing through hair to her scalp, buzzing in her ears, trying to force their way up her nose. She couldn't see anything and she was too busy flailing and beating them away to be able to think clearly. Undulating masses of flies coated her arms and legs, their feet prickling on her skin as they fought each other to bite into every inch of exposed flesh they could find.

Chandra slapped at them frantically as she staggered around trying not to fall or step outside the chalk lines, which she could still feel the hum of if not actually see. She wanted nothing more than to scream and run blindly away, but if she left the protection of the circle, the demon would have a field day with her. As it was, she was barely able to keep her wits about her. She ducked and weaved and her skin twitched at repeated bites in places she couldn't slap because she had to keep batting the foul smelling flies out of her eyes and ears.

"*Kneel to me, human, and I will call them off,*" the demon snarled as it turned to watch her with a knowing smirk and pitiless eyes. "*You will make a good thrall.*"

"Diana – I need your strength!" Chandra cried out as the flies began to bite her lips. A dozen at a time tried to crawl inside her mouth. Their stench and the sheer mass of heaving chitinous bodies began choking her. She spat them out as more followed, and Chandra knew she was on the very edge of hysteria.

The demon cackled with glee as Chandra went down on her knees under the onslaught. Covering her head with her arms, she struggled feebly against the unrelenting scourge.

OPEN YOUR EYES AND DO NOT SURRENDER TO MADNESS OR IT WINS. FIGHT THE DAUGHTER OF LIES WITH THE TRUTH OF ITS BEING, Diana whispered. A picture appeared in Chandra's mind, a hideous visage of a rotting corpse in grave cloth covered in maggots, the hair on its skin-covered skull lank and thin, milky eyes unseeing, and the snaggle-toothed mouth gaping in a soundless scream.

There was something about that image, something... something Emma had told her that Vera Hadley had said about not being dead. What was it? So hard to concentrate.

On a whim Chandra snatched up the compact, opened it, and gasped when the same hideous vision appeared within the little round mirror. Realizing what it was, she leapt to her feet and quickly turned it toward the one attached to the dressing table while still batting flies with the other hand.

"See yourself as you really are and begone back to the Void!" Chandra shouted triumphantly while holding the compact as steady as possible with it facing toward the larger mirror.

In a moment the flies cleared away, dropping to the floor with the pattering sound of a hard rain. She could now see the image of the succubus, and it was riveted on the smaller mirror. No longer fearful for her own safety, Chandra stepped forward out of the protective circle, her feet crunching on dead flies, as the demon recoiled in what appeared to be shock. Its form wavered as it pointed at the compact, its more grotesque death visage reflected repeatedly in the larger mirror; first a few times, then a dozen, and then hundreds of times more as Chandra closed in.

"That is not me – it's *not* me!" the succubus howled as her hands and arms, suddenly no more than dry skin stretched over bone, went up to her weathered face in shock. She covered her sightless eyes and screamed, but nothing came out of that empty, toothless mouth except a dry rasp that rattled the skeletal image into fragments, which faded into shimmering dust motes that drifted out of the larger mirror and swirled around until they were drawn into the compact.

Chandra remained steadfast as grave dust and prana – the essence of otherworld energy that gave the unseen world of spirits a chance to enter that of everyday reality – drifted back into what had become both their vehicle and tomb.

When it was over, Chandra snapped the compact shut and tucked it back into her black box. She pushed the dead flies away and smudged out the chalk lines before wearily gathering her things and heading downstairs. There would be some cleanup for poor Vera Hadley, but for the most part the house was now safe to enter once more. Most of the lost souls had been drained away when the succubus had finally made its appearance, and what was left of them seemed to have faded with the death of the carrion flies.

She was exhausted and used the house phone to call a cab, locking the door behind her and waiting on the front stairs outside. Emma would understand if she went straight home, had a long soak and a scrub in the clawfoot tub, and then took a nap.

* * *

"What did you learn from Vera Hadley about the compact?" she asked Emma over takeout food purchased at a chop suey joint on the way home.

"Oh, that's a no-brainer. She said her daughter found it in the dressing table that her father gave her for her Sweet Sixteen birthday. It was tucked into the back of one of the drawers, likely left behind when the piece was repo'ed, I guess."

"Interesting. I wonder how it picked up the demon?"

Emma shrugged. "No idea. They wouldn't let Donna keep anything like that in the asylum because the patients fight over them, and the glass could be used to... uh... to cut yourself." That someone could become so despondent as to willfully cause herself bodily harm was a disturbing thought to a young woman as upbeat as Emma Gilbraith. She shook her head before picking up another bite of her meal and chewing thoroughly. Chandra gave her time to finish her thought. "I guess Mrs H picked it up when she was cleaning her daughter's room, and tucked it into her purse for safekeeping, where it had been ever since. She hadn't really looked at it before today."

"I see," Chandra said slowly. There was a good chance the succubus had not left the house with Donna, and so it had pestered the mother about primping until the compact came out and it had entered it once more. She would have to see that it was locked up somewhere safe. She had friends in New England who collected such things, studying them and keeping them out of the hands of the public. Chandra supposed she could send it to them – though it might be better if she dropped it off in person.

"Emma dear, if your classes are done for the week and you haven't much studying to do, we need to take a road trip. How do you feel about driving to Connecticut this weekend and meeting some fellow spirit chasers?"

"Swell! Sounds like a blast to me," Emma said with the enthusiasm of youth.

Chandra simply smiled and nodded wearily.

THE SPIRITS IN THE AIR

AIDAN HAYES

"I'll have the chicken pesto, water to drink." I snapped my menu closed and handed it to the waiter.

"The house salad for me, water too."

I was in a small cafe on the south side of the city. It was dusk; the streetlights had just come on and were shining in through the wide windows. We were the only two customers left, everyone else had gone home. I would have felt bad for keeping the place open, but I made it a point to tip so well that the staff didn't care.

I was sitting across the table from a young girl with long hair. She had a nose ring and wore a loose blouse with a pair of khaki capris. Her arms were coated in bracelets from the wrists to the elbows. Each bracelet was unique, some made of metal, some twisted out of string.

"Let's start with the basics," I said. "How old are you?"

"You shouldn't eat chicken."

"Oh? Why's that?" I had my notebook spread open in front of me, a pen in my hand.

"When the bird dies the spirit binds to the flesh, and when you eat it, that sets the spirit free. Then it imprints on you. Chicken spirits are a bitch to remove."

"Good to know. Now back to my question, how old are you?"

"Twenty, but my birthday's next month."

"Where did you grow up?"

"What's it matter?"

"These questions are a sort of baseline, they help me get a feel for you," I said. It was true, but I didn't mention that I was checking her aura for changes, trying to get a feel for when she was lying.

"I kind of bounced around the system, I didn't really have a place to call home 'till I was sixteen."

"Tragic. Is that when you learned to lie?" I had known that what she said about the chicken spirits was true, and no one who lies about their age claims to be 20. That was all the truth I needed to pick out her lie like a bad tooth.

"Fine, I grew up in the Bronx. My family was well-off, rich really, but they never qualified it that way. I'm kind of the black sheep of the family, they don't like my politics."

"Just your politics? Not the fact that you see things?" I jotted down what she told me in the notebook as she talked. Writing things down was always good; words have power even when they're sealed up in a notebook.

"I didn't always see things. Even when I started to see spirits I didn't know what was going on at first. I thought I was crazy, it fucked me up pretty bad."

"What's the first thing you remember seeing?"

"I was walking to the bodega at the end of my street when I heard a crash. An SUV had T-boned a coupe. It had a family in it, just coming home with their new kid. They hadn't been married long, two years. They had a life ahead of them. I was just walking down the street and then they were dead. I was frozen, I wanted to help, I wish I could have done something. I saw their spirits leave the wreck. Those spirits, they never went away. Those were the first, and they still haunt me. Not literally of course, they stick to the site of the crash, but when I close my eyes it all comes back."

"That sort of accident is usually pretty powerful. You say the spirits stick to the site of the crash? How long ago did you last see them?"

"Christmas. I went home at Christmas, that's when my family cut me off, I haven't been back since. I used to see them every day."

The waiter brought out a tray with two waters on it. She set one in front of me and one in front of the girl.

"I'm sorry to keep you open tonight, tell the chef I appreciate it," I said to the waiter, while I pulled out a hundred from my cash-stuffed wallet to give her. The waiter took the bill and put down two straws.

"It's no problem, we're always happy to have you."

"You come here often?" The girl asked, taking a sip of her water. She didn't even look at the straw, leaving it wrapped on the table. I pressed the bottom of my straw on the table to push it out of its paper.

"It's the only place in the whole city that makes decent chicken. I doubt you care about that though." A lot of people who see things tended to avoid animal products. An awareness about those sorts of things came with the territory.

"I'm vegan, but I'm glad to hear the food's good."

"How long have you been a vegan?"

"About a month after I saw that family die I started to see other things, animals mostly. I ignored it at first. I thought it would get better, or that I was going crazy. I don't know what I thought, but you can't imagine the sort of toll it takes on a person to see what they eat come out of the flesh. I began by avoiding meat, which helped at first, but then things got bad again, so I cut out all animal products."

"Does it make the spirits go away?"

"No. It doesn't make them go away, but it keeps them off my back. They don't keep me up at night when they know I'm not the one who made them. And that way I never have to risk a particularly vengeful animal."

"Vengeful?"

I knew what she meant about the spirits never going away. Even when you don't eat meat other people still do, and the spirits tend to float around rather indiscriminately. I knew what she meant about vengeful spirits too. Most of the time a meat spirit was weak and didn't do anything other than float around your head showing off its mutilated corpse; sometimes, though, you got one that would attack your soul. The attack usually caused vomiting and sickness.

"Mean spirits. They kind of come after people they don't like. I had one make me horribly sick. That's when it really clicked that I need to avoid all animal products. I wasn't eating meat at the time but a spirit out of a piece of steak came after me while I was walking next to a diner in my leather jacket. It was a nasty spirit, one of the biggest I've ever seen; I was hospitalized for three days."

"It came after you because of a jacket?" Spirits clung to remnants of their physical form. It's possible that the cow the jacket came from was related to the steak. It wasn't something that happened often, and even when it did happen most of the spirits weren't strong enough to act. It was just bad luck that she got hit so hard.

"That's the only thing I can think of. Spirits don't attack people randomly, you have to do something to piss them off."

"What about haunted houses and stuff? Aren't some spirits just angry?"

"Not that I know of. You have to do something against them, sometimes it can be as simple as walking through the wrong part of the house."

She was right. Spirits were touchy things, but you do have to affect them in some way for them to take interest in you. There have been a few cases of spirits attacking people who didn't do anything, but those cases always had something else going on. The only time I had ever seen it, someone had been manipulating the spirits into attacking people.

The waitress carried two plates of food to the table – my pasta and the girl's salad. The plates were still warm; the kitchen had probably already washed all the dishes by the time I showed up. I pulled out another hundred and handed it to the waitress. My pesto was only seven dollars and the salad was six, but I would happily have paid any price.

"Take your time, we're gonna start to close up. Unless you need anything else," the waitress said.

"I think we're good." I gave a glance to the girl and raised my eyebrows.

"I'm good," she said.

"Thank you though," I added. The waitress left, and I unrolled my silverware.

"Please don't eat that chicken. The spirits float around even though I'm not eating it."

"Don't worry, like I said this is the only place that makes good chicken. They clean it with a special ritual; it binds the spirits into a crystal they keep in the back." I took a bite of the chicken pesto to prove my point. Like she said, usually when someone bites into a piece of meat the spirit – or a fragment of it – flies out of the food. This time, nothing happened. I loved meat, but I never got to eat it, so this restaurant was a great pleasure of mine.

She looked shocked.

"I told you," I said.

"That's not possible. Where's the spirit?"

"As I said, it's in the back."

"That's incredible. I didn't think I'd ever see someone eat meat without a spirit again. It's really kind of relaxing."

"No point in lying anymore – I can see things too," I admitted. She'd probably guessed that by now.

"If you can see spirits, then why did you ask me all those questions?"

"I was trying to get a grasp of how much you know. A lot of people think they can see things, but they can't; I'm sure you've met plenty of people who claim that they can see things but are just making shit up."

"I'm not lying this time."

"I know you aren't. You've got most of it right, an impressive amount really. I haven't heard you say anything incorrect yet, but I can probably elaborate on some points. The jacket probably was the issue with that cow. I know a few things that can keep it from happening again."

"Really?" The girl had abandoned her salad and was staring straight at me.

"Really." I continued to eat, letting silence fall between us. She needed to take the next step. If she was interested, she'd keep talking. She took a bite of her salad and chewed it pensively.

"So, what's the catch? What do I have to do? I don't have much."

"I don't want money, I want your help. I'm a journalist. I try to learn as much as I can and then I write it all down."

"Sounds lucrative." The girl was suspicious, or at least sarcastic. Journalists don't usually carry the kind of cash I did.

"I work for Hollywood, as a sort of consultant. They pay me to make their depictions of the occult more accurate. I do the opposite; I make sure that they don't do anything too genuine. That way no one gets hurt for a movie. And people don't start getting scared in real life."

"So, what exactly do you want with me?" The girl had once again abandoned her salad, her fork beside her plate with a piece of lettuce still on it.

"I want you to let me help you. You have a rare skill, and it's rarer still to be able to cope with it. I think you could do great things, with my help."

"So, you want to teach me?"

"Yes, seeing things is a powerful skill, I want you to make good choices with your gift. I'll give you a monthly stipend and you can leave at any time. I'm offering you an opportunity for hands-on experience dealing with spirits."

"I've spent a lot of effort avoiding demons since I started seeing them; what makes you think I want to deal with them?"

"You don't have a choice, you know that. Even if you walked away from me right now and tried your damndest to avoid the spirits you'd still see them. It never goes away, you're stuck with this for life. The best thing to do is to take ownership of it and use it. No one wants this gift, but it is a gift." I knew where she was coming from, I had run from myself for years. I did everything I could to hide from the truth. No matter how much I drank, or how much I ran, the spirits were always there.

"I don't want to hurt them, it's not their fault."

"The spirits don't want to be here anymore then you want them here. Spirits are restless, they don't want to exist, but they need assistance to get there. I'll teach you how to help them. It doesn't make it easy, but it helps. I'll teach you how to send that family to where they belong."

"Where exactly is that?"

"I don't know, but it can't be worse than here."

"Ok, when does the internship start?"

"It already has. Another part of the internship is telling me your life story – I catalog everything I can about those who can see. We can't afford to lose what precious little knowledge we have. That's lesson one – write everything down. I don't care what it is, write it down. When you put pen to paper it binds things, keeps them from being lost in the aether." I pulled out a blank notebook from my bag and handed it to the girl. I dug through my pockets and handed her one of my spare pens.

"Everything?"

"Anything you learn, anything you see, put it in the book. I find that it clears my mind and helps me connect dots I might miss otherwise. A big part of the job is investigating. Some spirits, like meat, are easy to dismiss; we know what caused them, so we can remedy it easily enough. Other things aren't so easy, you have to search for the reason why the spirit exists. They have unfinished business of some sort; I have to find it to help them pass on."

"So, can you help that family on my street?"

"Maybe. You said that they had just had their first kid, right?"

"Yeah, they were on their way home from the hospital."

"That's probably what's keeping them there. I could probably sort it out, but it would be easier for you to do it."

"How?"

"You take something that was important to them, something with a strong memory attached to it, then you write down what happened and speak it into the world. You acknowledge their business, and then you forgive it. If you can't find something that mattered to them you can use a quartz crystal, but it won't work with stronger spirits."

"So just say what happened and they get to move on? Plenty of people have said what happened to that family."

"Not everyone can do it — like I said, it's a gift. You have to know what you are doing for it to work. Stronger spirits also need stronger voices."

"Is that why you're a journalist?"

"Yes, it gives me a voice. Words have power. You'll see in time, most of us who see things end up writing for a living. It really does help."

"Anybody I've heard of?"

"Edgar Allen Poe, Stephen King, Ernest Hemingway, Philip K. Dick."

"That's quite the list."

"It's a gift, but it isn't something I would wish on my worst enemy. Drugs and alcohol are far too common. I can teach you how to cope without turning to substance abuse. Do you have any questions for me?"

"Where is this internship? In the city?"

"Yes, I have an office where you'll spend most of your time."

"How did you learn so much about spirits?"

"I had a mentor, she taught me everything she knew. It's been like that for five generations. She had a mentor and now I'm a mentor. Each generation adds to the knowledge gathered by the one before. I have a rather large library that, if things go well, will one day belong to you."

"When did you start seeing things?"

That was a touchy topic for me. I didn't like to talk about it, but this girl deserved to know if she was going to take over for me.

"I had an older brother. He was smart, driven, the sort of person that everyone loved. His teachers loved him, students loved him. He never made a mistake in his life, no one had a bad thing to say about him. I was no exception – I loved him deeply." I put down my fork and leaned back in my chair. "It was his senior year, I was only in the fourth grade, and he had just been accepted into Columbia. It was his dream, and he deserved it. He never got it.

"Our mother was out of town, a work conference, and he was watching me. We had a movie on, the first Scooby-Doo movie, I'll never forget it. He heard a knock on the door and he got up to answer it. The next thing I heard was a scream. It cut through the air and stopped the breath in my lungs with the sound of blood flowing into his. He had been stabbed in the chest twice. I held him as he died. I saw his spirit leave his body and stand there."

A tear threatened at the corner of my eye. It was a long time gone, but I could still hear the bubbling of the air in his chest cavity as he struggled to breathe.

"Every day I walked past him when I left the house. I thought I was seeing things, I didn't really know how true that was at the time. We found out after the funeral that he had been stabbed over eighty dollars that he didn't even owe the guy. The drug dealer had the wrong address and my brother looked just enough like the guy who owed him money to get stabbed."

I picked my fork back up and took another bite of the chicken.

"Did you ever help him move on?"

"He was the first one I helped, once I learned how."

"One more question: what's your name?"

"Lesson two: no names. You don't have a name if you take this internship. Names can be used against you."

"By what?"

"Not everyone who can see is a good person. The gift doesn't discriminate, there are plenty of bad eggs out there and they manipulate spirits. If they learn your name, they can twist it and use it to batter your soul. No names, ever." I wrote an address on a blank page of my notebook. I tore the page out and handed it to the girl. "See you tomorrow, 9:00am."

I walked out of the restaurant with my bag across my shoulder and my notebook in my hand. She had been telling the truth when she said she was in, but that didn't mean she wouldn't change her mind in the next twelve hours. I'd find out if she was my prodigy in the morning – no use worrying about it now.

She was waiting at my door at 8:55am.

CONAN AND CARNACKI: ROBERT E. HOWARD AND WILLIAM HOPE HODGSON

BOBBY DERIE

In the three-volume set of his *Collected Letters*, Texas pulpster Robert E. Howard (1906-1936) makes no mention of William Hope Hodgson (1877-1918). In the inventory of his library at the time of his death, recorded by Steve Eng in *The Dark Barbarian*, none of Hodgson's books are listed. A reader might

well suppose there was no evidence that Howard had ever heard of Hodgson – who was, after all, a fairly obscure British author most known for his sea-stories, occult detective, and weird novels.

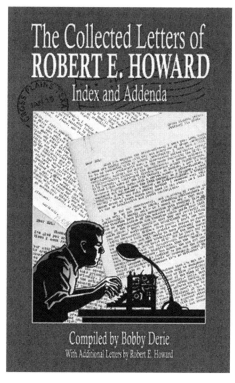

Yet if you put on your detective cap and dig a little deeper... while it is still not absolutely certain that Howard had heard of Hodgson, he was actually well-placed to have done so.

While not extensively published in the United States during his lifetime, Hodgson had success in publishing fiction in pulps such as *Adventure*, *The Argosy All-Story Weekly*, and *The All-Around Magazine*, which Howard was known to have read from at least the early 1920s. It would not have been out of place for the 19-year-old Texan to have read "Merciful Plunder" in the *Argosy All-Story* of 25 July 1925, and simply not have mentioned it in print. In 1917, Robert E. Howard may even have noticed the letter Hodgson had published in *Adventure*, or the notice of his death at Ypres that appeared in its pages in 1918. (*The Lure of Adventure* 8).

At the time the Great War ended, however, Howard lived in the small town of

HODGSON:
A COLLECTION
OF ESSAYS
Sam Gafford

Burkett; his access to pulps is unclear, and his letters don't start until 1923 – so it could be he missed Hodgson's contributions to literature up to this point in his life. He would be far from the only one. The bulk of Hodgson's work, especially his really notable weird fiction, was never published in the United States during his lifetime, except for a series of pamphlets to establish American copyrights. ("The Copyright Volumes" by Sam Gafford in *Hodgson: A Collection of Essays*). Even those well-read in the weird might know little or nothing about Howard in the early 20s.

An exception is the Rev. Henry St. Clair Whitehead (1882-1934), who would go on to become a writer for *Weird Tales*, and was familiar with Hodgson from the pages of *Adventure* (where he was also a contributor), and from British books and magazines obtained in the Virgin Islands. Whitehead mentions William Hope Hodgson and Carnacki in his letter "Editorial Prejudice Against the Occult" (*The Writer* Oct 1922, republished as Appendix F in *The Thing's Incredible! The Secret Origins of Weird Tales*), and in the article "The Occult Story" (*The Free-Lance Writer's Handbook*, 1926, reprinted in *Studies in Weird Fiction* #6). His story "The Shadows" in *Weird Tales* (Nov 1927) also mentions Hodgson in passing.

Around 1932 Whitehead and Howard corresponded very briefly (see "Conan and Canevin" in *Weird*

WILLIAM HOPE HODGSON
THE BOATS OF THE
GLEN CARRIG
"A variety of malign marvels..."—H. P. Lovecraft
Introduction By Lin Carter

Talers: Essays on Robert E. Howard & Others) and Howard himself admitted: "I had no regular correspondence with Whitehead beyond a few brief notes exchanged in a business way." (*Collected Letters* 3.47)

It seems unlikely, though not impossible, that Howard could have heard something of Hodgson's Carnacki stories from Whitehead – or would at least have run across the name if Whitehead had sent copies of either of his articles. However, later in his correspondence with H.P. Lovecraft, Howard admitted to having never heard of British ghost-story writer M.R. James (*Collected*

Letters 2.240), and James features in Whitehead's articles, so it seems very unlikely that Howard would have read either of those two articles.

Someone who *did* indisputably hear about Hodgson from Whitehead was H.P. Lovecraft, who visited his fellow *Weird Tales* author in Florida in 1931, and learned of the Carnacki stories from him. (*Letters to J. Vernon Shea, Carl F. Strauch, and Lee McBride White* 246, *O Fortunate Floridian! H.P. Lovecraft's Letters to R. H. Barlow* 163-164, *Essential Solitude: The Letters of H.P. Lovecraft and August Derleth* 2.656). The Carnacki tales, however, did not make a great impression on Lovecraft. The Providence pulpster would not be exposed to Hodgson again until 1934, when his friend and fellow Robert E. Howard correspondent, Clark Ashton Smith, lent him a small collection of Hodgson books that Smith had in turn borrowed from fan H.C. Koenig. (*Dawnward Spire, Lonely Hill: The Letters of H.P. Lovecraft and Clark Ashton Smith* 564).

Lovecraft was enraptured by *The Boats of the Glen Carrig*, *The House on the Borderland*, and *The Ghost Pirates*, and though he felt Hodgson's stories were poor in spots – particularly the quasi-archaic 18th century diction in 'Glen Carrig' – he quickly decided that Hodgson was a major weird author and deserved a mention in his long essay "Supernatural Horror in Literature" (*O Fortunate Floridian 168*, *Letters to F. Lee Baldwin, Duane W. Rimel, and Nils Frome* 100, *Dawnward Spire, Lonely Hill* 565-566). This essay had first

DAWNWARD SPIRE,
LONELY HILL

*The Letters of H. P. Lovecraft
and Clark Ashton Smith*

Edited by David E. Schultz and S. T. Joshi

been published in 1927 in *The Recluse*, an amateur literary journal published by Lovecraft's friend W. Paul Cook, a copy of which Lovecraft lent to Robert E. Howard in 1930. (*Collected Letters* 2.88).

In 1933, a revised and expanded version of "Supernatural Horror in Literature" began to be serialized in *The Fantasy Fan*, a fanzine produced by Charles Hornig and featuring a number of Weird Tales regulars as contributors, including Lovecraft, Clark Ashton Smith, and Robert E. Howard, the latter of whom began a subscription in late 1933. (*Collected letters* 3.136) Lovecraft had intended for Hodgson to feature in Chapter IX,

but the fanzine folded in 1935 in the middle of Chapter VIII. Lovecraft's notes, "The Weird Works of William Hope Hodgson," would eventually be published in another fanzine, *The Phantagraph* (Feb 1937) – but by that time Howard was dead.

Clark Ashton Smith sent Lovecraft two other Hodgson books (from Koenig, again): *Carnacki, the Ghost Finder* and *The Night Land*, in 1934. (*Essential Solitude* 2.661) Lovecraft sang the praises of Hodgson to many of his correspondents, and as with his unpublished manuscripts began a circulation list for those who wanted to borrow Koenig's books – starting with August Derleth and Duane W. Rimel, but including Bernard Austin Dwyer, F. Lee Baldwin, Emil Petaja, William Crawford, C.L. Moore, and Fritz Leiber. While Howard was on

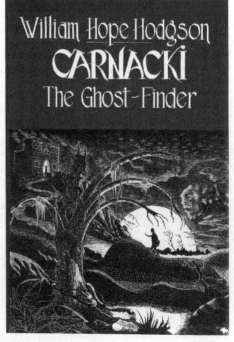

William Hope Hodgson
CARNACKI
The Ghost-Finder

several other circulation lists for Lovecraft's manuscripts and other items, there is no mention of his being considered for borrowing the Hodgson books... not that he would have survived to do so; the books were still 'lent out' into 1937, when Lovecraft himself died.

It is a curious quirk that in all of the surviving correspondence between Lovecraft and Howard (and, for that matter, Howard and Clark Ashton Smith, Howard and August Derleth, etc.), that Hodgson is not mentioned once. Their letters are incomplete, so this could well be a matter of the relevant letters or portions of letters not surviving; bad luck for the scholar instead of any genuine failure on Lovecraft's part to mention his re-discovery of a master of the weird tale. But this does bring us to something that Howard would have read, where he would almost certainly have 'discovered' Hodgson, if he was ignorant of him before from any of the other sources.

There remains another, sketchier avenue by which Howard might have heard of Hodgson, outside of *Adventure* and the crowd of weird fiction aficionados: physical culture. Both men were interested in the early trend of physical fitness and what would become contemporary body-building culture, Howard from at least 1928 (*Collected Letters* 1.165) and Hodgson since 1899 when he opened his first school. It is not impossible for Howard to have heard some reference of Hodgson through physical culture magazines, but without further evidence of what Howard was reading in this vein and when, we may only speculate.

The Fantasy Fan for December 1934 contained, among other things, another portion of Lovecraft's "Supernatural Horror in Literature," a prose poem by E. Hoffmann Price, an interview with Howard's friend, E. Hoffmann Price – and Koenig's article "William Hope Hodgson". Howard, who had a poem in the very next issue, could hardly have missed it. Which may be as close as we come to stating that Robert E. Howard read anything of William Hope Hodgson, at least until some new evidence comes to light.

MAMA G

TANYA WARNAKULASURIYA

I was roused from my sleep by a gentle fluttering around my neck. A moth or a butterfly? Surely not in the middle of a freezing November? The warm air inside Brixton Tube Station blew some much needed heat onto my body and provided a brief respite from the bitterly cold early morning. I opened my eyes, trying to look up and focus on the large rounded figure that loomed over me. It was her fingers that were dancing around my neck. Lightly fingering my mother's gold chain…

I gasped, shrinking back between the cardboard shelter that had been my home for the night and the wrought iron gates that prevented me from seeking refuge within the bowels of the station.

"Y'alright yeh, me not tryin' to hurt ya sweetie," the gentle Caribbean lilt crooned soothingly from the old lady as she straightened up and stared down, her gold tooth winking at me through a broad white smile. "Me, just takin' a peek at ya fine Indian gold. You Indians, you make de best gold. Pure. Dat lovely buttery yellow colour. Mmmm… mmmm… mmmm…"

She licked her lips like she intended to eat it. Her sharp eyes scanned me up and down, taking in my sleeping accommodation and the two carrier bags that carried everything that mattered to me at this point in my life.

"Is it Sunday?" I asked. As much as she was scanning me, I was doing the same to her. She wore a red winter coat, with a dragonfly brooch at the lapel, over a floral purple and white dress whose hem poked out underneath, modestly covering thick black support tights and cheap patent heels. A large wide brimmed hat was being held in place against a bitter morning wind, and beneath that was a shiny silk headscarf, further insurance against the cold. This was church-going apparel.

"Yes me darlin', am going to pay the good Lord a visit and pray for forgiveness for all us sinners," she nodded, "Would you like to join me? They be serving that nasty-tasting coffee that they get cheap from Mr Singh's but that Merleen, she make that lovely banana cake hot hot from de oven. Me thinks she put a lickle bit o rum in dere, to warm us up you know." She chuckled at her revelation and her ample bosom jiggled with laughter.

That's how I met Mama Gloria, the doyenne of Brixton Manor. Known to most of the community as Mama G, she was loved and feared in equal measure. Taking in waifs and strays, her little council flat on Coldharbour

Lane always had a crowd of people on their way in or out, and the door was never locked. Mama G was also one of the best fences in the area, well known for giving a fair price for stolen merchandise. She always managed to find the perfect customer for all manner of items, mostly from her fellow church-goers, or her ladies dominoes group or the police-community liaison group, where she was a valued and notable member.

I once saw just how fearful she could be. A young Polish kid tried to steal from her, pushing her back on the sofa and grabbing the gold necklaces he had brought to fence plus the cash she was counting out. In a deceptively swift move for such a large woman, Mama G slammed her walking stick down on the boy's hand, pinning him to the coffee table, and with her other hand she unsheathed a long blade from within the confines of the cane, slicing down. At the same time her dog Tommy, the old pit-bull she had rescued from the dog fights, flew across the room and tore a chunk of flesh out from the boy's side. As he reeled out of the flat spraying blood all over everything, Mama G calmly skewered the severed hand with the tip of her blade and plopped it into the pedal bin. She let Tommy gorge on the other piece by way of a reward,

"Ain't no way me gonna get that out of his jaws now, 'ee taste de blood," she cackled as she propped herself back in her seat and took a slurp of tea.

Her funeral was one of the last of its kind. A community commemorating the loss of one of its own. Paid for by the reviled and the revered alike, everyone who was anyone in Brixton wanted to show their respect for Mama G. Politicians, town councillors and police chiefs sat quietly alongside the Jamaican market stall holders, Indian shopkeepers, Polish coffee shop waitresses and Chinese delivery men. Wiping heavily mascaraed eyes, teenage mothers who were no longer teenage brought their children to say goodbye to the grandmother who loved them even though her blood was not theirs. Rastas, rude boys and raggas sat with hoodies up and heads bowed, so the world could not see the tears shed for the Mama who had fed them and loved them and also 'box dem ears'. When her body was lowered into the ground to the strains of Amazing Grace sung by her beloved church choir, we threw our handfuls of earth onto her, knowing that there would never be another Mama G.

* * *

Old Tommy decided to join me back on the streets. He didn't seem to mind the cold and I was glad to have someone warm to cuddle up to on the winter nights. Tommy also became my guardian, keeping me safe from others who were interested in my carrier bags, or my necklace. He was especially helpful when I had to leave my body through the tear in my personality.

On the night of the funeral, I felt the monsters trying to come through me. Clawing at that tear inside me, telling me to open up and let them come out to play. I rummaged in one of my bags and found the last of my pills. I would need to get to a doctor for a repeat prescription but I couldn't take all the hassle of being referred to a psychiatrist or run the risk of being committed again. Been there, done that.

Without the pills, the street light in my head was getting dimmer. The street light which shone that circle of light in which I could stand and be safe from the darkness where they lived. I could see them pressed up against the edges of the light, like they were squashed up against a window pane. Tapping with their dirty nails, mouthing obscenities, making lewd gestures. They knew that pool of light was shrinking and it was only a matter of time before they would have me in their darkness. That's when they would pry open my tear and climb through it into our world, wreaking their evil. The light began to dim, and I heard myself moaning in terror as I descended into their darkness. Suddenly, in the darkness, I felt familiar big hands pulling me away from the others.

"Not for you..." I heard her voice, so clearly. I sat up and looked around the empty high street.

"You hear that, Tommy?" I could see he had because he was looking at me with his head cocked, his sharp tail swishing from side to side like a whip.

"You stay hay'way from de girl... she all mine." The voice from nowhere spoke again. It was unmistakably hers.

I felt her hands grab my tear and wrench me wide open. I had to gasp for breath as she hauled her large dark form out of me. A few smaller entities scuttled after her taking the opportunity to come out and feast on our energies. She stood there before us, stretching her back and raising her head to sniff the night air. Tommy let out a low growl punctuated with a half-hearted bark, unsure if he was to defend his new owner from his old one.

Mama G, if that's who this was, and it certainly felt like it was, turned to look at us. Her eyes were black, pupils red. They seemed to cover most of her chubby round face now, leaving barely enough room for her nose. I don't suppose she needed one where she was now. Her mouth seemed to take up the rest of her face, the gold tooth still there amidst a host of glistening dagger-teeth through which tiny insects were crawling in and out. As she smiled at us, I heard her in my head,

"T'ank ya, darlin'.....you always was a good girl."

A slimy green tongue darted out of her mouth and endlessly travelled the distance between us to my face. I pressed myself against the tube station wall and shut my eyes. I smelt the stench from it as it licked the side of my face slowly, its rough warty surface travelling from my jawline up to my eye socket where it lingered on my closed lid, like a worm, trying to bury itself into the inner corner, tasting the frightened tears that were streaming from there. It only stopped when Tommy barked and leapt forward, swiftly returning to its toothy lair. She hissed at Tommy, who stood his ground, ready to fight. Then she was gone.

It was Tommy who had noticed the petrol bomb flying through the sky, the night after Mama G's funeral. Well, that's what we thought it was, having only just come out of the riots last spring. I watched him growl quietly, his body standing stiff and alert as he traced its flame, arcing through the sky, like a deadly comet. His tail wagged a little and he whimpered stepping back, as though this unfamiliar thing was somehow strangely familiar. It was not like the old war-horse to be so unsure, but then after yesterday's apparition we were both still on edge. I had decided whatever it was had taken the form of Mama G because she was someone I had loved. Loved and lost – leaving the most delicious pain for Evil to prey on. It was not the first time Evil had done this, in order to feed on me.

"Yep Tom, looks like the boys might be kicking up again." I gave him a pat, remembering previous riots and demonstrations. "Solomon told me another black kid died in the cells today. Mama G's not even cold in her grave and it's started."

But after that first ball of fire, nothing else followed. No gangs in balaclavas with baseball bats ready to fight and loot. No riot police with shields and batons. Nothing. Just a clear, cold November night. We settled down and went to sleep.

"Oi, Sleeping Beauty, this your dog?" The sharp nudge from the copper's boot, elicited a growl from Tommy, who lay next to me on the cardboard.

The policeman said he needed a sample of Tom's fur.

"To help us with our enquiries – been a dog attack in the manor. Someone saw a pit bull running out of the vic's house. Mind you, round here that's not saying much."

The attack had happened in the flats in Effra Road. I went to the doctor's surgery there for some more pills. The attack was all anyone could talk about.

"The little O'Toole girl it was," said the woman next to me, "Beautiful child she was, lovely golden curls, always laughing."

I asked her if their dog was a pit-bull.

"Well that's the thing," she said, her voice lowering to a whisper, "they didn't have a dog. The mum couldn't stand them, she'd been bit herself when she was a young. And the girl was allergic to 'em."

"So a random dog just ran in their flat and attacked the child?" I asked, "That doesn't sound right..."

"Well not just that," she leaned in, her stale cigarette breath laced with peppermint for good manners, "but the door was double bolted from the inside. Well you have to be bolted round these parts, don't ya? Doors and windows all locked and yet a dog gets in and rips the poor girl's throat right out. They said her head was clear across the other side of the room. Total blood bath."

The next night another murder. This time in the flat above the Kebab shop on the high street. A boy of eight mauled to death, with wounds resembling dog bites, but his body almost completely exsanguinated, as though the animal had sucked every last drop of blood from him. The family owned no pets. Police rounded dogs up. Dog owners were asked to report to the local police stations to help with inquiries. The Sus Law went into overdrive again, as young black men with pit bulls were stopped and searched in the street. Tension was rising in the community. Two children were dead and the police seemed to be doing nothing about it. When the third child was murdered, the media descended into Brixton in droves. This time a Nigerian baby only a few months old was found dead in her cot, her body drained of blood, and her throat savaged. The parents had heard nothing in the night. As with the previous cases, the home had been secured from the inside and the family had no dogs.

"Why don't you put your stinking mutt on a lead!" a young mother shrieked at me as she steered her pushchair away from Tommy, "You need a licence for them dogs you know!"

I was back on my meds and keeping the monsters at bay well enough by now. Tommy and I decided that under the circumstances we ought to keep a low profile, so we headed to the outskirts of town and slept in Brockwell Park at night. That's where I saw Jacob.

Solomon at the deli had given us some coffee and leftover sandwiches. We were finishing up our dinner when he appeared before us, shining and sparkling like a sort of human Catherine Wheel.

"She's a firerass, you know," he said with a strong Caribbean twang, even though he looked blond and beatific, more like Archangel Michael.

He obviously read my mind because in an instant he transformed himself into a shimmering Rasta, his radiant dreadlocks floating and dancing around his beautiful face, like benign snakes. I still had no clue what he was talking about.

"Your Mama G... like Ol Higue," he said, "they didn't bury her right."

"Oh, you mean she's a jumbie?" Poor Mama G, I thought. Left to wander the earth as a demonic hag feeding on the young, "But why? She was a good woman. Maybe she bent the law a bit, but she did more good than harm and everyone knew it. How could this happen to her?"

"Ours is not to question why, girl! Ours is to do or die, ya know." Jacob replied, waxing lyrical and relishing his new ethnic form. "Ya needs to come home and get to work."

* * *

As I sat in meditation that night, connecting with a consciousness that was beyond me, I let myself be transported to higher realms where answers could be sought. This was the other side of being 'torn'. The real reason why people like me have mental illness. I had been shown many years ago that it was my destiny, to see and hear things that 'normal' people could not. I was one of the chosen few tasked with the mission of maintaining balance in our world. Though darker forces wished to use my tear to climb into our world, I learned to use it to cross into other realms. Higher realms taught me how to clean up the dark energies that are created and attracted into our reality.

Jacob, and others, instructed me on how to catch the firerass that had taken Mama G's form and was now terrorising the community as an evil spirit-dog.

"You need to burn her skin with salt," they said, "By day she will exist as a quiet member of the community, inconspicuous and barely noticeable. At night, she will remove her skin and fly through the air in her true form – a ball of fire, in search of children's blood to feed on. She will hide her skin in a mortar. You must find it and burn it with salt. Then she will be unable to change back and must return from whence she came. We will guide you, so listen to our voices and see our signs."

* * *

Tommy and I began next morning. Returning to Mama G's flat, we tried to see if the firerass was there. We looked for anything resembling a mortar in the kitchen, but most of the flat had been picked clean of all her goods. Things don't hang around for long in these parts. As we scanned the living room for anything that might help, I felt something under my foot. A domino piece. We set off to the community centre where she used to play dominoes every Thursday.

The ladies had known Mama G for an eternity, coming to England together during the Windrush days,

"Ha, we swore faithfully we'd be going back home in a few years," old Lilian chuckled as she surveyed her hand and delicately picked up a tab to lay down.

"'Aint dat de truth!" agreed Florence, "Jus' a few years working in dis cold, grey country, den, back to me palm trees and me calypso and me rum punch!"

The ladies whooped in agreement.

"But not Mama G," said Sylvia, "She always like it 'ere. Always said there was work to be done. Communities to build. Young ones being born who needed teachin' 'bout our ways."

They all nodded and sighed in remembrance. No one here looked like a firerass to me.

That night a fourth child was killed. A twelve year old boy. This time, the family did have a dog, a docile mongrel named Ben who was promptly taken in by the police and destroyed. Ben apparently was the assailant of all four attacks. But, when the fifth child was killed the statement was retracted. Young men walking the streets these days did so with two or three ferocious canines straining on leashes ahead of them. They weren't about to let themselves be savaged by a rogue pit-bull no matter what restrictions the police put on dangerous dogs. Things were escalating and we were nowhere nearer finding the firerass or her skin.

"I thought you said you would guide me," I asked Jacob, as we sat on the park bench watching children playing football in the mud. Jacob was a sweet old Indian lady today, her sari bundled up in a thick camel coat that was three sizes too big. The woolly muffler wound around her head made her look as though she had a toothache. She cupped her hands around a steaming polystyrene cup and blew into it.

"We are trying my dear, but it is most difficult," she said between blows. "This firerass seems to be getting stronger and stronger with each feed. The tension and anger in the community is also not helping. Negative energies are building up here. The deceiving politicians and counsellors, the fear amongst families, the violence and blaming between community leaders and the police, it's fragmenting everyone."

"I know," I said, "I can feel the dark forces, building up, eager to come out."

"These are the conditions that are ripe for evil. When will humans learn that focusing on a problem does not solve it? The solution does not vibrate on the same frequency as the problem." Jacob slurped her tea, swilling it around her mouth as though it was mouthwash. "You may have to visit the darker realms, where I cannot pass, and ask there. Take these with you".

Placing her cup on the bench she reached into her coat pocket and after rummaging for a while brought out a disgusting clump of old tissues. Removing old bus tickets and an old furry boiled sweet from the clump, she handed it to me. I unwrapped it to reveal a colourful mass of sports ribbons. They looked like the type that are handed out at a children's sports day, but they weren't. These were merits. Blessings that help to remove the suffering of one's karma and move one closer to the realms of non-suffering. Demons would do anything for these.

As I sat in meditation and stepped through my tear, I felt the darkness envelop me like a cold fœtid cloak. I had to work hard to calm my breathing and remind myself that I did not need to succumb. Almost immediately they were upon me, sniffing me, touching my hair, licking my skin. I fought hard not to recoil, to stand my ground and regain my composure. Closing my eyes I took my mind to lighter places inside me, and as I did, my body emitted a gentle glow, a small casing of light from which they shrank back snarling and confused.

"Now, who here knows about the firerass that has come to my world?" I demanded.

"Why should we tell you?" cackled a twisted being, its misshapen head bent upside down.

"I know... but won't tell... won't tell... won't tell," sang a little girl as she chewed on her teddy-bear's face, tearing it off with her teeth and licking at the flesh and viscera underneath.

I removed the merits from my pocket and let them sit in my open hand, glowing and gleaming with good light. A gasp rippled through them, followed by whimpers of longing and shivering grasping hands. I had no intention of staying here any longer than I needed to.

"Who wants to know?" boomed a voice from the distance, "Let it pass. Bring it here."

The sea of bodies parted, making a path towards a red serpent that lay coiled on a rocky outcrop. Nestling amongst its coils was what looked like a deformed fœtus. Its oversized head sported delicate human features though there seemed to be the remnants of another face to the side of the skull too. Its body was curled in an embryonic position but that didn't stop it from scuttling around the coils of the snake, stopping occasionally to turn its head upwards and sniff the air like a dog.

"I have merits," I said calmly, "Looks like you need 'em." The comment caused a series of snorts and giggles from the crowd. It drew all manner of swearing and cursing from the fœtus.

"I don't need your stinking merits. Your blood is far more interesting to me, bitch."

"Well then, don't waste my time," I turned to leave.

"Wait, human!" It scuttled closer to the edge of the coils and painfully leaned its body to one side so that it could look at me. It was salivating. Drools of spit dripped onto the snake's scales, "Show me..." it rasped.

I held out my hand and let the merits work their magic. The thing whimpered lasciviously as it feasted its eyes on the pretty ribbons.

"She's a good God-fearing sort... just like the rest of us," it said, which brought peals of laughter from the others. "You won't find her mortar in a home kitchen. She's smarter than that. Leaves it in a catering place, in plain view for all to see. She's clever like that. Feeds them first, then feeds on their babies." Another burst of laughter and cheers erupted from the crowd. They were beginning to get frenzied – out of control. I needed to get out of there.

"Now GIVE ME!" the baby's voice boomed.

* * *

The next morning I headed to the church. Father Brady welcomed me and Tommy inside. He knew the dog from old and had been instrumental in re-homing him with Mama G. He told me they did not have a kitchen area in the church.

"But what about all the coffee and cake on Sunday, Father?"

"Well, we have a kettle to make the coffee in the vestry and Merleen brings the cake with her. I don't know where she makes it. At home I presume. She's here today, you can ask her directly."

Just then Merleen walked into the church carrying a tray of her famous banana cake. The minute she saw Tommy by my side, she hissed and backed away letting the tray crash to the ground.

"You can't bring those stinking animals in here," she glowered.

"This church is welcome to all God's creatures, Merleen," the Father said calmly, "Now let me help you."

I made my excuses and left. So, the firerass was now the quiet, unassuming Merleen – and the real Merleen, her spirit, would be long gone. But where did this thing hide her damn skin? Not in her own house, the baby-horror had said...

We walked down the road, past the hardware stores and the barber shops. It was getting close to lunchtime and I needed to eat. I set my bags down and taking a cardboard piece and a plastic cup, sat on the pavement to beg for some change. Tommy settled down next to me. As I watched the passersby going about their business, I tuned into the music blaring from the Rasta shop on the corner next to the community hall. It was an old Marley song that I hadn't heard in a long time, 'Duppy Conqueror'.

"That's where she is, Tom." I cried as the revelation hit me, "Come on, we need to see if the community hall has a kitchen in it." As I hoisted myself up from the ground I raised my eyes upwards, "Thanks for the sign, J," I said gratefully.

Duppy was the Jamaican word for a Jumbie.

Sylvia at the hall confirmed my suspicions. "Yes, darlin'. She uses the kitchen in 'ere to make us dem cakes. Says her kitchen at home is too small."

Merleen had keys to the community hall and would come in through the week to bake the cakes. This was the place we needed to stake out tonight.

After talking to the ladies, and getting a packet of crisps and a cup of tea from the centre, I went back to my place across the road and set up for the night. The bright lights and bustle of the high street into the late hours were such a contrast to the quiet of the park that it easily kept me awake for my mission. At about ten I saw her. The tiny bird-like woman that used to be Merleen hurried along the road, her head bent down and coat pulled tight against the cold. I saw her rummage about in her purse for the keys to the hall and let herself in.

"Tommy!" I suddenly cried, "We haven't thought this through!" I'd been so focused on finding the firerass's skin that I had forgotten that when she peeled out of it, she would be off in search of another victim. Another child might be killed.

"We can't let that happen, Tom, but we can't follow her, not and get back here in time! Jacob! Where are you? I need you!"

Tommy and I crossed the road and headed for the hall. We went around to the side of the building where a small alleyway took us to the back where the kitchen windows were. As we approached the alley, we saw a dispatch rider sitting astride his bike waiting for us. The ethereal light emanating from inside his crash helmet told me it was Jacob. He raised a gloved hand and gave me a thumbs-up. Tommy and I hurried down the alley-way. I up-ended a dustbin quietly and climbed on top to get a look through the window. Tommy snuffled through the rubbish, munching on scraps.

Inside I saw Merleen take her coat and clothes off, neatly laying them on the counter. Once completely naked, she reached around the back of her head with both hands and began to peel her skin off, first from her head and then continuing down her body, as though it were just another layer of clothing. What was left behind was a nebulous mass of searing fire, the flames so bright and hungry that they bathed the whole kitchen in a throbbing red glow of evil. The firerass lifted the heap of skin from the floor and rolled it. Round and round the skin went until it was a tightly wrapped ball, no bigger than a golf ball. The ball of skin then floated up to a mortar and pestle that sat on the top shelf and popped inside. Then she was gone. Out through the kitchen door and high into the sky.

"Quick," called Jacob at the entrance of the alley, revving his engine, "We need to get to Furzedown Flats before she does. That's where she's going."

How he knew that was a mystery, but not one he was going to let me in on. Those like Jacob would hint and help, but for some reason, it was up to poor sods like me to get their hands dirty.

We sped through the streets, Tommy keeping pace via cut-throughs and short cuts. We saw the firerass sailing through the sky and managed to overtake her but only by a few minutes. Jacob briefed me on the way. There were three houses with young children that were potential targets and we had to protect each one. When we reached the flats, I reached into the pannier and took out a bag of rice. Racing to flats, 3, 12 and 28 in turn, I poured a pile of rice at the front door of each home. Delirious from running and drenched in sweat, I leaned against number 28 to catch my breath. I looked down at Tommy, who seemed to be having a great time, tail wagging excitedly at this new game. I could hear Jacob's voice in my head,

"Chop chop, no time to dawdle. Now you need to burn the skin."

Breathing in deeply I set off at a trot back down the urine-soaked stairwell, doing my best to avoid the used condoms and hypodermics. As I passed the third floor, I saw her. The mass of fire was heading for flat 12. It started to shrink itself, ready to pass through a crack in the door, but then it seemed to notice the rice. The fire immediately solidified into a human mass of flesh and sinew. Merleen, without her skin. Transfixed with the rice, she crouched on the floor and with her bony fingers delicately picking each grain, she started counting. I heard Jacob again,

"That will keep her busy for long enough. Let's go, let's go."

I was halfway down the steps when I realised Tommy was not there. Looking up I saw him standing taut and alert, staring in the direction of the firerass.

"Tommy," I hissed, "Here, Tommy. Now."

It was no good, I heard his snarl, and raced up to grab him, though I knew I was not strong enough to restrain him. I got to the top of the stairwell to see the firerass turn and hiss at the dog. As she transformed into a large black pit-bull, Tommy lunged; the dogs met almost in midair, jaws crunching on bones, teeth tearing into flesh. The commotion caused lights to go on in the surrounding flats.

"It's his destiny, not yours. Now move!" Jacob's voice was firm.

He drove me back to the hall at speed. Smashing the backdoor lock with a brick, I entered and pulled the mortar, with the ball of skin inside, down from its shelf. Taking salt from the cupboard, I unscrewed the cellar and poured the contents into the mortar, covering the skin completely. The salt ate into it, making it fizz and bubble, emitting a foul stench as it reduced into nothingness.

The moment the salt hit her skin, she knew. I could see the scene – and her anger – in my head, and I knew that Jacob was sharing this with me. As she pinned Tommy down, preparing to rip his throat out, she let out an agonising scream. She leapt up onto the ledge of the balcony and off. Onlookers ran to the edge to see, but there was no body below.

Tommy lay on the ground, bleeding badly, panting heavily.

The shouts started. "This is the killer dog. This is the child killer. Shoot it. Shoot the bastard."

"Nah mate, it was the other one." A muscle-bound Jacob emerged from the shadows, "I saw the 'ole thing. That black one was sniffing outside number 12, trying to get in. Then this one went for it. He was trying to stop it."

Jacob marvelled at the fickleness of humans. The crowd murmured its approval. "Quick, get him to a vets, he's bleeding badly. Get some towels."

* * *

As we sit in our usual spot outside Brixton station, Tommy receives his fans with a wag of his tail and a friendly lick. He's put on quite a bit of weight with all the treats he gets from the community, now he's a local celebrity.

"I've got a nice bit of liver for ya, Tom," the local butcher calls. "Pop round this afternoon."

The killings have stopped of course, and the feeling of fear that had plagued the town has lifted. Just like his previous owner, Tommy seems to have brought the community back together again. Maybe Mama G did too, in her own inimitable way... as a firerass.

DASH THY FOOT

JULIE FROST

The day I trekked into the bowels of Hell started with me setting my phone down gently rather than flinging it across the room like I wanted to. It was well past its warranty and I couldn't afford a new one. Reaching into my desk drawer, I pulled out a flask of hundred-proof rotgut I kept for emergencies, uncapped it, and took a giant swig.

The current emergency had taken the form of the police commissioner's call. Landon Vickers, the man convicted of the home-invasion robbery that had killed my mother, was dead – shanked in prison, before he ratted out his accomplice, who was in the wind and likely to remain so now. I slumped in my chair and swore. As a private investigator, I didn't have to jump through the same procedural hoops the cops did, but I'd nevertheless had the same bad luck tracking the bastard down as they had.

I had a different motive, as well. The cops just wanted to put him in jail and possibly give him a lethal injection after fifteen years of legal wrangling. Justice delayed, if ever dispensed at all. I wanted to beat him to death with my bare hands and dispense justice *right then*.

It was enough to drive me to drink. More drink.

So I wasn't in the best mood when the lady walked into my office. I knew she was trouble the second I saw her. Rich, elegant, beautiful young women like that do not hire scruffy, down-at-our-heels, clearance-rack gumshoes like me for mundane crap, and I gazed at her sourly from the top of her expertly-coiffed head to the bottoms of a pair of black pumps that would cost me three months' salary if the months were very, very good.

Her white London Fog trenchcoat rode up her thighs as she had a seat, revealing nothing but more dark-smoke stockings, and I wondered for a wild moment if she was wearing anything else under it. She leaned forward and twisted a strand of brown hair around her finger, giving me a shy smile and a guileless blink from baby blues that didn't fool me for a second. I caught a whiff of understated and over-expensive floral perfume, and noted that the diamond on her left hand would choke my office cat if she got careless with it.

Yep. She was trouble, with a capital *"ouble"*.

However, just because she was trouble didn't mean I could afford to turn down a client – if I didn't get new work soon, I'd miss rent. Again. I hastily capped my flask and put it back in the drawer, shoving my personal problems to the side, at least for now. "May I help you, Miss?"

"Oh, I do hope so." She didn't even twitch at the flask. Score one for her, anyway. "Are you Clifton McDermott?"

"That's what it says on the door. All kinds of private investigation services, at your beck and call." Mainly because I didn't have any other clients right now. My wallet moths had starved to death long ago.

"My name is Jessica Denning. May I assume you do process serving?"

"Oh, sure, all the time."

"This one might be a little more... difficult. Than you're used to."

"I've served people who didn't want to be found before, Ms Denning. It's not as hard as you'd think, if you know where to look."

She smiled. It wasn't a nice expression. "Well, Mr McDermott, my client isn't exactly suing a 'person'." She reached into her voluminous purse and came out with a manila folder, sliding it over to me. I flipped it open—

And sputtered. I didn't get surprised often, but she'd managed it. "Your client. Is suing Satan."

Mirth danced in those blue eyes of hers, which were no longer guileless. "Lucifer. The Morningstar. The Prince of the Power of the Air. That's him." She lifted a delicate eyebrow. "Is there a problem?"

"Is he even in our jurisdiction? You know what, don't answer that." I pinched the bridge of my nose between my thumb and forefinger, squeezing my eyelids shut. "Is this a joke?" It wasn't quite a question.

"I can assure you, we are quite serious, and prepared to pay triple your normal fee, up front, if you will do this."

"And I would normally be all over that." I opened my eyes but kept pinching my nose. "But. Your client. Is suing. *Satan!*"

"Can you do it, or can't you?"

"*How?*" I slammed my hands down on my desk. "Last time I checked, Rand McNally doesn't make a road atlas to *Hell*."

"That's why I brought you a GPS unit. It will direct you right to Lucifer's throne room." She reached into her purse again and set the device on my desk. "Be sure to follow it exactly. Otherwise you can get into all kinds of trouble."

I stared at it like a rabbit eyeing a rattlesnake – but I didn't have anything better going, and rent was due soon. "Fine." I grabbed my battered leather attaché case from beside my desk and stuck the folder inside. "Three times my normal fee, up front, and then twice my normal fee when I finish the job."

"You're a hard-nosed man who drives a hard bargain." She smiled, and handed over the entire fee. In cash. "Godspeed, Mr McDermott."

I wanted my flask again. "Something like that."

* * *

I rubbed Flossie, my longhaired black and white cat, under her chin before I left, and made sure she had plenty of food and water, and a clean litter box. I also emailed my neighbor, asking her to please check on Flossie if she didn't hear back from me within a couple of days. I didn't want to leave her an orphan.

Sadly, that was all my affairs in order. I set the GPS in the cupholder of my third-hand two-colored-if-you-didn't-count-rust-as-a-color-three-if-you-did sedan and followed its directions to the letter, taking Jessica's word that even a minor deviation would put me in a world of hurt.

As the neighborhood got worse and worse, I thought I might be in a world of hurt anyway. The GPS sent me down a stereotypically sinister alley with nastily-moving shadows—

And then my car died with a hideous *thunk* from under the hood, along with a curl of smoke. "Fantastic," I muttered. Grabbing my attaché case and the GPS, I climbed out, leaving the keys. Maybe I'd get lucky and someone would steal it.

The GPS took me around a corner the car wouldn't have made anyway. I felt a moment of disorientation, during which my stomach had a hard time deciding if it really wanted to keep hold of my lunch or not – lunch won; it stayed put, but it was a near thing – and when the world stopped tilting I found myself confronted with what could only be described as an enormous demon, right down to the goat legs, the dark red bat wings rising from his back, and the horns sprouting from his forehead. He was furred from the waist down and naked from the waist up, and had muscles where most people didn't even have places. I took a rapid step back, making a strangled sound and trying to get my breathing under control.

The demon laughed, a booming sound that I could swear flattened my eardrums "Not what you were expecting, Clifton McDermott?"

I clutched my shirt over my heart, still panting. Great. He knew my name. "Actually, you're exactly what I was expecting. That's why it was so unexpected."

He grinned with way too many pointy teeth. "You have a sense of humor, little human! Good, you'll need it. Follow me, please."

I balked. "How do I know you won't kill me and steal my soul?"

"How do you know you have a soul to begin with? Especially one I'd be interested in?"

"Isn't that what you guys are all about? Tormenting souls?"

"I am Gaap, a great President and mighty Prince, and I command sixty-six legions. In other words, I have people who do that for me." He cast a look over his shoulder. "Also, the boss gets cranky when we actually kill humans, just so you know. Something about 'the greatest trick the devil ever pulled,' which means he's more subtle than I like to be, but he's the boss. So, since you're a living human, you've got safe passage. Don't you feel special?"

I felt intimidated and out of my depth, was what I felt, but I wasn't going to tell him that. I squared my shoulders and looked down at the GPS unit, which appeared to have me meandering all over the place before depositing me at my destination, looping back on itself about four times. I frowned at it, and Gaap craned his neck to have a peek.

He snorted. His breath stank of rotten fish and brimstone, and I tried not to gag. "Your device is taking you by the longest route possible. You don't want to do that, do you?"

I shuddered and wondered exactly what I'd see along the longest route possible. "I just need to meet with Lucifer. The sooner the better, honestly."

"Ooh, impatience. Well. Luckily for you, I am a demon of transport as well as my other duties, so I can escort you to the Throne. Perhaps the Morningstar will find you amusing."

I didn't particularly want to know what a demon, especially Lucifer, would find amusing, but it was either trek all over Hell for God knew how long, or let Gaap take me on a more direct route. I picked the direct route. "So how come Dante got Virgil, and I get a demon?" I asked.

"Why they let *him* down here in the first place," Gaap muttered, "is a question for the ages. Short answer: Dante saw what he expected to see. So did you. Long answer: it's complicated."

"Complicated," said an acidic voice behind me. "Is that what you're calling it Below, these days?"

I turned to see who the newcomer was, and my jaw dropped. Gaap just made an impatient noise, and said, "Khatuliel, put the sword away, you look ridiculous."

The newcomer looked utterly magnificent. Shining white feathered wings with silver tips bristled from his back, and his sword glowed with unearthly (of course) light. He too was shirtless, wearing soft brown cowhide trousers tucked into calf-high boots of a darker brown hue. An enormous scar bisected his chest from his left collarbone to the bottom of his ribcage on the right, and his muscles were just as impressive as Gaap's. Shoulder-length black hair was

tied back with a band of leather, and his skin was dark bronze.

I immediately felt better, and closed my mouth with a snap. If demons were real, then it made sense that their opposite numbers were too. I had no doubt that my brain would fall apart into a gibbering mess once I was safe back at home, but for now I was rolling with it.

"Do you really expect me to go unarmed into your vipers' pit with my Charge?" Khatuliel demanded.

"I don't expect you to come along at all," Gaap snapped back. "This is hardly the place for one such as you."

Khatuliel glowered. "It is hardly the place for one such as my Charge, who yet lives and over whom you have no authority."

"He came of his own Free Will. You flout that at your peril, you great feathered twit."

I raised a timid hand. "Do I get a say?"

"Your folly has brought us to a pretty pass," Khatuliel said, "but what is your wish?"

"I have a job to do, but I'd feel a lot better if you were with me. Just as, you know. A precaution."

"You've already thrown caution to the winds by taking this job to begin with." His sword disappeared, and he pointed at Gaap. "You will answer for it, should any harm befall him."

"He has safe passage to Lucifer's throne. What may happen after, I cannot say. Shall we proceed?"

"You will be far better off if you follow your GPS, Clifton," Khatuliel said, jerking his chin at it. "You were given that for a reason."

"Gaap knows a shortcut?" I didn't mean to inflect it like a question, but the angel was intimidating. "I really don't want to spend more time here than I have to. It smells like burning carrion and sulfur."

He gusted a sigh. "I suppose you have a point. You're taking it all remarkably well."

"Oh, I'll drink a fifth of Jim Beam when I get home, because this is *crazy*!" My hand flapped at the end of my arm as I waved it.

"You are not wrong." He glared around at nothing in particular. "Lead on, Gaap. Let's get this over and done with."

Gaap gave him a mock bow and turned down a side path. "As you wish, little brother."

"Don't call me that," Khatuliel snarled to his retreating back as we followed him.

"Some history there?" I asked.

"Nothing you need concern yourself with." His hand came up and rubbed the scar across his chest in an automatic gesture, and I suddenly had a pretty good idea where it came from. "Family feuds are the worst."

"Well, maybe if Daddy hadn't thrown us all out on our ears—" Gaap started.

"Maybe if you hadn't listened to the preposterous rantings of a complete lunatic," Khatuliel shot back. It sounded like an old argument.

"*Recalculating!*" interjected the GPS unit. I barked out a startled laugh and looked at the screen. It showed a new route, and Khatuliel frowned at it, frowned at Gaap, and light dawned on his face.

"So that's how it is. Both you and Ms Denning are craftier than I gave you credit for," he said to the demon.

Gaap tried for an innocent look and failed spectacularly. "I have no idea what you're talking about."

"This is my skeptical face, *big brother*. Get used to it."

"What's going on?" I asked, mystified.

"Ms Denning programmed your GPS so it would take you on a tour, as it were." He glared at Gaap's retreating back. "And my erstwhile brother is bypassing all that because he doesn't want you to see the horrors down here. Lest you re-evaluate your life choices and they lose you completely."

"Wait." I stopped dead. "They have me?" I may have squeaked.

"If they 'had' you yet, I would not be here." He snorted, and we continued on. "Considering the fact that you're about to meet the Prince of Darkness himself, I doubt that Gaap's attempt to... *spare* you—" An eye-roll. "Will be successful. Lucifer has a less-than-sunny disposition."

"You're not as holy and reverent as I'd have expected."

"We are meant to blend in." I eyed him. He wouldn't 'blend in' anywhere except, maybe, at the sort of bodybuilding competition where they got their muscles by actual work rather than at the gym. "It doesn't always work. And I thought this guise might make you feel more at ease."

"*Recalculating!*" the GPS said again. It sounded put out. "*Take the next left.*"

"Can't you turn that off?" Gaap asked sourly.

"I never turned it on. It just does its thing."

He growled and pointedly did not take the next left. "*Recalculating!*" the GPS squawked after several steps. Gaap sped up after that, while the unit got more and more exasperated and finally shouted, "*Fine! Get lost. See if I ca—you have arrived at your destination.*" This as we stopped outside an enormous wood-timber double door strapped with bronze and flanked by an equally-enormous pair of demons.

I squinted. "Pitchforks? Really?"

Gaap gave me a toothy grin. "Would you like them stabbing around among your intestines?"

Khatuliel's sword reappeared in his hand, and he took a wide-winged stance. "You can *try*."

"Yes, I'm sure you'd do very well with three-to-one odds on our ground. Unruffle your pinfeathers, pussycat; it wasn't a threat."

Khatuliel glowered. "You will be the first to taste my blade if it is, Gaap. And don't call me that either."

"Of course." He opened the doors and led us into Lucifer's Throne Room. I took two steps and stopped short. Whatever I'd been expecting, it wasn't this.

To describe the room as 'opulent' would be a laughable understatement. Precious metals and rich silks in red and black adorned every surface. Incense swirled toward the ceiling several stories overhead, fighting a losing battle with the charnel house stench overlaying everything in this place. The throne was an elaborately-carved marble-and-gold bejeweled monstrosity that would have dwarfed any human rear end.

That's because it wasn't built for a human rear end. I cursed Dante, because I was not prepared to be confronted by an iridescent black dragon coiled upon the seat in sumptuous luxury, idly toying with a human skull. He was at least forty feet long from nose to tail, with a grinning head at the end of a long, sinuous neck that swiveled around the moment we entered, golden slit-pupiled eyes zeroing in on me. He ran his forked tongue out – and *laughed*, a bright, happy sound almost childlike in its simple cheer, and all the more awful for it.

"It has been long and long since a living human dared enter here. Come in, Clifton McDermott, and tell us your business."

He was the most beautiful and terrible thing I'd ever seen, and I was frozen to the spot. Well. Not quite frozen, because my legs decided they didn't want to hold me up and I fell to my knees before him. His grin grew wider, revealing rows and rows of needle-sharp teeth as long as my forearm running all the way to the back of his mouth. He stretched out his neck and sniffed at my face, while Khatuliel stood stone-like beside me, the sword shining in his hand even though he must have known he didn't stand a chance against something like that. Rough cackles sounded in the background, and sibilant voices whispered things I couldn't quite make out, but might have driven me mad if I could.

"That is the proper place for you, yes. On your knees. Soon all of humanity will follow your fine example." Lucifer's tone was musical, with just a hint of dissonance. I felt like an ant under a magnifying glass, vulnerable and insignificant, who had just come to the attention of something that would barely notice while it burnt me to a crisp. His tongue slithered out and caressed my face. I shivered; the touch was hot and freezing at the same time. Lucifer turned his attention to Khatuliel. "You would do well to follow it also, Khati. You will in the end anyway."

"I do not kneel before any but Father." I marveled at Khatuliel's steadiness. "And neither should my Charge."

"Hn. So you say. For now." Lucifer fanned his wings and reared his head up, staring down at me. "I quite like him like that. Perhaps I should keep him."

Khatuliel's wings bristled. "He is not yours. He yet lives, and your minion pledged safe passage."

Gaap was actually on his face before Lucifer, but he made an offended noise at the 'minion' remark. Lucifer sniffed me again. I tried not to gag; his breath stank like a plague-ridden morgue left out in the sun. "Not mine, no. But not Father's, either. What a curious state your soul is in, Clifton." He settled back on the throne. "Now, tell me. Why is a living human in my demesne for the first time in centuries?"

I unstuck my tongue from the roof of my mouth after a couple of tries and fumbled at the clasp of my attaché case, finally getting it open and delving in for the paperwork. I was acting in the capacity of an officer of the court, dammit, and that stiffened my spine. I clambered to my feet and held out the envelope. My hand hardly shook at all. "Lucifer, you are hereby ordered to appear in the Fourth Judicial District Court of Nebraska, in Omaha, on July the twenty-seventh. You've been served."

Satan tilted his head, then reached out a giant talon and speared it through the file, narrowly missing my hand, which I snatched back as Khatuliel let out a warning growl.

"Someone. Is suing. *Me*?" The Prince of Darkness ripped the manila envelope aside to reveal the papers within. He laughed again, and this time it was a chilling sound that froze me in my shoes. " 'Negligent rebellion.' 'Subsequent existence of Hell.' 'Origin of everything awful in the universe.' " More laughter, high and horrible. "Do they understand that Father created the Tree of Knowledge of Good and Evil to begin with? He made the rules. Not me."

"That is so not my concern," I managed to squeak out.

" 'Damages of a billion dollars and the court to order him to repent of his misdeeds and stop being a raging asshole.' " He got back in my face. "They do realize that I'm the first lawyer ever, right?"

"I don't know. I'm just the process server. I'll see myself out?"

"Do that. Good luck. Try to keep your Guardian out of trouble; he looks like he's about to detonate in a flurry of feathers and pique."

And we quite suddenly found ourselves on the other side of the closed doors, without the faintest idea how we'd gotten there. I let out a breath I didn't even know I was holding, and Gaap clapped me on the back, almost sending me to the floor. "That went well. He didn't devour you out of hand. Or Khati."

Khatuliel pointed his sword at Gaap's Adam's apple. "Do not touch my Charge, Hellspawn. And don't call me that either. You haven't earned the right to use a brother's nickname."

"You are tightly wound, Khatuliel. It's a wonder you don't give yourself ulcers."

"It is not I who causes ulcers." The sword didn't move. "But be assured I will give *you* a sore throat if you touch him again."

"*Recalculating. Recalculating. Recalculating.*" I pulled the GPS out of my pocket to find the screen swirling around in circles. I'd never seen one do that before.

"Uh."

Gaap's lips stretched into a parody of a smile. "Getting into Hell is easy. Getting back out again, not so much. And unless your Guardian wants you to be trapped here for far longer than you counted on, he will put his little pigsticker away and stop annoying me with it."

"You promised me safe passage," I pointed out.

"True. I did not, however, promise you *rapid* passage." His eye grew a glint. "And that safe passage does not extend to the feathered fool currently pointing his blade at me." The GPS picked that moment to burst into flames, and I let out a yelp and dropped it. Gaap's enormous cloven hoof stamped down, and it expired with an agonized "*Recalc—!*"

Khatuliel huffed, but his sword disappeared. "Get him out of here, Gaap. As soon as may be."

"Of course, little brother, your wish is my command." Gaap gave him a mock bow and turned to lead us out.

I balked. "That's not how we came in."

"Do you think you can find your own way back? You're more than welcome to try."

"I hate you," I muttered.

"That's the first sensible thing you've said since this entire ordeal began," Khatuliel said.

"You may sing a different tune once you see where we're going, Clifton. I have a gift for you."

"A gift. From a President of Hell." My voice dripped with irony. "I'm touched. You shouldn't have."

Khatuliel scowled. "Hell's 'gifts' come with strings, Clifton. Tread lightly, and be wary."

"And Heaven," Gaap countered, "is full of stick-in-the-muds who don't want you to have any fun. Ah, here we are." He stopped outside a much less impressive door than the one to Lucifer's throne room. A faint scream threaded its way between the joints, but it was enough to make all the hairs on my arms and the back of my neck stand at attention. He opened the door and gestured me grandly inside. "After you."

With some trepidation, I stepped forward. A pair of ginormous (everything in this place was ginormous, why should they be any different?) black dogs with matted hair stood over a naked man curled up on the rough wood floorboards, their snaggle teeth dripping saliva that smoked when it hit his already-torn flesh. Blood spatters painted the walls and floor, even the ceiling, and a puddle of the stuff pooled under him. His back had the appearance of raw hamburger; a chain scourge dripping more blood lay discarded in a corner. Iron sconces held flickering torches that gave off noxious smoke.

A demon looked on indulgently, leaning against the wall with his arms crossed. Implements of torture, some obvious, some less so, lay scattered across a table, and a river of lava bisected another corner of the room, passing under the stone walls. The man made inarticulate whimpering noises, covering his head with his arms, or trying to. The radius and ulna of one arm poked through the skin at an angle usually reserved for horror movies and medical photos.

"Hello, Ronwe," Gaap said. "Your turn with the wretch today, I see."

"I've barely begun, and already he begs," the other demon replied. "Disappointing, really, I'd've thought he'd be made of sterner stuff, seeing what he's here for."

"What *is* he here for?" I couldn't help but ask, morbidly curious.

"This one." Gaap placed a cloven hoof on the man's ribs and rolled him from his side onto his shredded back. The victim let out a stifled moan as the broken arm fell away from his face. "Liked breaking and entering and murdering helpless old women in their houses."

The man stretched his unbroken arm out, trying to grasp my ankle. "Help me." He could barely speak; it sounded like someone had taken a rasp to his vocal cords. "Please, you gotta get me outta here, man, please—!" He broke off with another scream as one of the dogs grabbed the outstretched limb and chomped enthusiastically, wrenching its head back and forth and growling.

But I'd recoiled already, because I recognized this man, yes I did. Landon Vickers – who'd slaughtered my mother in the home invasion robbery. A red mist covered my vision for a moment; I staggered and nearly fell, before Khatuliel caught me. "I have you, Clifton. Be eased."

I rounded on him, furious. "Be eased? That sonofabitch killed my mother! Like hell am I going to be eased!"

"And he is receiving the just recompense for his many crimes, while your mother enjoys a mansion in the Heavenlies."

"Do you really think that pie-in-the-sky bullshit makes me feel better?" Tears streamed down my cheeks. I let them. "I was supposed to be there that night, but I blew her off, figuring I could see her any time. Maybe if I *had* been there, I could have stopped them."

"And perhaps you too would have died. You don't know that you could have made any difference at all."

"She wouldn't have died alone," I whispered, suffocating on rage and loss and guilt. "She would have died knowing her son loved her."

"Oh, Clifton." He enfolded me in arms and wings both. It was enormously comforting. I didn't deserve it. "She knows. Of course she knows."

Gaap intruded. "The accomplice yet escapes justice, however." I turned to look at him through Khatuliel's sheltering wings. Gaap smirked through all his teeth and picked up an elaborately-wrought iron poker, dipping it in the lava until it glowed. "Would you like a turn with him? He doesn't need his eyes down here anyway. Go ahead."

I turned away from Khatuliel and stepped toward Gaap. Khatuliel made a protesting noise. "This is unfair even coming from you, Gaap. No mortal man but a saint would resist such a temptation placed in his path."

"Why, Khati," Gaap looked shocked. "hasn't Father promised that He will not suffer them to be tempted above that they are able to bear?"

"Do not mock the Scriptures, Gaap; blasphemers never end well. This is not Father's temptation, but yours. Your side does not play by such rules."

"Why should we be constrained by something so arbitrary?" Gaap placed the poker in my hand and wrapped my fingers around it. "If you do this just right, he'll beg to tell who helped him. And then you can go after him, too, and he can join his companion in this very room."

The other dog had grabbed the broken arm, and they were engaged in a vigorous game of tug-of-war while my mother's murderer shrieked and thrashed between them. I stepped forward, almost automatically, and Ronwe rapped out a command. The dogs released their prey and sat beside him, panting.

I knelt beside Vickers, fisted my hand in his hair, and yanked, waving the poker in his face. "How about it. Who helped you." They weren't really questions.

"Oh, God, I'm sorry, I'm so, so sorry, please, please just take me out of here, I'll tell you anything you want to know, man, please, they won't even let me pass out..."

"No rest for the wicked," I mused, and slid the poker down his ribcage. The odor of burning flesh filled the room, and he flinched away from it.

"Clifton," Khatuliel said. "There are better ways of handling this. Don't stain your soul on the likes of him."

"Pft. Your soul. You're not using it anyway," Gaap pointed out. "And really, Vickers is here for a very good reason. You would simply be one more instrument of divine punishment, so, really, you'd be carrying out Father's vaunted Will anyway, right?"

"That is not how it works," Khatuliel said, "as you know very well, Gaap."

"It might as well be, however. Everyone has a price, Clifton. What's yours?"

"I don't know." The poker weighed heavy in my hand. This man had slaughtered my mother for a few trinkets. I moved the tip closer to his face; he tried and failed to turn away as I tightened my grip in his hair. "Don't move, asshole."

"He's not worth it," Khatuliel's voice sounded like it was coming from far away.

"No, but your mother was." Gaap's voice was much louder. "And you know, we can make sure that if you kill the accomplice, no one ever finds out. Her blood cries out for justice, does it not?"

"The accomplice will get his justice, whether by your hand or no. Your sainted mother would not want you to be a monster on her behalf, Clifton. For her sake if not your own, step *away*."

I'd dreamed about what I'd do if I ever got my hands on this man. Thought about it at great length. Killing him slowly had been at the top of the list, but he was already dead. Gaap saw my hesitation and waved his hand at the table. "We have other implements if you'd rather use them. Spiked brass knuckles are a perennial favorite."

Vickers closed his eyes and shivered. He was at my complete mercy, and I wasn't feeling too lenient. I knew exactly how much my mother had suffered as this man took her life – I'd seen the autopsy report – and my hand moved almost of its own accord, shifting the poker toward his eye. He tried to shrink away from the heat, but I still held his hair fast. Staring gleefully down into the abyss, I found... myself. Staring back.

"Clifton." Khatuliel's words were an anguished whisper. "Please."

I dropped the poker—

And punched Vickers viciously in the face. His nose crunched under my fist, and his eye socket, and his cheekbone. His lip split, and I raised my arm again, breathing heavily. Gaap laughed in the background, while Khatuliel choked.

I stared at Vickers' shattered body, trapped here for an eternity of torment. Did I want to be trapped with him? Would I be, if I took this further?

And did I want to be the same sort of person he was? He'd taken his time with my mother. Become the monster to defeat the monster, or find another way?

It took physical effort, but I let go of his hair with a wrench and a gasp and backed away from him, burying my face in my bloodied hands. A moment later, a pair of feathered wings covered me. I wasn't sure why, but I'd take it.

"How disappointing," Gaap said. "I don't suppose they'll ever catch his accomplice now."

"Corey. Harmon," gasped Vickers. "Warn him. Please. Warn him. About this..."

The demon hissed angrily; my head came up as Vickers lowered his, and the wings tightened around me. "Come, Clifton," Khatuliel said. "You won this round, for certain values of winning. Let us go from here."

I nodded, unable to speak just then, and he drew me to my feet and out of the room. Gaap huffed impatiently and followed, but had no more words about much of anything as he led us to the place where I'd entered. "Perhaps we will meet again," he said, and disappeared with a dramatic puff of horrible-smelling smoke.

"He seems annoyed," I said. I'd found some of my equilibrium on the trek. "Thank you, Khatuliel. You're right. I don't want to be a monster. That would be a terrible legacy."

"What will you do now?" he asked. "You have your name. With your profession, you can find him easily, and you know enough to hide a body where it will never be found. Can you restrain yourself?"

My lips tightened. "I don't know. Might be best to just give Harmon's name to the cops and see what they can do with it. And, if they fail? Then I can decide."

"That is fair. I'm proud of you, Clifton. Not everyone would have stepped back from that."

I felt oddly humbled, that an angel would be proud of me. "I'll try to live up to it. What will you do now?"

"Continue with your Guardianship. It is my Purpose, and my Joy. You will not see me, of course, but I am with you always." He laid his hand on the hood of my car, which was untouched, exactly where I'd left it. The engine purred to life, sounding better than it had when I'd bought it, actually. "But if you would listen, more often, to that still, small voice? 'Twould ease my task."

"I'll try." I ducked my head. "At least now I know what it sounds like."

"Indeed." He embraced me. "Go with God, son of man, and know He loves you." He faded out...

And left an enormous feather in my no-longer-bloodied hand. Later that evening, I placed it on the mantle beside my mother's ashes.

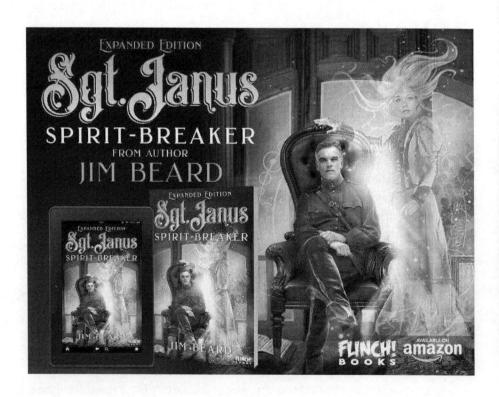

BEYOND THE FADED SHRINE GATES

BRANDON BARROWS

When I was a little boy, I was very angry. The world seemed wide and terrifyingly huge and I wanted to take in every centimeter of it that I could grasp and make it mine. Not out of any malice or desire to rule or anything like that, but because I was filled with wonder and curiosity, and it was there for the taking, so why not? As someone living on this big blue ball, it belonged to me as much as it did to anyone. But when we're young, our ambitions often outpace our reach and stymied wonder becomes frustration. That frustration, in turn, becomes anger more easily than most of us would like to admit. Standing before the paint-cracked, weather-faded *torii* of *Ankokuishi* shrine, it's easy to remember that. No, more like it's hard to forget.

I grew up in a town at the foot of a mountain in Nagano. The name doesn't matter. What does is that, while the world at large seemed immense, my personal world was very small. The town was small, my school was small, my few friends content with what they had. No one was interested in the things I was, the places and people outside of our little home. Talk among my peers mostly ran to whatever comics or TV shows were popular, and while those things are fine, it just wasn't enough for me.

Adult interaction wasn't much better. My parents were distant. My mother loved me, as much as she dared, but she always treated me as if I was somehow something that didn't quite belong to her. I was of her body, and she wanted me in her heart, but something was in the way. I realized that thing was my father, though it took me a long time to understand why.

My father was... distant, is the best way to put it. I never felt that I was unwanted but nor did I feel from him love or warmth, or any of the things a parent supposedly feels by default. We were more like cohabitants of a too-large house than family. He didn't ignore me, we just didn't speak often. When we did, it was usually in the form of one-sided admonishments: don't do this, don't do that; this isn't proper, that isn't fit for someone of our status. I had no idea what that even meant. What was our "status?" I asked him more than once. He never explained. I suppose that was beneath him, too.

I grew up in that small, lonely town, craving more, but I wasn't born there; we moved when I was very small – young enough that I didn't really remember anywhere else. That was part of my frustration: I thought maybe if I'd been born into that place, I'd have fit better. Talking about it was useless; my mother was mute on such subjects and I assume my father had made the decision in the first place, so I never even tried with him. And it must have suited his purposes quite well, because once we'd moved into our new home, he hardly left it – though he did have a lot of visitors. They would arrive in the evenings mostly, enter my father's private den, stay for minutes or hours or anywhere in between and then disappear. I wasn't allowed to speak or even look at them if I could avoid it. My mother never greeted them or served refreshments. They were like passing ghosts we did our best to ignore. On the rare occasions that my father did leave the house – always, it seemed, prompted by a visit – he would be gone for days, or even weeks. My mother was happiest during those times and that made me very sad, though I only understood why in the vaguest terms. I just knew it wasn't normal.

By the time I was ten years old, I'd mostly gotten used to not having a father in the traditional sense. It didn't make me any freer or feel any less angry, but I'd learned to hide it better. My world was small and so was I, but I had something to drive me – that directionless anger – and I let it propel me as far as I could go.

Small as my world was, there were still places to explore. I touched every square millimeter I could reach and did my best to make them mine. The little park where couples walked, hand in hand, while old men snoozed in the sun. The abandoned hospital built during the war and left to crumble afterwards. Mountain trails behind my school and bike paths by the river. I was careful to never cause trouble for anyone or go into places where I'd be found out, but somehow, my father always knew.

I don't know *how*, but he did.

The first time I was called to his den, I didn't know why, and expected something terrible was about to happen. I received a lecture about keeping out of places I didn't belong and that was that. It wasn't particularly harsh and it wasn't at all effective. The second time was worse: it was the first time my father ever struck me. Just a slap across the bare bottom, but still a shock. Even so, it only drove my anger a little deeper and made it just a little hotter.

I didn't hate my father, but I hated that he kept secrets from me. The state of my world was solely his fault, as far as I was concerned. Why did we have to live in some rural mountain town where nothing happened or ever would? How did he always know where I had been? I resented him for those things. I was angry and I defied him because I wanted to make *him* angry. I never heard him raise his voice and, except for that one slap on the behind, he'd never raised his hand against me or my mother (that I knew of), but I'd also never heard him say things like, "I love you" or even "good morning." I wanted some sort of reaction beyond indifference or admonishments. Defying him was the only way I knew to get one. The third time I was summoned, I knew that I had gotten what I wanted, but, kneeling on the *tatami* before him, eyes fixed on the floor, palms sweating, I was still afraid.

My father stared at me for a long time, utterly silent. When he finally spoke, he surprised me. "I think I understand you a little better, Azuma, than I did before."

I risked a glance up, from under my bangs.

"Believe me, when I say," my father continued, "that I am sorry that I can't give you every little freedom you desire. There are reasons that I don't care to share with you because they simply don't matter. This place," he gestured around us in a vague sort of way, "is safe. That I can guarantee. Out there..." he motioned towards the window behind him, unshaded but darkened by the night, "I do my best, but there's only so much I *can* do. I know you don't like being told what to do, but believe me, too, that I tell you these things for your own good." He sighed, something else I'd never heard from him. "Look at me." I lifted my eyes and met his squarely. "Azuma, you aren't going to stop wandering, are you?"

I said nothing.

"It's all right," he prompted. "You may answer."

I just shook my head.

"Azuma," he stood, moved to the window, looked out for a moment then drew the shade before turning back to me. "Azuma, whatever you do, do not go into *Ankokuishi*, do you understand?"

I didn't. *Ankokuishi* was an old shrine at the very edge of town, abandoned long before I was born. Before even my father was born, I guessed. I'd been there before, briefly, but found nothing of interest. I almost told my father that, but something stopped me. Maybe it was that, for once, he didn't seem to already know.

"Do you understand, Azuma? Under no circumstances are you to enter *Ankokuishi*. That place..." He sank slowly to his knees, sitting closer to me than he had before. "That place is the end of this world." His eyes met mine. "Promise me that you will never, ever cross through that gate."

I had no choice. I promised.

I broke my promise the first chance I had.

I didn't participate in any after-school activities. Sports and so forth didn't appeal to me at all. I was fit enough and chasing a ball seemed pointless. A few friends were in clubs, but no one ever asked me to join them. That suited me just fine. School let out at three o'clock, but I didn't need to be home until five. I used those hours to wander. The day after my father's warning, there was no need to wander. I knew exactly where I was going.

Ankokuishi shrine stood atop a hill, northeast of town, at the edge of the forest that blanketed the base of the mountain. There was no proper road to get there, only an old pathway of beaten dirt, partially overgrown by scrub brush as the forest reclaimed the land. It was lined by stones that might have once been statues, eaten down to anonymous gray blobs by wind, rain and time. And that was the reason I first found it. Weathered as they were, they still formed a pathway that was irresistible.

The walk from town took nearly forty minutes, but the walk up the pathway took only another ten before I stood before the first *torii*, the gateway from this world to the world of the gods. As a kid, I was never quite clear on what that meant. I knew the gates signified our passage into a holy place, but the distinction was lost on me. Nothing seemed to change from one side to the next, no matter how often you passed through them. Now, my father's words, *the end of this world*, bounced around my skull and a little shiver crawled down my spine.

I took a deep breath and stepped through the gate.

Nothing happened.

I allowed myself to breathe and forced a smile. This was nothing. Just an old place nobody came to anymore. I hiked up the pathway as it grew steeper and stepped through a second, smaller *torii* into the shrine itself.

The grounds were even more overgrown than the pathway had been. The rough-hewn stones used to pave the courtyard had been pushed aside by thick, hearty grasses. Brush crowded in around the edges of the space, and around the one remaining building. A few trees grew tall and shaded the grounds, here blocking the late-afternoon's slanting sun and casting deep shadows, there splitting its beams into dapples strewn across the earth and stones and grass. I looked around, heart thumping in my chest. I hadn't come this far before, but I was an explorer, I told myself, and nobody could stop me. Even so, I wasn't sure what I was looking for; I wasn't certain I wanted to find anything at all. What, I wondered, would be worse? My father being right? Or my father being wrong?

Wind, down from the mountain, had blown gently all afternoon, a soft breeze that grew stronger the higher I climbed, but all of a sudden, it gusted and raged, whipping the long grasses back and forth and pressing my clothes against my body. It only lasted a moment and when it faded, its roar was replaced by a thin, high keening from somewhere nearby.

A flute, I realized, but who was out there besides me?

Following the sound, I crossed the court, long grasses slapping gently against my legs, and, around the corner of the tumbledown shrine building, I saw him – a boy about my age, wearing traditional clothes: *kimono*, *hakama* pants, and wooden *geta* sandals. His hair was dark and shaggy, but his skin, even in the shadows of the trees crowding the edges of the grounds, was startlingly white. His features were delicate, his eyes closed as his pursed lips blew on a reed flute. His thin arms ended in long, nimble fingers that danced over the instrument's holes. His fingers somehow reminded me of ballroom dancers I'd once seen in a movie: elegant and beautiful, moving together with a purpose greater than any alone could.

Mesmerized, I listened to the boy play for two or three minutes. He seemed not to realize I was there. Then he stopped, lowering the flute as his eyelids rose, and pinned me in place with his gaze. I probably gasped. I know I took a step backwards and I know my heart seized in my chest. The boy's finely-shaped features and pale skin were strange, but his eyes were absolutely eerie: completely colorless and seeming almost to glow with an inner light that had nothing to do with the sun stippling the grounds around us.

"Wh-who are you?" I asked.

"Who are *you*?" the other boy replied.

The boy's outdated clothing and unearthly appearance and my father's words all rattled around and combined in my brain and I blurted out, "*Yokai!*"

The stranger with the flute cocked his head, considering me, maybe trying to see me from another angle. Then his lips twisted into a smile and he burst into laughter. "You're a *yokai*?"

"No!" I shook my head, irritated and a little embarrassed to be laughed at. "*You're* the *yokai*! What else would you be, dressed like that way out here?"

"Huh?" The look on his face seemed genuinely confused.

"Don't come any closer." I dug into my pocket, searching for my good luck charm: an *o-fuda* I'd carried since I began my explorations. It was just a simple 'good health' charm, inscribed with the characters for 'health' and 'luck' and the name of *Ooyamatsumi*, the deity of the town's still-occupied shrine, but I'd won it at the fall festival in the luck-guessing game and when I went into the darker corners of my little world, holding it always made me feel safer. Now, I held it out towards the strange boy and said again, "Don't come closer. Don't come near me," as I backed away. I wasn't sure what my plan was. Should I run? I needed a moment to think and distance seemed like a good idea. I took a step backwards, my dark eyes locked on the other boy's strange, colorless ones, and never saw the rock that turned my ankle and sent me tumbling down to the grassy, stone-pocked earth.

The back of my head cracked against a paving stone and the wind rushed out of my lungs with an *oomph*! Red and black and green exploded behind my eyes and for a moment, I felt a crushing weight on my chest. I struggled to open my eyes as a shadow fell across me. I wrenched one eye open and stared directly into the stranger's delicately-beautiful face and weirdly-empty eyes.

"Are you okay?" he asked, extending a hand to help me up.

Clenching my jaw against the throbbing in my head, I tried to roll away from his grasp, but the other boy grabbed my hand and yanked me to my feet with ease. "C'mon. You're being silly." He turned me around, examined my head, announced that I'd probably be fine, then brushed my clothes off. I couldn't meet his eyes so I watched his hands, long-fingered and deft, as they worked.

When he was done, he looked me over again and said, "There. Except for the bump, good as new."

"Thanks," I said and, in a whisper, added, "I'm sorry."

His eyebrows lifted, making his odd eyes seem very large. "No need. It was no trouble."

"I mean," I forced myself to look up, to meet his gaze. Up close, his eyes looked like pure mountain water, absolutely clear, though I could see nothing behind them. I wasn't sure what I *would* see if I could. I had never seen eyes like those before, but, despite appearances, the boy seemed perfectly normal otherwise. I was ashamed of my outburst. "For calling you a *yokai* and, you know…"

He smiled. "It's fine. You surprised me, though. How long were you listening to me?"

"Not long," I admitted. "You're good." I motioned towards the flute the boy still held, half-forgotten, dangling from loosely-grasped fingers.

He held the flute up, smiled wider. "Oh, thanks. So, what are you doing out here?"

"Um…"

"Are you maybe running away from home?'

"What?" As angry, as unhappy, I was with my life, the thought had never even occurred to me. "No, I'm not running away. What are *you* doing out here? This isn't a place for kids, you know."

He burst into laughter. "You know what? You're great. You're really funny. Did you come out here just to tell me that?"

"Of course not." Embarrassment colored my cheeks and I squatted, pulled up a handful of the long grass, then let it flutter away, blade by blade, caught by the wind. "My dad says I'm not supposed to come out here. So…"

"I was practicing my flute." The other boy crouched down, matching my stance, and plucked his own handful of grass. "I'm supposed to perform the music offering at a festival soon."

"You are?" The festival at *Ooyamatsumi*'s shrine wasn't until the fall, still months away, and I'd never seen this boy before. Maybe he was a relative of the shrine family, moving to town to learn the family business?

"I know!" The boy stood and clapped his hands together, around the flute, making a muffled slapping noise. "Why don't you practice with me?"

"What do you—"

Before I could finish the question, he'd pulled me to my feet and begun arranging my limbs into an unfamiliar pose. He said, "Come on. Stand up! I know the song, but I've only seen the dance a few times and I want to make sure I have the rhythm down. It'd really help me out if you could practice with me."

"I'm not sure…" My face went hot again. I didn't even know this boy, but I'd already embarrassed myself in front of him and now he was putting me on the spot.

"C'mon, it'll be fun. I'll show you." He struck a pose similar to the one I awkwardly stood in and did a few simple steps, then repeated them, then once again. "Now you." He waved a hand then brought his flute to his lips and began to play. The same thin, ethereal sound I'd first heard flowed from the instrument, filling the courtyard, seeming to wrap itself around me. I began to move and it was as if I'd already been practicing for days or weeks. My feet and arms moved almost effortlessly, the pain in my head and shoulders where I'd struck the ground became distant, then disappeared entirely as my body grew more limber, more agile. The music swirled around us, the notes of the flute seeming to sway up and down, back and forth as my limbs followed it, carrying me around the area, around my strange, new friend. It was less like I'd learned the dance and more like he'd simply released something that had already been inside me.

I don't know how long he played, how long I danced, but when the other boy finally finished the tune, I was flushed and sweaty and smiling so hard my cheeks hurt. I glanced around and realized that the shadows had grown very long as the sun dipped low behind the mountain.

"Phew! That was fun." The other boy grinned. "You've got a lot of talent. You're so graceful."

"No, it was nothing…" I shuffled my feet, suddenly awkward again and more than a little confused. I'd never really danced before in my life and that had felt so effortless.

"You should come to the festival with me." The other boy stepped closer, grasped my hands in his. There was something in his transparent eyes that hadn't been there before. "You'll be the star of the whole festival. You and me."

"B-but," I stammered, "the festival isn't until after the summer. It's—"

He shook his head, making the shaggy mane sway back and forth. "Not the harvest festival. A better one, much sooner than that."

"A better one?" Odd and humiliating as our meeting had been, I was having fun with my new friend. With those words, though, something changed between us.

"You hate your father, don't you? You came here to make him worry. Think about how worried he'd be if you came to the festival with me, if we left right now and didn't even tell him."

It was like being struck across the face. "How did you—"

"How did I know that you hate your father?" He smiled and it was no longer the warm smile he had shown me so many times already.

"No!" I shook my head vigorously. "I don't hate my father. But he's..." I struggled. I'd never put it into words. There had never been anyone I *could* talk to before. "It's just that he keeps things from me. Everything is a secret with him. I don't know why we live in the middle of nowhere or who those men are that come to our house almost every night. I don't even know who my father really is. I only know that he only tells me what I can't do, but never *why*. I'm not even supposed to be here. He said *Ankokuishi* is a forbidden place. He called it—"

" 'The place where this world ends'?" The boy's smile grew wider and thinner. Chills so sharp they were almost painful raced down my arms and through my belly.

I nodded. "Your parents say it, too, huh?"

The other boy crouched and gently laid his flute down on the ground, then stood back up and moved a step closer, his eyes never leaving mine. "And that's why you thought I was a *yokai*?"

I shook my head, turned away. "I'm sorry. Forget it. That was a stupid thing to say."

"If I was..." He moved closer still and grabbed my arms. He was close enough that I should have been able to feel his breath on my cheek. "If I was a *yokai*, what would you do?" I turned and our eyes, only inches apart, met. His eyes were no longer transparent or colorless, but absolutely empty, as if I was looking through him into somewhere else entirely, somewhere I still couldn't quite see. "Would you run away screaming? Would you try to destroy me with that charm in your pocket?"

I shrugged out of his grasp and tried a smile that I didn't feel. "That's silly. You're not a *yokai*. And even if you were, we could still be friends. You seem..." I didn't know how to finish the thought. I wanted to say *like a nice guy*, but I was no longer sure. I realized something then. "Oh, hey. What's your name, anyway? I'm—"

"Azuma Kuromori."

"What?" It came out a whisper.

"Don't move." As he said the words, I realized I couldn't. My feet were rooted to the ground and all my muscles locked in place. Had he done something to me when he grabbed me?

The other boy, if that's what he was, stepped back and averted his eyes from mine. "I'm going to tell you something, Azuma Kuromori." He started to walk around me in a circle, gesturing to the space around us. As he did, the final traces of the sun slipped behind the mountain and darkness fell all around us. I wanted to scream, to run, so badly that it hurt, but my eyes were the only thing I could move and all they showed me was blackness as the last of the light disappeared.

"Living all around you, here, in this town, and everywhere – anywhere – else you might go, are things that aren't like you. *Yokai, ayakashi, oni, yurei, obake* and more other kinds than even I know, I suppose. The Other Shore is a crowded place. There are places where we can come into your world and also places where we can bring you to ours. *Ankokuishi* is just one of them. Most of the people who were born here, who have roots here, know this. Your father knows this. That's not his only secret, but it's the one you should be most concerned with right now."

"*Under no circumstances are you to enter Ankokuishi,*" my father had said. "*That place is the end of this world.*"

I felt a tear roll down my cheek. When we'd last spoken, my father told me that he understood me a little better than he had before. Just then, I thought maybe I understood him better, too, but I was sure I'd never get a chance to tell him that.

The thing completed its pacing, stood before me and held a single, delicate finger to its lips. "Can you keep a secret, Azuma?" He winked and with a jolt of electricity, I could feel my body again. I gasped, sucking in great heaps of air. Sweat rolled down my forehead to mix with the tears that now flowed freely from my eyes. His eyes moved up and down my face. "Well?"

"You *are* a yokai." I needed to say it out loud.

His smile was thin. Though his features were still beautiful, they seemed somehow terrible, now that I knew for sure. Even so, there still didn't seem to be any malice in the way he looked at me. "Are you afraid, Azuma?"

I was. I didn't want to admit it, but it was the truth. I didn't think I needed to actually say it, though. It was clear from the way he looked at me that I was right.

He continued: "You don't need to worry. I won't eat you. I like my meals a little more mature. A little meatier, if you will. You're very lucky it was me who stumbled across you, though, and not one of the others." His smile grew very wide and something in the back of his throat gleamed, like another set of eyes catching light from some unknown source. I looked away, falling to my knees like a puppet whose strings had been cut. I was suddenly exhausted. Exhausted right down to the bone. Down to the *soul*, if it was possible.

The thing I'd been chatting with all afternoon sighed then turned on its heel, moving through the darkness towards the entrance of the shrine grounds, towards where I'd originally come from, putting itself between me and escape. It stopped, looked over its shoulder at me and said, "Make sure you do as your father tells you from now on. Whether you believe it or not, adults don't just tell children things to hear themselves speak. I've enjoyed spending time with you, Azuma, but you really shouldn't come here again. Now, if you'll excuse me..." He turned and continued moving forward again, disappearing into the night.

I don't know how long I knelt on the ground, chest heaving, weeping softly, arms clutched around myself. When I finally found the strength to rise, the moon had also begun its climb across the sky. I slowly, carefully, made my way out of *Ankokuishi* shrine and then, when I reached the path towards the main road, I began to run. I didn't stop until I was inside my own home. My father was nowhere to be seen, cloistered in his den with visitors, I supposed. My mother fussed over me to the extent she always did, wondering where I had been. I didn't tell her. I never have. Before long, though, she gave up, put me in the bath and then to bed. I expected consequences from my trip to the shrine, from my father, at least, if nothing else. There were none. He never said a word to me about the shrine ever again. I wondered if perhaps that was the one place he couldn't know I'd been. I didn't want to find out.

You might think an experience like *Ankokuishi* would cure me of my curiosity, make me more content with the idea of a quiet life. How could it, though, when that thing in the shrine had said that its kind were all around me? Maybe there was no such thing as a quiet life, only the illusion of one. In a way, meeting that strange boy was a blessing: it was proof that there really *was* more to the world than I knew. And with that revelation, my anger disappeared and the curiosity was all that was left, stronger than before. My wanderings only stopped for a few days before the urge overcame me again, but I found that they carried me to *Ooyamatsumi's* shrine more often than before. In time, I became good friends with the head priest there and I learned a lot from him.

In almost thirty more years of life, I've seen more of the world than my ten-year-old self could ever imagine. There are some things I wish I didn't know and some things the knowledge of which I wouldn't trade for anything. I understand my father pretty well now and I know more about *yokai, ayakashi, oni* and all the rest than is probably necessary.

There's one thing I've never learned, though, and it's bothered me for a long time. That strange, pale, fine-featured boy with the dark hair and colorless eyes knew my name, but never told me his.

I reach into my pocket, rub my thumb across the characters on a battered old 'good health' *o-fuda*, and step through the *torii* into his world.

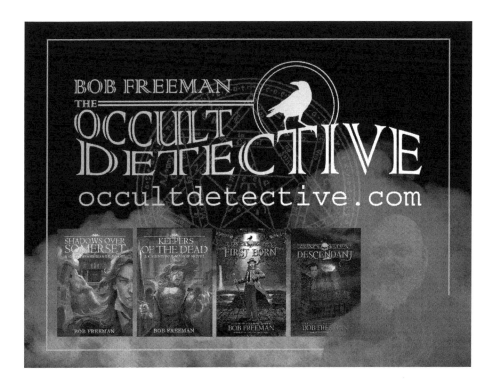

A NIGHT IN GORAKHPUR
A Tale of the Occultress

COLIN FISHER

Sinclair could not have lied, for the simple reason he had no imagination. He could no more have submitted a falsehood than I could have hit a double century at Lords. Such a thing was simply impossible.

So when I inform you that every word of the following story, which Sinclair relayed to me after dinner in one of the Club's private dining rooms, is true, I expect you to believe me. And indeed to feel the same frisson of terror, of ice-tipped fingers upon the spine, that I felt that evening as he paced, gesticulating, by the window – as my cigar, untasted, burned to a stub in my numb hand. Dear God, would he or I invent such a fable?

Makepeace was of the Faversham Sinclairs. A family raised to minor nobility under the Tudors by virtue of the sizeable quantity of iron discovered beneath their land, which lent a Kentish weight to the wars of Henry and Elizabeth. Their fortunes took a downturn under the Commonwealth, but the Restoration, and a dose of fiscal prudence, saw them regaining their former estates, which they held to the present day.

Sinclair was, therefore, a solid, dependable scion of a solid, dependable family. I knew him at Oxford. When we went down, my feet inclined naturally to the Law, whilst his followed the generations of his predecessors who had marched, dependably, into the military, where he gained the unimaginative sinecure of a minor commission in the Lancers.

After ten years unimpeachable service in the various reaches of Empire, he was rewarded with the governorship of an unimportant province in East Punjab, and he quickly settled into the routine of a British colonial administrator, expected to do no more than maintain his staff's efficiency, quell the occasional native unrest in the northern tribal areas, and prevent his men from outraging the honour of too many native women. He fulfilled all these duties with the diligence and lack of note required, and enjoyed a cordial relationship with the native officials and rulers. Polo and cricket were a mainstay of his tenure, and there was little civil or military action required, relations between the natives and the state having improved considerably following the transfer of power from the East India Company to the Crown. He was, in short, an ideal functionary of the British presence.

All that changed when he had been in post a little over two years. Owing to Sinclair's lack of experience, he leaned a good deal on the advice of his assistant, a retired Major by the name of George Linklater. The Major was a bluff, no-nonsense individual who was known for speaking his mind, but was also unusually sympathetic to native religious and social customs and thus respected in both British and Indian circles. He had lost a leg during service, but this hardly hampered his energy and commitment. Sinclair relied on him thoroughly.

The topic on which Linklater was most forthright was that of Sinclair's marital status, and he often urged the younger man to take a wife. It was seen as a necessary adjunct to his social standing; without one, he was not only at a disadvantage with regard to the number of invitations he could accept, but was in danger of becoming the target of chatter. Tongues will wag, after all, and the colonial administration was, if nothing else, a hotbed of gossip. An eligible bachelor was not expected to remain in that unhappy condition for long.

At that time the English craze for seances, for spiritualist mediums who claimed to speak with the dead, was beginning to spread across the Empire. "Just a lark," was how Sinclair described it to me, "Just a lark, old man. Table rapping nonsense." There was a sense that the Indians themselves took a slightly dim view of the practice – dangerous meddling with supernatural forces – but, naturally, that carried little weight.

"It was simply boredom. Not to be taken seriously," Sinclair said, pacing nervously, and he had the curious habit of drumming his fingers against the walnut panelling, gazing as he did through the window into the square outside, bathed in the evening sun of summer. "Not my sort of thing at all, I don't mind telling you. But the season's thing, you know?

"Anyway," he said, "nonsense it may have been, but Linklater persuaded me to take up the invitation when it came in. *'There'll be an unattached young filly there, old man,'* he said. Friend of the spirit medium apparently. I wasn't particularly keen, but knew I needed to show willing or risk social ostracism. It was held at the Fitzwater's – you know the family?" and he broke off, turning to me with a quizzical eyebrow. I shook my head, and he continued. "Well, it was a fairly intimate gathering. A half dozen husbands and their wives, the Harrises, Tristram and Marjory Gainsworth, Colonel Beynon and his wife. George and Charlotte Linklater. A few others whose names escape me. That sort. There was an American, J. Pickering Crowningshield, whom I most remember for his extravagant moustaches. Nobody you would look upon twice. That all changed when the medium,

Madame Eusapia Hardinge and her companions arrived.

"Let me tell you, Edward, she made an extraordinary sight. Not a small woman by any stretch, she was swathed in blue silk robes, rich as a Maharanee. She wore a black turban wound with golden thread, and her eyes were hooded, dark, though I noted her gaze dart about the room as our small group was introduced. Those eyes were calculating, but somehow distant. She was imposing, carried a definite authority, however bizarre her appearance. The same couldn't be said of her husband, Clive. A shrewish, servile fellow, hovering at her elbow and bobbing his head at each introduction. Wore a starched suit, collar and tie, which in that heat must have been hellish. His hands were damp and limp, as sensationless as the touch of a feather. He gave the impression of wanting to shrink inside his wife's shadow, and his watery eyes peered from behind circular black-framed glasses with an expression of incipient panic. I didn't take to him, frankly.

"The third member of the group was different again, and my breath caught as I was introduced to her. A young woman, barely in her twenties, as tall as myself and easily a head taller than either of her companions, with the palest, porcelain skin I had ever seen. Almost bloodless. She wore a high collar, which failed to conceal an extraordinarily long neck, and her hair, in bun and barley curls, was quite remarkable. Quite remarkable, old man." He shook his head, and fell silent. His eyes took on a distant aspect, as if gazing into the past.

"Howso?" I prompted, taking the opportunity to pour myself a generous measure from the decanter of Garrafeira he had provided.

"I'm not sure what colour it was. Some form of blonde, of the very lightest kind, but with a silvery sheen, like a young birch. It almost shone in the light. Her face, too, was striking. Narrow, tapering, but with broad, predatory green eyes like the golden cats that curled about the walls of the temple at Gorakh Nath. Her nose was straight as the prow of a ship, and brought to mind the fierce unblinking aspect of the hawk-headed god of the Egyptians. She radiated intelligence."

"Sounds like quite a creature," I interjected. "And this was the girl Linklater was all for pairing you off with?"

"So I surmised," he said. "I don't mind admitting, I was riveted, along with every other man in the room." He chuckled, "Much to the dismay of the *memsahibs*.

"Anyway, we all stood about sipping our sherry and making polite conversation. Madame Hardinge was steered to an armchair, and I almost expected her companions to take up the position of courtiers at her sides.

Only her husband joined her, however, bobbing his head at each proffered hand like a deferential maidservant. The wives graduated towards them, keen to hear their guest's experiences of the world beyond.

"Our hostess, Mrs Fitzwater, guided the final member of the triad around the room. When they reached me I could already feel myself heating under the young woman's penetrating gaze.

" 'Permit me to introduce our esteemed Governor, Makepeace Sinclair.' Mrs Fitzwater waved her hand, and added 'and the only bachelor at tonight's soiree. Mr Sinclair, this is Miss Lucy Godolphin.'

" 'Oh, that's my favourite *nom de plume*.' I said the first thing that came into my mind, stupidly referencing – as if she'd know – an author of abridged classics my parents had made me read. But the comment had an extraordinary effect.

Her smile froze on her face. 'I'm quite afraid I don't know what you mean,' she said frostily. Mrs Fitzwater looked dismayed at the unexpected tone the conversation had taken.

" 'Oh, no, I meant no disrespect,' I stammered, 'I was thinking of that novelist woman, Aiken. Her name was Lucy and she wrote under the name Godolphin.' The girl continued to stare at me, and I felt myself reddening. I waved my hand vaguely at my head. 'It was just, you know, erm... an association.'

" 'I see.' She offered me a thin smile. 'Yes, a most curious coincidence. I never thought to meet a reader of children's literature at such a place. Congratulations on an association well made.' But her tone remained cold.

" 'Oh, you're familiar with her work?' I said, trying to steer the conversation in a less contentious direction. 'I enjoyed her *Robinson Crusoe*, but I'm afraid I've always found Aesop absurd. Talking animals, ridiculous.'

"But I'd lost her attention, and cursed myself. Mrs Fitzwater and I chatted, while Miss Godolphin's gaze wandered the room, and she made only the occasional polite murmur. Her attention seemed more drawn to the conversations that her friend and husband were having. Making one last attempt at conversation, I asked if she had known Madame Hardinge long. She shook her head without even looking at me.

" 'Just since Lucknow,' she said. 'I rather imposed on their hospitality.'

" 'Lucknow?' I was nonplussed. 'The state capital? I'm sorry, I thought you'd all travelled over from England together.'

" 'Not at all, no. We met in the hotel last week.'

" 'But surely,' I coughed, 'for a refined young woman such as yourself...' I was unsure what to say. 'Well, to travel this far north alone might be considered inadvisable.'

" 'Yes, certainly,' she said, clearly not listening to a word I was saying. She finally looked at me, 'Do excuse me,' she said, and walked off to join in a conversation with the moustachioed American.

"I shrugged at Mrs Fitzwalter, and pulled a wry face. She patted my arm. 'Never mind, Governor. The night is young.' I drained my glass, and placed it on the tray of a passing servant, waving away the offer of another. I wanted to maintain a clear head.

"Soon it was time for the evening's entertainment – for such I privately labelled it – to begin. I liked to keep an open mind – I'd seen some strange, unaccountable things in places the white man rarely treads – but spiritualism, well, fakery and fraud if you asked my opinion. However, it would have been discourteous to our hosts to admit to such.

"We were ushered into a dining room in which a circular table sat, dark wood aglow with the warm light from the mantles, and we stood, waiting for the servants to seat us. By accident or design – I suspected the latter – I had been placed next to Miss Godolphin, and I was astonished when she waved away the servant behind her chair and sat, pulling herself forward with a scrape of wood. Gainsworth coughed into his hand, and I heard a muttered 'I say,' from the Colonel. The American chuckled. To cover the embarrassment, Mrs Fitzwater made a discreet gesture, and with a rustle of clothes we were quickly seated.

"I noticed Mrs Hardinge had a different, more solid chair, one with a high back and a strange veil-like attachment affixed to the top. Her large, manicured hands grasped the arms like a hawk grips the sleeve of a falconer. Her husband sat to one side, dabbing his sweating forehead with a silk handkerchief.

"The servants had already drawn heavy drapes across the windows; now they turned down the mantles, and a shroud of darkness settled across the room. Only the table, illuminated by the sepulchral glow of a chandelier, provided a reassuring anchor. A shiver of anticipation ran round the group, and it seemed the air grew close and heavy."

Sinclair turned, and raised a hand as I opened my mouth to speak. "Yes, I felt it too. Chicanery surely, I was aware of that, but the mood, the whole tone of the theatre, was such that it was impossible not to be drawn in."

"Please continue," I murmured, my port as forgotten as my *figurado*.

He stared at the floor, and there was a moment's quiet as he assembled his thoughts. "Mrs Fitzwater nodded at Peshaman, her Hindoo butler, and with a gesture he directed the other servants to leave. He closed the door on them, and stood to one side, a shape barely discernible in the gloom. When I returned my attention to the table, it was to see Mr Hardinge draw the chair's veiled attachment about his wife's head and body, for all the world like a corpse shroud. Despite the humidity of the evening, I felt cold. Her head, dimly seen through the veil, bowed and her breathing slowed. Only her hands emerged, clutched now by her husband and Gainsworth, presumably to divert accusations of subterfuge.

"Once he was again seated, Mr Hardinge addressed the group.

" 'Please join hands. I shall lead us in a short recitation of *Captain and Conqueror* whilst my wife attains the proper mental state to contact her spirit control.'

"And in a quavery tenor he began to sing, *'Join all the names of love and power, that ever men or angels bore'* and after a moment's hesitation we joined in. *'All are too mean to speak his worth, or set Immanuel's glory forth.'* Felt rather a fool, don't mind telling you. Happy as the next man to raise my voice in church, but seated round a dining table holding hands? Not my cup of char, at all. But the others seemed enthused enough, and besides, I was, as I remarked, sat next to Miss Godolphin, and thus more than happy to feel her cool fingers entwined in my own.

"In fact, I tried to catch her eye during the hymn, perhaps with a slight smile to show I was a man of rationality and didn't take the entertainment seriously. But she was merely mouthing the words and her head was bowed, as if looking at the table. Her eyes, though, those extraordinary green eyes, were staring from beneath hooded lids directly at Mrs Hardinge, and they bore a look of—"

Sinclair broke off, running his hand through his hair. "You know the district court at Ghaziabad?" I shook my head, but he continued anyway, his eyes focused on something distant. "The judges, when they're hearing a case, have that mixture of concentration and calculation, coolness mixed with... malevolence. Like a cat sizing up its prey."

"She seems to have made quite an impression on you," I noted, but he waved his hand irritably.

"What? Oh, never mind that, there was something wholly... antique in her expression, in her eyes." He began pacing, chewing his lip. "She was a young girl, barely out of her adolescence, but the look she directed at the medium was one of age, experience and dispassion. As if she were about to pass sentence."

"I see," I murmured. I did not see at all, but he was becoming agitated, and I had no wish to provoke him. "Please continue."

"The hymn ended. Hardinge took his place at his wife's side and, gazing around the circle with his moist eyes, intoned 'By the power of the Saints and by the Lord Jesus Christ, we are gathered here to respectfully request and require contact with those who have passed on.' A shiver of expectation passed around the table, particularly among the women. The atmosphere became, if anything, heavier and more intense. Madame Hardinge's head dipped forward, her veil brushing the edge of the table. Her breathing achieved a slow, even rhythm. Then she spoke. It was a rich baritone. A man's voice. 'I am Brother Marcus,' it intoned, to hushed gasps and intakes of breath. 'It is dark.'

" 'Welcome Marcus.' Mr Harding spoke warmly, with a tone of familiarity. He didn't look at his wife, instead shifting his grip on her hand and that of Mrs Beynon, who sat to either side. I could see his eyes glittering beneath lowered lids as he looked at the table in contemplation. 'It is a while since we heard from you. Are you well?'

"His wife's eyes were closed, her face impassive. I suppose she had a gift for voices. Some have, you know. I wasn't taken in, but I could see many of the others were riveted, staring at Mrs Hardinge with wide eyes.

" 'God keeps me well,' the supposed spirit replied. 'But your knee troubles you again. You must reduce your drinking or suffer the worse.'

"How very canny, I thought. No doubt his wife had attempted to curtail his habits previously, and was now enlisting the spirit world in her endeavours – and to provide some easy verisimilitude. I saw Hardinge incline his head with a slight smile.

" 'Thank you, as ever, for your wisdom, Brother Marcus,' he said, before glancing around the circle. Next to him, his wife's breathing was slow and steady, a slight rasp speaking of unhealthy lungs. 'And will you be materialising tonight? We have a circle of new friends who would delight in your appearance.'

"There was a pause, then the supposed spirit spoke again, 'I shall not manifest.' I could sense a collective sigh of disappointment, as if the circle were a single organism. Clearly some had been hoping for the more advanced chicanery of an actual apparition. 'Not all here are attuned to the spirit world. I feel negative vibrations that would not be conducive to my appearance.'

"I felt a twinge of guilt, I don't mind telling you. I hadn't wished to spoil the fun for the rest of the crowd, but clearly the dashed woman had picked up on my disbelief, or perhaps someone had let slip earlier I was a firm sceptic in such matters and she did not wish to be challenged."

Sinclair looked across at me. The sun was setting, casting the room in chimeras of gold and orange. His eyes glowed, and his face was thoughtful. "I had nothing against them, you understand, but really just wished the theatre to be over, that I might attempt to repair my relationship with their travelling companion. I wouldn't have challenged any of it."

"Pray continue," I said, stubbing out the remains of my untasted cigar. I snipped a fresh one and rolled it around my fingers. "Did further revelations proceed from Brother Marcus?" Belatedly I offered the box to Sinclair, but he waved it away.

"Oh, the revelations came thick and fast. Hardinge took the news that we were too negative for a manifestation in his stride. 'Then perhaps you have some messages for those who are willing?' he said, 'Some communications from departed loved ones?'

"Miss Godolphin shifted in her seat, and I wondered if she had travelled with them in the hope of contacting some dear departed. I had no idea of the etiquette on such occasions. Did the spirit world take requests? I need not have worried, for it seemed that between them Hardinge and his wife – in the guise of 'Brother Marcus' – intended to lead the proceedings. 'I have an older man here,' intoned the spirit, 'he is tall and spry, but was not always so.' There were glances around the table. Hardinge spoke in his timid voice, 'Are there any here who recognise the description? Perhaps someone who was an invalid in life? Perhaps one who was frustrated in their confinement?' At this, Mrs Gainsworth's eyes widened.

" 'Oh!' she said, with an expression between joy and alarm, 'My brother! Poor—'

" 'Wait!' interrupted Hardinge. 'Let us see if the spirit gives the correct name. Brother Marcus, who is it that speaks to you?'

"His wife breathed heavily into the silence, and the voice resumed, 'Algernon is his given name. He is happy now, in God's presence. He has no more need for the clutter of chairs and sticks.'

" 'Oh!' wailed the poor woman again, 'Oh Algie. My brother, you know, he crossed to the other side last year. I am so glad.'

"Of course, we did know. We all knew Viscount Ashworth had been seen off six months previously by the condition that had afflicted him ever since he reached his majority. And I'd no doubt that wretched woman and her husband could have found out the same with ten minutes research in Lucknow library."

"Dashed poor," I murmured, tasting the pungent leaf, "playing on the woman's credulity."

"I thought so too," Sinclair replied, "and the only thing that stopped me getting up and walking away from the whole charade was that – as the fakery proceeded – it seemed to provide a modicum of comfort to the assembled group. We heard from the Linklater's son, killed ten years before in the Sepoy Mutiny, as anyone reading casualty lists could have determined. Mrs Fitzwater was visited by her late husband, and Colonel Beynon's wife got a favourite aunt. And as if to demonstrate that the fair sex have no monopoly on credulity the American, Crowningshield, was offered a visitation by his niece, who had apparently died in childhood – although he seemed vaguely amused throughout the exchange, and the ends of his moustaches curled upwards with not infrequent smirks."

"Nothing for you?" I said. "No visitant from the spirit world?"

At this, Sinclair's fingers, which had been drumming on the windowsill, became still. I watched them curl into a ball, like the legs of a dying spider.

"I was coming to that, old man," he said thinly, before continuing, "It had become oppressively hot. More so even than one expected in that damnable climate. The gas in the mantle seemed to be declining, since the pool of light about the table had diminished considerably. The assembled guests had shrunk to dark outlines, only their faces lit as they leaned forward into the pool cast by the overhead light. There was an intensity to the glow, as if something predatory peeped through from a world of shadow. I wanted to loosen my collar, but dared not break the grip I had on the hands of Miss Godolphin and Mrs Fitzwater, the one curiously cool, the other hot and clammy.

"After we had dispensed with Ada Harris's father – drowned when she was ten – who had even brought along the family dog, as evidenced by some very convincing whimpering from the corner of the room, I felt Miss Godolphin suddenly stiffen and sit up. At the same time there came a draft, as if something rank blew toward me from Mrs Hardinge. I'd smelt something similar when travelling through the slums in Kathputhli, a mixture of body odour and curdled milk turning to paneer. It seemed overlaid with the smell of freshly turned earth. On the edge of the light I saw her garments billow, rippling up her arms as if she were herself caught in a breeze, although I knew the windows and all the sounds of night were shuttered out. Her veil parted and I glimpsed her face, rapt with concentration.

"That voice, that dashed queer voice, came from her again as the supposed monk spoke up. This time, however, the tone was markedly different. 'I can taste blood,' it said. 'I can taste iron. Iron in the blood, iron in the line. Oh, and the name, too, is iron. Or should I say, irony.' And then, weirdly, it laughed, a horrible chittering noise like the raucous song of the red-eyed *coucal*. Iron, of course, immediately made me think of my own family fortune, founded in our Kentish mines. And his next words confirmed it. 'The irony of a name in a bloodline made for battle.' He was mocking my own name, Makepeace. I frowned. None of the others had been so mocked. Was it because I was Governor? I determined to speak out. I couldn't have some mountebank couple scorning my family name, certainly not in front of servants.

"Before I could do so, the charlatan monk continued, 'oh, but there was another Sinclair, wasn't there? I forget, I forget. I see so many crowding souls, the pleading and the bleeding. Veins are hot, spicy. What was the other, what was the other?' The woman's head turned from side to side, as if she were looking about her, although her eyes were closed and she still appeared to be in her trance state. Was it my imagination, or was she expanding, her voluminous robes larger than before, billowing as if blown from within? Alarmed I looked about to see if anyone else had noticed. Then I felt a sharp stab of pain. Miss Godolphin's fingernails dug into my palm. I glanced at her, and she gave the slightest shake of her head. I looked from her to Hardinge. What was going on?

"I pressed my lips together. I did not like the direction the Hardinge woman was taking the session. Meanwhile, her husband inclined his head, and spoke in an obsequious tone. 'Governor, do you perhaps recognise any aspect of Brother Marcus' statement?'

"I spoke through gritted teeth. 'I'm afraid not, Mr Hardinge.' But my hands were sweating and my heart was beginning to pound.

"Mrs Hardinge actually *hissed*, like steam escaping from an engine. Around the circle people were beginning to look alarmed. Crowningshield glanced between myself and Mrs Hardinge in consternation, and from the corner of my eye I saw Peshaman take a step forward.

"Then the woman – the monk – spoke again. It was almost discursive. 'There is a fragrance in abjection, the waft of bitterness that sits and strokes the tongue, like the touch of rose petals on skin. Scarlet hearts start, consume the ruddy moon.'

"I shrugged. 'Gibberish, old man,' but Hardinge glared at me, eyes a-glow in the lamplight.

" 'Don't interrupt!' he hissed, all trace of deference gone. 'Marcus must have his say.'

" 'The Devil he must,' snapped the Major, but the billowing figure of Mrs Hardinge was already continuing.

" 'Swept away, kept away. For fish to strip and crabs to rip. How fine, how gay, a summer's day.' Madame Hardinge's head snapped up, 'Did you intend to kill him?'

"My throat was dry, my heart hammered in my chest. Rivulets of sweat that owed nothing to the Indian heat burned into my eyes. My brother, Heston, my twin. You probably don't remember, old man. It was before Oxford. He fell from the cliffs at Portreath. There was a brief mention in the press, obituary, condolences. A brief stir about the family tragedy. But I wasn't there, I swear it. I wasn't even there!"

Sinclair banged his hand on the windowsill, staring into the street. He was completely lost in his memories.

"It was conceivable that she had read something of the story, researched my background. Yet it was nearly twenty years before. But there was something else. I couldn't breathe, it felt like air was being sucked from the room and replaced with the stench of the grave. I gasped at the monk's words. I expected the others to break ranks, to fling each other's hands down in anger and stand, but there was stillness, faces swimming white, ghastly, in darkness, staring across the table in a sheen of sweat. What had happened? Some visitation seemed to afflict us all.

"And then, while we were all transfixed, Miss Godolphin cleared her throat and leaned forward, her eyes on Madame Hardinge. 'Perhaps you have something for me, Brother Marcus? Some netherworld dispatch?' Her tone was ice cold.

"Mrs Hardinge looked at her. The voice that emanated from her throat had sunk to a rasp. 'Oh, I have nothing for Miss *Godolphin*. Is there another name you'd like me to use? A name of the graveyards? Corpse dry. Out of the earth, out of the earth. Fledgling of the occult. Dabbler in the dirt. Yes, yes. Miss *D'Urfe* is it? Come to me, let me sniff you out. Steeped in blood. Blood for honey, blood for milk.'

"Miss Godolphin, or whoever she was, seemed undaunted by the venomous speech. 'I'm afraid you may find this wine too aged for your palate, *bhuta*. Where did you find them? In the cemetery at Nishatganj? Mrs Hardinge was interviewed in the Atlanta Weekly and mentioned it in passing. I suspected her intentions immediately. Grave dirt is so *de rigueur* for the progressive necromancer. Did she summon you deliberately, or were you just skulking, waiting to abandon a dead body in favour of a live one? I found the disturbed grave you know. There weren't many murderers buried there. You can end this clerical masquerade.'

"Mrs Hardinge's jaw sagged open, wide, almost as if she were a snake about to devour a rat. Wider, wider. The rank odour was overpowering. 'Little *occultress*. Miss Ven D'Urfe. Clever morsel, clever *shikaar.*'

" 'I am not your prey,' said Miss Godolphin. 'I'm afraid you have our roles quite reversed.' And with that she let go of my hand, hitched up her dress and plucked a revolver from her undergarments. Then she shot Eusapia Hardinge through the head.

"The report echoed around the room. For a second there was silence, then pandemonium erupted. Ada Harris screamed and her husband fainted. There was a clatter of chairs as Colonel Beynon and the Major sprang to their feet. At a nod from Miss Godolphin – whom I supposed I now had to call Miss D'Urfe – and before anyone else could move, Peshaman leapt forward and wrapped his arms around Mr Hardinge. He slumped in the bigger man's grasp, staring in horror not at his wife, but at her assassin.

"The gun remained unwavering, the shot still ringing in my ear. Across the table Eusapia Hardinge sat motionless. I stared, mesmerised by the thin wisp of smoke that curled from the neat hole between her eyes and rose like an undulating snake to the flickering orb of the gaslight above. Then she collapsed.

"When I say collapsed, I don't mean she slumped forward across the table, or fell backwards out of her seat. I mean she *collapsed*, like a punctured bladder of air. Her head simply folded into her neck, flapping like loose linen as her turban tumbled to the floor. Her clothes lost their voluminous bulge and her arms shrank to her side, like an empty jacket. Then the whole simply subsided into a misshapen pile of garments bereft of an occupant. Her face lay like a discarded canvas on the empty robes, eyes staring upwards side by side like those of flatfish. Then – and I shall never forget it – they blinked, once, and closed.

"Miss D'Urfe stood, and with one hand lifted her chair away. She moved her gun to cover Hardinge, though it seemed scarcely necessary. "I found her remains in the *bhuta's* grave, Mr Hardinge. I assumed you'd planned that exchange, to offer it life. She'd been stabbed in the back. It would have severed her spine, but not killed her. It devoured her slowly, from the inside."

" 'That bitch,' Hardinge jeered, his weasel face screwed up, 'I *hated* her. I enjoyed watching it. Years of her rubbish, waiting on her hand and foot, day and night—'

" 'Nobody cares,' Miss D'Urfe waved her pistol, 'Save it for the courtroom, it's terribly dull. Thank you, Peshaman, such a relief knowing I could count on you.' Then she looked across at the American, Crowningshield. 'And thank you for the recommendation,' she said, offering him a dazzling smile. 'Moderately effective.' Despite the horror of the situation, I found myself wishing it were directed at myself.

"He inclined his head. 'A pleasure, Ma'am. Colt Sidehammer, never let you down.'

" 'So you said, and so it proved. That, and a small concoction of salt.'

"Then she looked down at me. 'I'll leave further niceties to yourself, Governor. I daresay you have a nice cell somewhere you can offer as accommodation.'

"I stared at the pile of clothes, and shuddered. 'On what charge? Dirty laundry?'

" 'Why, murder of course. His wife is buried in a shallow grave back in Lucknow. That should hold him, even if necromancy does not.'

" 'And the... that thing that spoke to us. What was it, and, more importantly, has it gone? Did you kill it?'

"She pursed her lips. 'It's a *bhuta*, a murderous revenant. It feeds on fear and guilt, then, when it has weakened its target enough, it will fasten onto them, entering and devouring. I've driven it off. It can't be killed for it has no life.' Seeming to sense my thoughts, she said 'Pay no attention, its words are designed to weaken.' Then her smile flashed again, 'Though I quite liked "occultress." I might use that.' "

Sinclair fell silent, staring into the street. Two floors below, the longcase clock outside the library began its sonorous chime. I sat, counting unconsciously. Seven, eight, nine. Nine pm. Not quite the witching hour, but a tale of witchery such as made my hands tremble and sweat run down my back. I poured myself another generous measure and sank it with one gulp. "What happened then? You stayed in India another decade, didn't you? Was she there too?" I asked.

Sinclair shook his head without turning round. "We all agreed to keep quiet about it. Hardinge was found dead in his cell the next day, so it never came to trial and was easy to keep out of the papers. Miss D'Urfe left the following week, as did the American. Life returned to normal. I married one of the Pargeters, she came over from England specially."

"I didn't know you were married," I said, moving to join him at the window. I offered a glass but he just looked into the twilit street.

"She died," he murmured, "childbirth. Such fragile things."

"Did you see Miss D'Urfe again?"

His eyes glittered, and a slight smile played about his lips. "The Occultress? I've seen her a few times, but I never spoke to her again." Shadows played about his face. It seemed to be growing warmer, although the day's heat was dissipating. I loosened my collar. Sinclair put his hand on my shoulder. "Are you feeling quite well, Edward?" and he looked into my face with a queer intensity.

Uncomfortable, I slipped out of his hand, and stepped around him to the window. "You've been gazing out all evening," I said, for want of something to break the uncomfortable stillness. "Are you expecting a guest?" I nodded as a hansom drew up below. "Perhaps that's him now."

The cabbie jumped down and opened the door. A tall, slender figure stepped out. Though dressed in a long coat, from the deportment I could tell it was a woman. She looked up, straight at our window, and the dying sun turned her hair into an incandescence of silver. She was young, hardly more than a girl, but her eyes glowed with a predatory flame. Then she walked with quick strides towards the alleyway that ran behind the club.

"I say," I murmured, "that's deuced queer. What do you think of that, Makepeace?"

Behind me, the door closed with a soft click. I turned, but the room was empty. Sinclair was gone, and the faint scent of earth was all that remained.

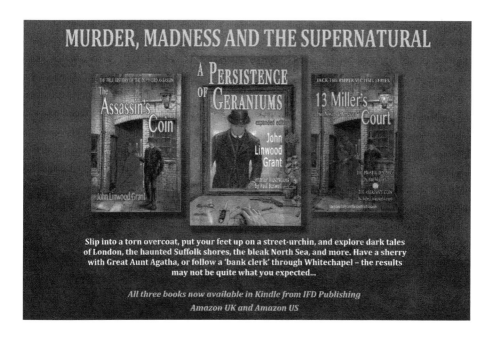

GRIMM, GHOST SPOTTER/DOCTOR

DAVE BRZESKI

The Golden Age of American comics in the 1940s featured quite a few occult detectives. One such, Grimm, Ghost Spotter, made his first appearance in *War Victory Adventures #3* (Harvey Comics, Winter 1944). The six page strip is credited to Don Weaver. Some believe the artwork at least might be by Rudy Palais. It's pretty stylish for the 1940s.

The strip opens with the following portentous caption...

"WE WARN YOU, THESE PAGES WILL TREMBLE BENEATH YOUR FEARFUL GLANCE. IF YOUR HEART IS WEAK, DON'T READ ANY FURTHER, FOR GRIMM IS RUBBING ELBOWS WITH... AH, BUT THAT'S FOR YOU TO FIND OUT!!"

I'll be honest, that didn't exactly fill me with hope, but I read on...

Grimm happened to be drinking in a tavern in a tiny village near the Black Forest where he found the old (and quite scary looking) barkeep's gossip intriguing. Apparently, the old caretaker at the

Tuber Castle had been murdered that very night, by the ghost of her own daughter! The girl, who was jilted by a 'Tuber Count' returns every night to seek vengeance on the woman he did end up marrying. Mistaking her own mother for her rival, she killed her.

At this point, Grimm sets off to investigate, politely refusing any more details the barkeep could offer. This is the first hint we get as to how good Grimm actually is at his chosen vocation.

Armed with his trusty 'ghost disintegrator' [i] he drives to Tuber Castle, but is waylaid on the way by a skeletal ghost who is trying to warn him of the danger he's heading blindly into. The ghost disappears at the appearance of the countess, who just happened to be taking a late-night stroll because she was "greatly disturbed". Someone shoots at them – we never find out who, or why – but somehow, despite the fact that Grimm was sure she was hit, the countess is unhurt. In the castle, Grimm helps himself to wine, but the countess tells him she never drinks... wine! The ghost appears again, just in time to knock the drugged wine out of Grimm's hand. Grimm, being evidently none too bright, assures the countess that he can deal with the ghost with his ghost disintegrator. He checks his pockets and finds that the ghost has slipped him a wooden dagger. Grimm still doesn't catch a clue! The countess has swiped his disintegrator, and while she pretends to help him look for it, he spots that she casts no reflection in the mirror. He finally realises she's... a zombie!

The countess throws his disintegrator on the fire, and while Grimm rushes to rescue it from the flames, the ghost grabs the dagger and dispatches the countess – who immediately crumbles to dust. The ghost transforms into a beautiful blonde. She is, in fact the real countess, whose material self was given to the caretaker's dead daughter, by black magic. She reveals that the 'zombie' [ii] had already killed all the servants and her mother and that she would have remained a ghostly prisoner forever if Grimm hadn't come along.

Quite what Grimm did that was in any way useful is up for debate.

That was the final issue of *War Victory Adventures*, but this first case was reprinted in *Bomber Comics #1* (Elliot, March 1944), which was followed by his second recorded case in *Bomber Comics #2* (Elliot, Summer 1944).

I couldn't help but wonder if someone had pointed out to Grimm that advertising his ability as a 'ghost spotter' didn't really suggest he was capable of actually doing anything about it once he'd spotted one. Despite the fact that the evidence so far rather suggested that he wasn't, he adjusted his byline to 'Grimm, Ghost Doctor'.

Grimm gets a call from a well-known psychiatrist friend, looking for help on a case that has him stumped. Margo 'the beautiful songstress' is being haunted by the spirit of 'the famous' musician, Martie Draw. When they arrive at Margo's estate, they find her collapsed from an overdose of sleeping pills. When revived, Margo asks to talk to her surly maid, Marie, in private, at which point she accuses the maid of trying to kill her. Marie tells her to keep quiet, or the doctor will think she's mad and put her in an asylum where she belongs.

While Margo is telling Grimm about her haunting, Marie fatally stabs the psychiatrist. Grimm decides to take a look around the house. While he's gone Margo gets another spectral visitation.

Having just discovered the body of his friend, Grimm finds a secret passage behind a bookcase and catches Marie in the process of faking the ghost with the aid of a record player and a cine projector. She has him covered with a gun, but he manages to throw a match onto the film in what seems to be an inexplicable bid to destroy some evidence. She cold-cocks him with the gun, and goes to beat Margo to death with a candlestick. It's revealed at this point that she holds Margo to blame for drawing Martie's attention away from her. Grimm recovers just in time and tackles her, then the police and fire service barge in to investigate the smoke Grimm caused. I underestimated him – there was a point to him setting the film on fire after all. I'm not convinced a short reel of celluloid would really produce that much smoke, but maybe the house was on fire by that point. There's only so much you can squeeze into so few pages.

So, in a nutshell, Grimm and his famous psychiatrist friend go to investigate an obvious fake haunting, and after the doctor is murdered Grimm just about saves the victim, before the authorities (alerted by the somewhat questionable method of starting a fire) burst in.

It was interesting to see him tackle a fake haunting case, but at this point, I really am thinking that Grimm wouldn't be high on my list of experts

to call in, should I ever need an occult detective.

This story gets two reprintings in *Haunted Thrills #3* [iii] (Farrell, October 1925) and *Witches Tales volume 1 #7* (Eerie Publications, July 1969) [iv].

Grimm's adventures continue in *Bomber Comics #3* (Elliot, Fall 1944).

Okay... here goes... An unidentified Japanese lady steps out of her coffin in the morgue and throws a dagger at the attendant, killing him. Now incorporeal and invisible, she makes her way to the office of an eminent plastic surgeon.

She's apparently visible to him, so obviously she can turn visible at will. She pulls a vial from her sleeve and drinks the contents, which make her corporeal again. Turns out the doctor is a German deserter, living in America under forged papers. She blackmails the doctor into performing plastic surgery on her, presumably so she no longer looks Japanese. After three weeks, the bandages come off, but there's a problem – she has no reflection.

Next thing we know is that the doctor – a disguised German, remember – has committed *hari kiri*! On reading the newspaper report of the doctor's suicide, Grimm suddenly realises that he should have taken a closer look at the dagger that killed the morgue attendant. We have to assume he was called in due to the strangeness of the murder and the missing corpse. Finding that the dagger is no longer in police evidence, he decides to do some research – in a local bookshop. Not one of those mysterious bookshops found in back alleys that so regularly have copies of the *Necronomicon* on its shelves, but an ordinary high street bookshop. He asks the pretty, new clerk (guess who?) for a book on Japanese mysticism. Naturally, he then takes her to dinner. They are interrupted by a blackout, but some bright spark of a photographer thinks it would be cool to take a flash photo of them during the blackout. The girl freaks out. She doesn't want her photograph taken "for personal reasons", so they give chase to the photographer, who refuses to hand over the film. She attacks the photographer with her dagger, but Grimm's disintegrator falls from his pocket. He turns it on the girl, claiming "The little fool! She played right into my hands!" and she melts into nothingness.

Kind reader, please forgive me if I don't actually believe Grimm! It seems pretty obvious to me that her knocking him to the side as she attacked the photographer, caused the ghost disintegrator to fall out of his pocket and catch her in its destructive beam, by pure dumb luck! Naturally, when developed, the photograph shows no evidence of the ghostly girl.

Bomber Comics #4 (Elliot, Winter 1944/45) brings us the final recorded case of Grimm, Ghost Doctor. This time Mr Hilt, a rich eccentric, has found a note pinned to the door of his private greenhouse by a dagger. He telephones the police – immediately getting through to the chief, as you do – who dismisses it as nonsense. But Grimm just happens to be sitting in his office at the time and volunteers to look into the matter. The note appears to be typed and unsigned, but Flint Hilt – I assume the Flint referred to in the note was his first name – is "certain no living person wrote it..."

Hilt has been nursing his pride and joy, a black rose, which will finally bloom at midnight. Grimm, being the occult expert that he is, also notes that

the moon will be full that night. Grimm sees what looks like a bloodstain on the floor, but Hilt shrugs it off as a flaw in the tile. Then the dagger disappears, causing the note to fall to the ground. Odd that neither Hilt nor Grimm actually took it down themselves for a better look. Grimm does have experience with neglecting to examine daggers properly, after all. They go back to the house and Grimm immediately lets Hilt out of his sight as he goes to fetch a warming drink. A cry for help sends him running to Hilt, who is being attacked by a ghost with the dagger. Hilt reaches for his ghost disintegrator (spelled incorrectly as 'disintergrator' for the entirety of this story) but the ghost beats a hasty retreat.

Returning to the greenhouse, at the insistence of Hilt, to witness the blooming of the black rose, they are admiring Hilt's life's work when the ghost attacks again. Grimm goes for his disintegrator, but he's managed to lose it – again! The ghost tells Hilt to confess that he tortured her for the secret of how to grow the black rose, which resulted in her death. Amazingly, Hilt actually does so and feels such remorse that he grabs the dagger and plunges it into his own heart! The ghost hands Grimm his disintegrator, which she apparently

183

purloined earlier, and promises that she will now go voluntarily to her eternal rest – leaving Grimm clutching the black rose – which he appears to have picked in total disregard for its rarity – wondering how he will explain it all to the chief of police.

That this was Grimm's final recorded case [v] comes as little surprise. Inept doesn't begin to cover it. He is in possession of an immensely powerful occult artefact in his 'ghost disintegrator', but has it pickpocketed twice! It's difficult to see where in any of these cases he actually achieved anything positive that didn't rely on blind luck.

I somehow suspect that Grimm may be currently residing in a forgotten corner of a dank, dark hell dimension with his 'ghost disintegrator' firmly inserted where the sun never shone.

Obviously, this article contains huge spoilers, but I suspect few readers will mind overmuch. Should anyone like to read these four stories in full (they are in the public domain) they should find downloadable copies on more than one website [vi].

[i] We are never told how this device works, or where he got it.

[ii] I'm going to assume here that the countess wasn't well-informed about matters of the occult and simply took Grimm's word for it that not drinking… wine, having no reflection in mirrors, and being dusted by a wooden dagger through the heart, suggested a zombie.

[iii] This reprint is actually given a title – 'Music Mayhem' – rather than the original 'Grimm, Ghost Doctor' heading.

[iv] Both reprints apply some clumsy additions at the top of each page, due to the fact that comics had changed proportions since the early appearances and pages were now slightly longer. The black and white magazine, Witches Tales, actually made some fairly major changes to the artwork, as can be seen in the accompanying illustrations.

[v] There is, I suppose, some slight possibility that further adventures were printed somewhere, but none have yet been uncovered. Bomber Comics ended its run with #4. Much of the contents of these four issues appear to have been picked up from discontinued runs in Quality Comics titles. Elliot appear to have only existed for a few years and only produced a handful of other comics.

[vi] I picked up my copies at Comic Book + https://comicbookplus.com/?cid=1507

REVIEWS

Title: Soul Breaker
Author: Clara Coulson
Publisher: Knite & Day Publishing
Format: Paperback, Kindle, Audiobook
Reviewer: Dave Brzeski

"There's a dangerous monster loose on the streets of Aurora, Michigan, and Detective Cal Kinsey is determined to stop it... or die trying." That's what the blurb said and as the ebook was free on Amazon, I decided to see if it was worth reviewing for ODM.

As it turned out, I thought it was, so...

Cal Kinsey was a rookie cop in Aurora, Michigan when he watched helplessly as his partner was torn to pieces by a rogue vampire – a vampire who has yet to be caught.

Now Cal is a rookie in an altogether different organisation – The Crows – or to give them their proper name, The Department of Supernatural Investigations, or DSI. On the other hand, the regular Aurora PD, which doesn't believe in the occult, refers to them as Kooks.

Here we hit the standard flaw in this concept, one that is common to so many other stories involving organisations that investigate the scary stuff. Most of the population do not believe that such things are real, despite the fact that the authorities occasionally send the DSI in to consult on the weird cases – obviously someone in the command chain is more clued up. It is rather hard to take such things as rival werewolf pack turf wars (an event which is mentioned in the book, but not actually a part of this story) seriously in a world where everyone else somehow manages to remain ignorant of the supernatural.

It's a common trope of the sub-genre, though. Buffy the Vampire Slayer got away with it for years, so we simply have to accept that the DSI can actually cover up mayhem on the level we see in this novel. And mayhem indeed is the word for it, as Cal Kinsey finds himself facing off against some serious demonic entities. We're not quite fully informed as yet as to why a rookie like Cal was brought into such a dedicated department as the DSI, but I'm sure this will be made plain in future volumes.

Cal is pretty good at what he does. He has some specialist skills, but he also has some, shall we say, technical problems with the weapons at his disposal. He is also very much outclassed by the people he fights alongside. What starts out as a quite explicitly gory series of murders, which the DSI are called in to consult on, soon develops into a major problem, where the DSI are forced to ally themselves with local witches and sorcerers in their bid to shut down what could become a very serious infraction from Everwhere. Everwhere is a catchall name they use for the extra-dimensional realms where all sorts of gods and monsters reside.

While the star of this book is definitely male, there are two engaging female characters, both of whom are somewhat more powerful than Cal Kinsey. It makes for an interesting dynamic.

This is one of those cases where the author has made the first book of a series free. This particular novel was published in 2015. According to Amazon, there are seven books, all of which are currently available, in the series. I have no idea if that means Coulson is now done with the character. It's certainly well-written and a real page-turner of a book. I shall make a point of checking out more of her work.

Title: Vigil
Author: Angela Slatter (Verity Fassbender Book 1)
Publisher: Jo Fletcher Books
Format: Paperback, Kindle
Reviewer: Julia Morgan

I must confess that my spirits fell a little when I first saw this book. "Not another parallel world where humans live side-by-side with supernatural beings in an uneasy truce", I thought, and then, "not another sarcastic half-breed heroine". This book has the usual drop-dead gorgeous ex-lover, and seemed to hint at yet another tedious love triangle. But it had a map at the beginning, and I always like to see those. Maps can give you a taste of things to come, without spoiling the plot. And it was unusually well-written. The next thing you know, I had finished the whole book in one setting, with only

one loo-break. Having trotted out all the cliches at the beginning, this book proceeded to side-step them, coming out with something original and engaging, and disturbingly dark.

The story revolves around Verity Fassbender, half-human and half Weyrd, her ex-lover and boss Zvrezdomir Tepes, known as "Bela", her mentor Ziggi Hassman, who has an eye in the back of his head, and her sparring partner Detective Inspector McIntyre, aka Rhonda. Verity is called in to investigate a series of child-abductions, and there is a suspicion that the children may have been kidnapped in order to eat them. The Weyrd of this story are not comfy-cosy; some of them are cannibals, and indeed, Verity's long-dead father once used to catch and kill children himself, to supply the city's illicit meat trade. Before long, Verity's caseload includes the murder of a Siren, and the missing adult son of a Weyrd billionaire – and she has to deal with a huge variety of potentially dangerous beings, including Norns, shapeshifters, a golem, angels (not the fluffy kind) and the drunken sister of her friend and neighbour.

This novel is a bit slow and confusing at first; the author has a world to build, and chooses to do so with a minimum of exposition. New words and concepts are introduced, and you will have to wait to find out what they actually mean. A good, strong opening chapter gives a clear indication that something sinister is going on, and I had fun trying to figure out who the nameless people in it actually were. The large cast of characters is interesting, and well-defined, so that you are rarely left confused as to who they are, once they have been introduced. The heroine's saltiness isn't overdone, and never descends into mean-ness. I found Verity Fassbender to be enjoyable company, and I particularly liked the banter between Verity and her Lestrade, Rhonda McIntyre.

Plotwise, this is convoluted, and not always easy to follow, but a little patience rewards you with explanations. I personally do not enjoy love stories, and I am grateful that the love story in this volume is kept low-key. This may be a bit of a disappointment to some readers, but then, this is an occult detective story, not a romance. Although in many ways this is a fun read, we can sense that Verity is trying to make light of the situation precisely because she is coming from a very dark place. Underneath it all, Weyrd culture is savage and carnivorous. The Weyrd characters mostly try to keep their dark side under control for the sake of co-existence, but there is a history of predation upon the human population, and of lethal retribution. In trying to resolve the various mysteries at hand, Verity has to live in a moral grey area, which sets up some interesting problems for future volumes. Never forget that many of the Weyrd enjoy the taste of human flesh, blood and tears.

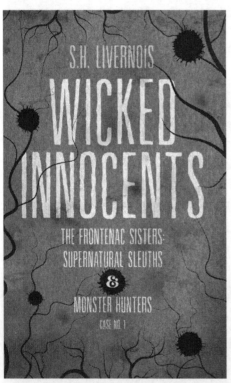

Title: Wicked Innocents
Author: S.H. Livernois
Publisher: Boonies Press (Self-Published)
Format: Paperback & Kindle
Reviewer: Dave Brzeski

I've seen the question brought up quite often recently: Can an occult detective story ever actually be scary? I grant you that when you are aware that the main protagonists will survive (because there are more books in the series), it does hamper the tension a teensy bit. S.H. Livernois manages something quite extraordinary, though. She proves that it is certainly possible to build up a high level of tension and fear in a book featuring investigators of the supernatural. She also proves without a doubt that an occult mystery story can successfully run to novel length.

This is the first book in a series, of which two more are already available and a fourth is on the way. The Frontenac Sisters: Supernatural Sleuths and Monster Hunters is the series title and I do wonder if that might not suggest the books are lighter in tone than they actually are. Indeed, Wicked Innocents is not only an occult detective story, it's also a horror novel.

Hyla and Liseth (I fear I found it nigh impossible to read that name without hearing 'Lisbeth' in my head) Frontenac receive a letter from ten year old Nelly Huggett, claiming that her mother has turned into a monster and chased her with some sort of weapon – and that her family has disappeared. Hyla is unsure how reliable these statements are, but the case reminds her of events in her own past – and her guilt over having once let her best friend down. Thus the sisters head out to meet Nelly, who has taken refuge with her aunt Emma, a woman openly hostile to their becoming involved; Liseth, who is an empath, has to work quite hard to hold back Hyla's angry reactions...

It gets very complex from here on and very dark. The detective element of this novel is very strong. There's no figuring out what is going on fairly early, then having to solve the problem. Livernois writes so well that we never get ahead of the Frontenacs in working out exactly what's up. Hyla really wants to believe the girl, but evidence suggests she might actually be the problem. I can't write too much about the rest of the book for fear of spoilers.

If I have one criticism it's that they eventually have to rely on a male friend they call in to tackle the Big Bad; I rather hope that the sisters manage to sort out some of their cases without such help. Having said that, I have no trouble in recommending this book and I will certainly be checking out future volumes of The Frontenac Sisters: Supernatural Sleuths and Monster Hunters.

That this book is self-published is a surprise. Don't get me wrong; I'm not one of those people who maintain that self-published equals rubbish, but this is so well edited and put together that it matches the output of traditional presses.

Title: PUNK MAMBO #0-#5

Author: Cullen Bunn / Pete Milligan
Artist: Adam Gorham / Robert Gill
Colourist: José Vallarrubia
Publisher: Valiant
Format: Comic Book / Trade Paperback
Reviewer: Dave Brzeski

Although I had both the collected edition of Punk Mambo and the original 6 issue (#0, plus #1-5) comic series on hand, for this review I decided to read the individual comics, in order. After the fact, when I looked through the

Artwork by Dan Brereton © Valiant Entertainment 2019.

trade paperback edition to see if there were any relevant extras, I noticed that they relegated the #0 origin story to the back of the book. This didn't really make much sense to me, as it was originally published around five years before the first issue of the mini-series.

In #0 we are introduced to Punk Mambo (daft name in my opinion, but whatever) in the Bayou, as a couple of young guys come looking for her in hope of securing an interview for their student magazine. And we soon discover that she's really not very nice.

Following a vision she has while consulting her spirit guide – Sid Vicious no less – she is drawn back to her punk roots in London. We discover in flashback how she graduated from being a pleasant girl at a posh boarding school, to a runaway punk rocker, to something else. When she first arrives in London, it isn't long before her new punk friends immediately sell her out to one Joe Mayhem – think John Constantine if he was even more of an arsehole. She is used and abused, but watches, learns and eventually escapes. Her vision revealed that Mayhem has a new punk band and she decides to make sure no one else ends up going through what she did.

We do get some evidence at the end of this issue that she's not quite as unpleasant a piece of work as originally suggested. Those two students, who I had assumed might be missing, presumed dead by this point, are shown to have returned, hopefully having learned their lesson.

Robert Gill's art is very good indeed, so good that I felt some disappointment when I saw that he didn't work on the mini-series. Nevertheless, Adam Gorham's art on the later issues is equally good, just different.

The main run of the comic, by Cullen Bunn, shows us a Punk Mambo who is still an anti-authority figure, very much refusing to be controlled, with a downright obnoxious attitude. Having said that, she is somewhat softened compared to Milligan's introduction.

Our 'Doctor Strange, but snotty', learns that someone is abducting the Loa (intermediaries between the Creator and humanity) to steal their power.

Robert Gill art from Punk Mambo #0

She's recruited, very much against her will, by the gods of Voudoun to find who the demon doing the abducting is working for, and put a stop to it. Despite her being about as disrespectful as it's possible to be when talking to actual gods, she does take the case – albeit she manages to piss off the Voudoun priest she's given to work with to the extent that he tries to quit.

It's no spoiler to reveal that she wins through in the end. We are left with a promise that Punk Mambo will return, but there's also a hint that she's not nearly as in control of her own destiny as she believes.

Being that it's a modern US comic book, it's no surprise that there are multiple alternate covers. #0 has three excellent covers by Russell Dauterman, Kalman Andrasofszky and Rian Hughes. Honestly, I couldn't choose between them. The individual issues of the mini-series have an insane number of variants – thirteen for #1 alone. Lots of great artwork for people who don't mind excessive duplication of content, but I can only speak for the main covers by Dan Brereton, which I love. The trade paperback,

Adam Gorham art from Punk Mambo #3

which reuses the main Brereton cover from #1 may, or may not, have variant covers – I don't know – but it does include a number of the series variants as extras. Much as I love great artwork, I really wish publishers would curb this habit of releasing endless variants.

I reviewed this series on its merits as a story told in comic format – on the quality of the writing and artwork. While I enjoyed the series and look forward to further adventures, hopefully with more Brereton covers, I can't not mention a rather obvious sticking point. Here we have a scenario where the powerful mambo is a white English girl who learned her craft from a white English man. She's so powerful that she has no problem disrespecting the actual gods of her adopted religion.

Be it martial arts, sorcery, or simply lording it over the jungle, there was once a seemingly endless flood of white (more often than not male) characters who seemed more gifted than the locals or the culture which originated an idea. Some of those stories are classics that are now part of fictional history – Tarzan being the most obvious example – and seem to have received a partial pass. Others tend to make us cringe, or are just downright wrong. For me, this falls somewhere in the middle. I recognised the issue, but it didn't prevent me from enjoying the overall story.

DESCRIBIN' THE SCRIBES

BRANDON BARROWS is the author of the occult-noir novel *This Rough Old World* as well as over fifty published stories, selected ones of which have been collected into the books *The Altar in the Hills* and *The Castle-Town Tragedy*. His next novel, *Burn Me Out* is coming September, 2020 from Black Rose Writing. He is an active member of the Private Eye Writers of America.

MATTHEW M BARTLETT was born in Hartford, Connecticut, and now lives in Western Massachusetts with his wife Katie and an unknown number of cats. As well as being a widely published short story writer, he is known for his striking and original collections of weird fiction, including *Creeping Waves*, *Gateways to Abomination*, and *The Stay-Awake Men*.

DEBRA BLUNDELL has won numerous awards, none of them for writing. She has a degree in Pre-Columbian art history and studied modern outsider art at The University of Memphis. Her shamefully neglected hobbies include astronomy, painting, perfecting the hand-pie, and collecting vintage box cameras. She spends her spare time with her cat Finn, composing third-rate ambient tunes under project name 'Auva'.

COLIN FISHER was born in London, and his poetry and short stories have been published by Egaeus Press, 18th Wall Productions, Wyrd Harvest Press, Fringeworks Press and Martinus Publishing. His weird fiction chapbook *La Ronde* will be published in 2020 by Eibonvale Press. In between writing he works in IT and studies for a Masters in Celtic archaeology, myths and history. He lives in Kent with his wife and two grown-up cats, and can be found at his infrequently updated website at www.colinfisherwriter.com. Somewhere, there is a Facebook page with his name on.

JULIE FROST grew up an Army brat, travelling the globe, but is now resident with humans and animals in Utah. Her short fiction has appeared in *Monster Hunter Files*, *Writers of the Future*, *The District of Wonders*, *StoryHack*, *Unlikely Story*, *Stupefying Stories*, and too many anthologies to count. Her novel series, *Pack Dynamics*, is published by WordFire Press.

NANCY A HANSEN is the author of various novel length works under her own Pro Se imprint, *HANSEN'S WAY*, plus a children's adventure series, *Companion Dragons Tales*, with Roger Stegman and Lee Houston Jr. She has contributed numerous stories to anthologies from Pro Se and other publishers. These include the *Sinbad: The New Voyages* and *Tales From The Hanging Monkey* anthologies from Airship 27, where she also has an ongoing series of the very popular *Jezebel Johnston* pirate novels, including a 4 book omnibus.
She currently resides on an old farm in beautiful, rural eastern Connecticut with an eclectic cast of family members, and one very spoiled dog.

AIDAN HAYES is an exceptionally loud North Carolinian. He currently attends UNC-Chapel Hill where a tenured English professor called him his "most annoying student in thirty years." Aidan can not be reached by telephone or by email.

PAUL STJOHN MACKINTOSH is a Scottish poet, writer of weird fiction and translator, primarily based in Hungary. In addition to writing dark tales, he is an active reviewer and critic. Following collections of both his fiction and his poetry, his novella '*The Three Books*' was released last year by Black Shuck Books.

JONATHAN RAAB is the author of *Flight of the Blue Falcon*, *The Hillbilly Moonshine Massacre*, *The Lesser Swamp Gods of Little Dixie* and more, and has had a number of his dark stories anthologised. He has written non-fiction for the New York Times At War blog, CNN.com, and other venues, and lives in Colorado.

DJ TYRER is UK based, and is probably best known as a horror writer, but has written in many other different genres and styles, including magical realism, Afromyth, and Holmesian pastiche – as well as being behind the Atlantean Publishing small press.

AARON VLEK is an American writer who works with the trickster, Jinn, and Coyote mythos. Featured in the *Miskatonic Dreams* anthology, she's also been heavily involved in the *Wicked Library* and other podcasts where she takes a deeper look at the denizens of Lovecraft's world. Her favorite topics there include The Deep Ones and the Mad Arab, Abdul al-Hazred.

TANYA WARNAKULASURIYA is an experienced freelance writer and journalist based in Sri Lanka, who has worked on issues such as the arts, disability, and the empowerment of women. She has had fiction published in venues such as *Selene Quarterly Magazine*, composes for the piano, writes lyrics, and enjoys working with animal welfare projects in Asia.

Printed in Great Britain
by Amazon